i 'den amongst ... ellers of an
...lerground Regency gentlemen's club, w...re
decadence, daring and debauchery abound,
the four owners of **Vitium et Virtus**
are about to meet their match!

Welcome to…

The Society of Wicked Gentlemen

Read

A Convenient Bride for the Soldier
by Christine Merrill
September 2017

An Innocent Maid for the Duke
by Ann Lethbridge
October 2017

A Pregnant Courtesan for the Rake
...Diane Gaston
... 2017

And l...

A Secre...nt

De...

Author Note

In every book I try to include a little bit of history that might be an insight into a world long gone but still beloved by so many. The panorama visit by Jake, Rose and Lucy is a description of a real place and event during the time frame of this story. Panoramas were a forerunner of the movies we love to watch today. The size of the building, the care with which the scenes were painted and presented, were a testament to human creative ingenuity.

Everyone flocked to the Leicester Square Rotunda to see the latest panorama offered by the owner Robert Barker for nearly seventy years. The painted views provided a window on other parts of the world, and were not only painted with painstaking accuracy, but decorated with artefacts to add to their realism. People viewing these vistas often became nauseous because of the realism and unaccustomed scope. Barker's Rotunda still exists in London today, tucked in between buildings in Leicester Square—and, fittingly enough, the only way it can be seen is from above.

I do hope you like Rose and Jake's journey to happiness, and enjoy reading the series as much as we authors have enjoyed writing it for you.

If you wish to know more about me or my books, visit annlethbridge.com. If you would like to dive deeper into the world of the Regency, visit my blog: RegencyRamble.blogspot.com.

Until next we meet, I wish you health, happiness and love.

AN INNOCENT MAID FOR THE DUKE

Ann Lethbridge

Published in Great Britain 2017
by Mills & Boon, an imprint of HarperCollins*Publishers*
1 London Bridge Street, London, SE1 9GF

Special thanks and acknowledgement are given to Ann Lethbridge for her contribution to The Society of Wicked Gentlemen series.

ISBN: 978-0-263-92608-8

Our policy is to use papers that are natural, renewable and recyclable products and made from wood grown in sustainable forests. The logging and manufacturing processes conform to the legal environmental regulations of the country of origin.

Printed and bound in Spain
by CPI, Barcelona

In her youth, award-winning author **Ann Lethbridge** reimagined the Regency romances she read—and now she loves writing her own. Now living in Canada, Ann visits Britain every year, where family members understand—or so they say—her need to poke around every antiquity within a hundred miles. Learn more about Ann or contact her at annlethbridge.com. She loves hearing from readers.

Books by Ann Lethbridge

Mills & Boon Historical Romance and Mills & Boon Historical *Undone!* eBooks

Rakes in Disgrace

The Gamekeeper's Lady
More Than a Mistress
Deliciously Debauched by the Rake (Undone!)
More Than a Lover

The Gilvrys of Dunross

The Laird's Forbidden Lady
Her Highland Protector
Falling for the Highland Rogue
Return of the Prodigal Gilvry
One Night with the Highlander (Undone!)

The Society of Wicked Gentlemen

An Innocent Maid for the Duke

Linked by Character

Wicked Rake, Defiant Mistress
One Night as a Courtesan (Undone!)
Secrets of the Marriage Bed

Haunted by the Earl's Touch
Captured Countess
The Duke's Daring Debutante

The Rake's Inherited Courtesan
Lady Rosabella's Ruse
The Rake's Intimate Encounter (Undone!)

Visit the Author Profile page at millsandboon.co.uk for more titles.

This novel is dedicated to CanadaLoneWolves, in particular Donmar, Lyon and Katz. Each and every day these awesome people provide me with laughs and smiles. Everyone needs folk like these in their lives and I hope you all have some of those too. I also want to dedicate this story to the other three authors in this series. Thank you, ladies, for being such a wonderful group to work with on this project.

Chapter One

Entering the owners' private quarters at the gentleman's club Vitium et Virtus, Jake, Duke of Westmoor, stifled a groan at the sight of the other two founding members lounging in heavy leather armchairs placed around a low table. One of the two empty chairs was his. The fourth supported a small gilded box.

'This was the reason you sent for me?'

Even seated, the brown-haired, brown-eyed Frederick Challenger had a military air. At Jake's words he snapped to attention and glowered. 'It may have escaped your lofty notice, Your Grace, but today is the sixth anniversary of Nicholas's disappearance.'

Jake tensed at the use of his title. The significance of the date had indeed escaped his notice, busy as he was with the affairs of the Duchy, but he wasn't about to admit it. 'I thought we were beyond all this.' He had enough reminders of loss at home without adding to them here. The one place he thought of as a refuge.

'Sit down, Westmoor,' Oliver, the other member of their group, said, his green eyes snapping sparks in his burnished face.

Jake sighed, but did as requested. Or rather ordered. If Oliver hadn't been such a good friend… No. Not true. He had no wish to alienate these men, his oldest friends. Without them he might not have survived the loss of his father and brother.

He glanced on the gilded box on the other chair. It contained Nicholas's ring, the last reminder of their missing founder of Vitium et Virtus. Could it really be six years since Nicolas's disappearance? It hardly seemed possible. Back then, they'd scarcely achieved their majority. Now look at them. All three of them reaching the grand old age of thirty. The intervening years had passed in a heartbeat.

Yet the shock of finding a pool of blood in the alley outside Vitium et Virtus and Nicholas's signet ring trampled in the dirt beside it wasn't any less raw.

Oliver leaned forward and laid his hand palm up in the centre of the table.

'You seriously intend to do this,' Jake said.

The other two glared at him. Grudgingly, he placed his hand on top of Oliver's, the warmth of another man's skin odd against the palm of his hand. Frederick added his to the pile.

'In vitium et virtus,' they chorused like the bunch of schoolboys they'd been when they started this stupid venture. In vice and virtue. Even after all this time, the words sounded strangely lacking without Nicholas's voice in the mix.

Withdrawing his hand, he picked up his brandy, lifting the glass towards the empty chair in a toast. 'To absent friends.'

The others imitated his action.

'Be he in heaven or hell—' Oliver continued with the words they'd been saying each year for the past six years.

'Or somewhere in between—' Frederick intoned.

'Know that we wish you well,' they finished together. As if anything so nonsensical could bring their friend back.

They threw back their drinks, staring at the empty seat.

'I was so sure he'd turn up like a bad penny before the year was out telling us it was all a jest,' Frederick said.

'If so, it would be in pretty poor taste. Even

for Nicholas.' Oliver said, his green eyes dark with the pain of loss they'd all felt since Nicholas's disappearance. A loss Jake didn't want to think about. There had been too many in his life. Each one worse than the last.

'It would have been like him,' Jake said, burying the surge of anger that took him by surprise. 'Nicholas always was one for stupid japes. This club, for example.'

Troubled, he rubbed at his chin and felt a day's growth of stubble. Hadn't he shaved this morning? Surely he had.

'I hear his uncle is petitioning the Lords to have the title declared vacant.' Frederick rolled his empty glass between his palms. 'Bastard can't wait to step into his shoes. I wouldn't be surprised if he didn't do away with him so he could get his hands on the estate.'

Inwardly, Jake flinched, though he kept his face expressionless.

Oliver's eyes sharpened. 'Don't be an idiot, Fred.'

Frederick's ears reddened as his glance fell on Jacob's face.

Apparently, his lack of emotion hadn't fooled his friends.

'Dammit, Your Grace. You know such a thing never crossed my mind.'

He made a dismissive gesture with his hand. 'Naturally not.' But others had whispered words like *murder* behind his back. And it wasn't as if he was entirely innocent.

The night his father and brother died came crashing back with a vengeance. The loss. The horror. The guilt. He leaned back in his chair, needing even that fraction of distance from the sympathetic glances of his friends.

A sympathy he did not deserve.

Oliver frowned at him. 'You look like hell, Jake. When was the last time you had a haircut?'

He couldn't remember. 'None of your business.'

The sound of catcalls and hoots came from behind the thick oak door that separated their private owners' quarters from the public rooms of the club.

Glad of the distraction, Jake raised a brow. 'What is going on out there?'

'It's choose-your-partner night,' Fred said.

Bell, the balding erstwhile butler, now manager of Vitium et Virtus, shot through the door. The noise level went up to deafening.

Bell's face screwed up into an expression of worry. 'Please, sirs. One of you needs to restore order. One of the gentlemen is insisting he wants five of the girls at once and none is interested. I've explained the rules, but he is being most uncooperative. Several other gentlemen have bet on his abilities and are insisting.' He disappeared back through the door. It closed behind him with the faintest click.

'Blast it all,' Jake gritted out. 'It really is time we closed this place once and for all.' It certainly didn't fit with his new position in life. He glanced at the empty place at the table. 'If this wasn't the one place that might draw Nicholas back, I'd be for closing it down.' The club had been Nicholas's idea. He had provided the largest portion of money to get it started.

'I'll go.' Frederick grabbed up his mask and cloak, the required uniform for all entering Vitium et Virtus. While people might guess at their identities, they had never admitted to owning the place.

On his way past, Frederick shot Jake a conciliatory look. 'Water under the bridge, right?'

'Right,' Jake said. He forced a smile. 'It's a good thing Nicholas wasn't here, or he'd be ribbing me about my thin skin for weeks.'

Fred picked up his pace as the door failed to keep out the noise of the rising mayhem beyond.

Oliver pushed to his feet. 'Nicholas would

have been ribbing you about your appearance, too. Take a look in the mirror next time you pass one. White's wouldn't let you through the door.'

Jake scraped a nail through his stubble. 'Good thing Vitium et Virtus isn't so fussy. Where are you going? Home?'

Oliver's green eyes sparked mischief. 'At some point. You?'

Jake grimaced, envying his friend his light-hearted grin. The idea of going back to the ducal town house caused his gut to clench. He hated walking through the door, let alone spending time there. He ought to go back, though. Duty called and all that. So much duty. 'Soon.'

He'd have to go soon. His grandmother was expecting him to bid her goodnight. And then she'd look at him with such sorrow in her eyes…

He picked up the decanter and poured himself another glass of brandy. The best money could buy.

'Want to talk about it?' Oliver offered, concern in his gaze.

Sympathy was worse than self-recrimination. 'I'm not in the mood for company,' he said, deliberately avoiding the question, but telling the truth all the same. He rarely was in the mood for company any more. Burying one's family did that to a fellow.

Only when the door clicked, did he realise Oliver had gone.

He swallowed the brandy in one gulp, poured another and headed for the office. These days, work and brandy were the only things that helped him sleep.

Rose stacked the last of the plates in the cupboard, removed her apron and stretched her back. Oh, it felt so good.

'All done, Rose?' Charity Parker, a middle-aged woman and housekeeper at the V&V, as the servants called it, swept a gimlet glance around the kitchen.

'Yes, Mrs Parker.' She hesitated, wondering if there was more to do.

The woman's stern expression softened a little. 'Go on, then, join your friends in the Green Room if you must, but don't be staying up all night sewing their dresses. And be careful, Rose. Things are still in full swing.' She bustled away.

Rose grinned at her back. Mrs Parker's bark was far worse than her bite. But she was right. At this time of the night the gentlemen members were often half-seas-over and could be a little too friendly to anything in skirts. Even someone as drab and plain as her was fair game in their eyes. She certainly didn't want to risk losing her position by breaking any rules. Mrs Parker and Mr Bell were very strict about the servants keeping to their proper places. For their protection as much as anything.

It was just one of the things that made her feel especially lucky to have found this position. The pay at the club was better than anything she'd ever received before and, best of all, she didn't have to live in as she did when working as a housemaid in a gentleman's home. Housemaids risked the advances of any lusty fellow under its roof. Men who couldn't keep their hands to themselves were the reason she'd left her last three positions. She knew the risks of a kiss and a cuddle under the blankets. She was likely the result of one.

No, she was better off going to her own place every night. Her own home, meagre though it was. No matter how kind and respectful the family might be to their servants, she always felt like an intruder. An outsider looking in on a happiness she had never known. Perhaps one day she would have family of her own. She was determined she would. The idea of it sent a chill down her spine.

Enough daydreaming. If she was to do a bit of mending for the girls before she went home, she needed to get going.

She slipped into the Green Room unnoticed. Not green at all, of course. Painted white and blue and lined with mirrors, the large open room was in the basement at the back of the house. It was here the girls who performed at the V&V changed into their costumes, practiced their acts and rested when not required on stage. Or wherever they performed.

It had none of the lewd pictures and murals covering the walls and ceiling of the rest of the place, or the statues and artefacts, thank goodness. She'd become used to them over time, even got used to dusting them, but at first she hadn't known where to look.

The Green Room was a whole different matter. She loved this room full of chatter and laughter and singing as the girls swirled around in their brightly coloured costumes. It was nothing like the stark cold rooms at the Foundling Hospital where she had grown up. Or the kitchens and servants' halls she'd worked in when she'd gone out into the world. In those places, everyone was afraid of their shadow and talked in whispers.

She sank into the old horsehair sofa in the corner and pulled out the needle case she'd made at the orphanage. A small embroidered book that safely held her few precious needles and pins. She sorted through the mending in the basket beside the sofa and pulled out pair of holey stockings. She loved helping the girls and if they occasionally slipped her a penny or two for her efforts, she was grateful.

From here, she observed the goings-on while she rested her poor aching feet before walking home. With a sigh, she unlaced her half-boots, rubbed at her soles for a blissful moment or two, then tucked her them up under her skirts.

Peace at last.

'I 'oped you'd come by.' Fleurette, whose real name was Flo, plopped herself down beside Rose. Her fair golden locks were arranged in the elaborate hairstyle Rose had helped her with earlier in the day.

It was Flo who had first asked for Rose's help with her hair. When the other girls had seen the result, they had begged for help, too. She did what she could, but Mrs Parker only gave her a few minutes off here and there during the evening. Still, she made a point of helping whenever she had a moment or two, as well as after work. It was these snatched moments that had put the idea into her head that she might one day become a ladies' maid or a dressmaker.

Flo cracked a huge yawn, then exploded in laughter. 'I'm so tired I could fall asleep right here.'

Rose had liked Flo on sight. Apparently the feeling had been mutual. For the first time in her life, Rose felt as if she had a true friend.

Making friends at the orphanage had been frowned upon. They weren't there for enjoyment. They were unwanted children and needed to learn how to make themselves useful as adults.

'Was there something you needed?' she asked after a moment or two of silence.

Her friend winced. 'I wore that new red gown for my first number and caught my heel in the hem. The old besom will fine me when she sees I've damaged it already.'

She looked so downcast Rose wanted to hug her. 'Give it to me. I'll fix it and take it up an inch and then you won't trip.'

'I feel terrible asking. You've been here for hours—'

'And you need it for tomorrow. I'm happy to do it.'

'I'll pay you.'

'No! What are friends for?'

Flo gave her a mock glare. 'You'll take a couple of coppers and like it. I'd have to pay a whole lot more if the old besom had her way.' All the girls called the wardrobe mistress 'the old besom.'

'It is not right that they fine you for rips and such,' Rose said. 'It is not as if the gowns are brand new when you get them. Don't worry, I'll do it before I go home.'

Flo leaned in and kissed her cheek. 'You are a dear. I'll go and fetch it. And don't be offering to sew anyone else's gown for free. Or style their hair, for that matter.'

'I do it because I like doing it,' she said to Flo's departing back. And because it gave her hope that one day she could be more than a scullery maid. A hope that people wouldn't look at her with disdain because she scrubbed floors and washed dishes, and was a bastard to boot.

Within moments, Flo was back with a gown of brilliant scarlet with silk roses adorning neckline and hem.

Rose let the silky fabric slide through her

fingers, careful not to let it catch on her work-worn skin and torn nails. 'Leave it with me. I'll have it done in no time.'

'Flo,' one of the other girls called. 'Your gentleman's waiting at the back door.'

A shadow passed across her friend's face, but then she shot Rose a cheeky smile. ''Is lordship's taking me out for dinner.' She glided away.

His lordship, as Flo called him, was Flo's gentleman follower. Rose sometimes wondered if he treated her right. There had been a couple of unexplained bruises that Flo had brushed off as falls.

The girls were allowed to walk out with the club members as long as they were discreet and did not ask for, or mention, any names. Flo lived in hopes her beau would ask her to marry him. Rose had offered dire warnings after seeing those bruises.

In her turn, Flo had instructed Rose on how to avoid unwanted children, just in case.

Rose pulled out the pair of thin cotton gloves she used to keep the silky fabrics the girls wore from getting ruined by her rough skin and set to work.

Slowly the noise around her dwindled to nothing. The wall sconce above her head contained the only candles left alight. A clock struck the hour.

Four in the morning! Already? The repair had taken far longer than she had expected because she'd also found three rips in the gauzy gown's side seams and some of the silk roses bordering the hem had been loose.

She snipped off the thread and held the gown towards the light. So feminine, like something one of the titled ladies who occasionally visited the club would wear, even if it was a little gaudy.

What would it be like to be one of those ladies? Living a life of ease and luxury. She didn't envy them the boredom that Flo said was the reason they came to the V&V, drawn there by the excitement of losing hundreds of pounds at the gambling tables or by the private assignations with one or other of the virile young men who were members.

She pushed to her feet, rubbing at the ever-present ache in the small of her back. Time to go home or she wouldn't get any sleep at all. She carried the gown over her arm to Flo's chest full of clothes. On top was a mask covered in red spangles shaped to cover the top half of the wearer's face. It matched the gown.

As Rose moved it aside, she caught a glimpse of herself in the mirror, tired, drab, plain.

Grinning at her image, she held the gown up against her and kicked out a foot, making the red fabric swirl around her ankles. The picture she created was spoiled by the sight of her ugly brown dress as she turned to view herself from the side. She stared at the neckline. Was it too low? Should she have added a bit more fabric? While the V&V was renowned for debauchery and depravity, Flo was a singer not a courtesan.

Perhaps she should try it on before she put it away. For Flo's sake, naturally. She shook her head. Who did she think she was fooling? She wanted to see what she would look like in such a gown.

She whipped off her frock and slid the whisper of a gown over her head. In the mirror, a magical transformation took place. Her eyes seemed to pick up the sparkles at the neckline and her figure seemed more shapely. If it wasn't for the plain Jane face staring back at her, she might have thought herself pretty.

The mobcap had to go. But with the severe bun still in place, it made little difference. She pulled the pins from her hair and let it fall around her shoulders, then, with a naughty smile, tied on the mask.

She turned this way and that, regarding her reflection. Better. Much better. Why, she might almost pass as one of the girls. And if she really used her imagination, perhaps as a lady. The neckline was not as bad as she had feared. It was a little low, showing the rise of her bosom, but not at all indecent.

Eyes half-closed, she twirled around humming one of the tunes she'd heard the musicians playing in the ballroom earlier that evening, pretending she was waltzing with one particularly handsome gentleman, who had no clue she even existed.

Sore feet and aching back gave her not one twinge.

Returning from seeing his grandmother, Jake passed a carriage standing outside the front door of Vitium et Virtus. Waiting for one of nobility's late-night revellers, no doubt. Usually it was the ladies who kept their carriages at the ready. He went around the side of the club, to the door out of sight of regular members, reserved for the owners.

The porter, Ben Snyder, bowed him in. 'Good evening, Yer Grace.'

Jake froze. The pain of loss held him rigid,

followed swiftly by a rage he could scarcely contain.

With a muttered curse Jake slung his coat and hat on one of the four hooks in the shape of aroused male appendages they'd bought as a job lot upon opening Vitium et Virtus.

Snyder handed him a mask and retreated to his chair.

No doubt the man had seen the anger and thought it was directed at him. Jake reined in his emotions. Built the wall of distance that kept him halfway sane. But, God help him, each and every time he heard those two words, his instinct was to glance around for his father. Only to realise it was he who was being addressed. He loathed it.

It was a constant reminder of his father and brother. Of their lives. Of their deaths. Of the reason he was now addressed as *Your Grace.*

It was also why he was here and not tucked up in the ducal bed in the ducal mansion. Here and only here did he seem able to snatch a few minutes' sleep. A slog through the ledgers with a brandy or two in the comfort of the owners' private rooms should send him into the arms of Morpheus. He hoped.

'Any one left above stairs?' he enquired of

the porter, trying to sound normal and coming off icily cold.

'A few, Yer Grace,' the man said warily. 'In the gaming room and upstairs in the private bedrooms. Want me to clear them out?'

'No. I am not in. To anyone. I don't care if the place burns down, I do not want to be disturbed, understand?'

'Understood, Your Grace.'

The porter also added a whispered *as usual*, but Jake decided not to hear. The porter would follow orders. He always did and that was all Jake required. He strode along the deserted corridor with its erotic statues and murals seeming to leer at him, the need for brandy an ache in his throat.

He took the servants' staircase down. It would take him to the other side of the house to another set of stairs leading up to where the owners' private quarters were located. Allowing him to avoid any lingering customers.

A sound of soft humming brought him to a halt outside the ladies' dressing room. He frowned. The girls should all be gone by now. They were certainly not supposed to entertain gentlemen here. There were rooms on the top floor set aside for such frolics. Rooms equipped with costumes and toys for every taste.

He donned his mask and opened the door a fraction, enough to see in but not be seen until he could figure out what was going on.

A petite woman in a glittering red mask was singing to herself, her scarlet gown swirling around her shapely ankles as she twirled in front of the mirrors, each one giving a different reflection of a gown moulded to every curve of a sinuously lush body moving in time to her humming. The smile on her parted lips was not the forced smile of a courtesan, nor that of a jaded widow, or yet the hopeful smile of a debutante anxious to please a duke. This smile was pure delight. Enjoyment.

Her joy at the simple act of dancing spilled over with an infectious feeling of lightness that unaccountably lifted his spirits. He found his own lips curving upwards in response. Even more surprising, he found himself wanting to be the one to waltz her around the room.

A movement in the shadows caught the corner of Rose's eye. She turned and gasped. It was him! The Duke. Though he was wearing his usual mask, she would know him anywhere by his height and breadth and commanding presence. By his dark stubbled jaw and firm chin. By his lovely mouth.

Too many times had she stopped to admire him as he passed her at her work. Of all the owners of the club he was the only one who had caught her attention in that way. He was impossibly handsome, but coldly unapproachable. A proper duke.

Or how one assumed a duke to be.

Not that she would ever mention that she knew who he was. No names were ever spoken. House rules.

Despite his lofty position, something about him had struck her as sad. As if some deep sorrow weighed him down and made her want to offer comfort. A foolish fancy. Someone of her lowly station had nothing to offer a man such as he.

But how often she had dreamed of feeling those strong arms curl around her while she laid her head on his chest. The very idea of it made her feel strangely weak.

Never before had she felt such a powerful attraction, despite knowing better than to get tangled up with a man. Fortunately, he was nothing more than a fantasy. A man who marched through her dreams like a knight in shining armour. As long as she kept him there, in her dreams, she was safe.

But this was no dream. The crushing realisation pressed down on her shoulders. She should not be here. It was against the rules. She glanced around for an escape route. But he was between her and the door and approaching slowly, his bright blue gaze fixed on her face.

His expression did not reflect anger. Indeed, the warmth of his smile, with a glimpse of white teeth, charmed her into remaining still. She released a breath she had not realised she was holding. A sigh really. Of appreciation.

His smile broadened and he bowed. 'I beg your pardon, my lady. I did not mean to startle you.'

My lady? Her heart fluttered strangely. If only she were his lady. She placed her hand below her throat and shook her head. 'Merely surprised.'

She'd responded with the careful diction she'd taught herself from listening to those of the upper classes as she moved unseen among them, cleaning grates and scrubbing floors.

'I have interrupted you,' he said, cocking his head to the side in question.

'Foolishness,' she said, peeping up at him. Heavens, he was taller than she had thought and broader. And so much more handsome close up. She could scarcely breathe and yet somehow the scent of his cologne filled her lungs and made her feel strangely dizzy. 'I should go.'

'Not before you give me the honour of a dance, surely?' His voice had deepened. His eyes, which had always seemed coldly reserved as he went about the business of the club, were bright, sparkling with mischief.

Dance? With a duke? 'I cannot,' she choked out.

He chuckled, low and deep. 'You certainly can. You waltz as beautifully as you hum.'

Heat rushed up from the neckline of the shocking gown, for now with his gaze upon her, she felt almost naked. Flirting. A duke was flirting with her and every particle in her body wanted to allow it. Nay, wanted to encourage it.

Wanton. Like your mother.

She must say no. But it would never happen again, this chance to dance with the man who haunted her dreams. When she was about her work, he never noticed her underfoot. None of the gentry did. They weren't supposed to. She had long ago realised it saved both the served and the server embarrassment.

What harm would one dance do? This was the first time she had seen the man smile since she started working here. If it would bring him a measure of happiness, and her, too, why not? It would certainly be something for her to dream about for the rest of her life and perhaps tell her grandchildren at some long-distant time in the future.

The night their old granny danced with a duke. The idea of that dream of a family made her smile.

'You know you want to,' he said, holding out a hand.

A moment later, she was in his arms.

The faraway gaze in eyes the loveliest shade of green Jake had ever seen sent blood humming through his veins. Those eyes were limpid and soft as she gazed up at him, as if this was all a dream. To his surprise, not only did their steps meld in perfect unison, it was if they were designed to be partners.

For months he'd been numb to everything around him, going through life by rote, fulfilling required duties and responsibilities hour after brutal hour. Keeping himself busy. But now, here, with this vision of loveliness, he could actually feel the blood coursing through his veins. It was as if he had left a cold dark place to enter a land of light and warmth.

Her light. Her warmth. He basked in it, even though he knew he did not deserve it.

He swept her around a turn at the end of the room, gazing down into her face. What did she look like beneath the mask? Her lips were lush and full, her eyes dreamy, her loose hair a river of thick gilded waves that curled in little tendrils on her faintly flushed cheek.

His body responded to that shadowed glow of pink on her skin. The blood in his veins beat a tattoo of desire.

Her lips parted as if she, too, felt the connection between them. The rise and fall of her generous breasts quickened with each indrawn breath. A pulse beat rapidly at the base of her throat. A place he longed to taste with his tongue.

Awareness sparked in the air. Their steps slowed. Their gazes locked. Hers dropped to his mouth.

With all the old reckless impulsiveness he'd been determined to curb these past many months, he drew her flush against his body. She tensed and, though he wanted to curse, he eased his hold, preparing to let her go. Unbelievably, she smiled up at him and relaxed into his embrace.

A brief kiss was all he intended, a thank you

for the respite she'd brought to the darkness of his world, but as the plush full mouth yielded beneath his lips, he lost himself in the pleasure of kissing a willing woman.

Deeper and deeper he delved the soft recess of her mouth, while he felt the warm breath of her sigh against his cheek. A tentative dart of her tongue into his mouth sent a jolt of lust ripping through him.

A groan rumbled up from deep in his throat and he pulled her hard against his body. Feeling pleasure as her belly pressed against his groin.

She gasped and pulled away, staring at him in shock, startled out of her daydream by the evidence of his arousal through the wisp of silk she wore. He cursed his stupidity. Lost in sensation, he'd forgotten the rules of the game. Never rush a woman, especially one he did not know.

He stepped back and bowed. 'I beg your pardon.'

Fingertips went to her lips, covering her mouth, her eyes wide behind her mask, wary, distraught, but also hazy with desire, which gave him a vague sense of satisfaction.

'I mean you no harm,' he hastened to assure her, taking another step back.

'I must go,' she said breathlessly, her glance finding the door. 'I should not be here.'

A married woman then, out for a night of discreet fun. A strange sense of disappointment filled him. Really? This was exactly the sort of entertainment his friends had been recommending would get him out of the doldrums. Before he settled down to find a duchess.

'Allow me to escort you to your carriage.'

She looked startled. 'My carriage?' She swallowed. Smoothed her hands down the front of her gown, caressing the lovely shape that only a moment ago had seared a memory into his skin. 'Oh, yes. My carriage. No need for escort, Your Grace.'

Inwardly he cursed. She knew who he was. Of course she did. There wasn't a person in London who didn't after all that had happened. No wonder she didn't want to be seen with him. To be seen leaving a place like this on his arm would create yet another scandal.

He schooled his expression into cool reserve and looked down the renowned Westmoor nose. 'As you wish.'

She cast him a shy little smile. 'Thank you for waltzing with me.'

That tiny upward curve of her lips, her soft voice with its odd little accent he could not place, caused a pang behind his breastbone. 'You are welcome, my lady. May I see you again?' He froze, startled by the words that had left his lips before his brain caught up to them. Yet he waited for her answer with a sense of hopeful anticipation.

Her jaw dropped a fraction. 'Me?' she squeaked.

He couldn't help but chuckle at her surprise. He took her small hand encased in a silky glove and pressed a kiss to the inside of her wrist. 'Naturally, you.' There was no denying it to himself. He wanted her. And since he hadn't desired a woman since the night of the accident, it came as something of a relief to know he could still feel desire. 'I would like to get to know you better. If it would suit you.'

Heart pounding strangely hard, he waited for her answer. God, he felt like a schoolboy all over again. Shy. Nervous of rejection, yet full of hope.

She looked wildly around as if expecting someone to leap out at her. 'I couldn't.'

She sounded so genuinely regretful, it made him all the more determined. 'You could if you really wished to.'

Her bottom lip drooped. 'It is not possible.'

He'd not flirted and bedded the most beautiful women in London without learning a trick or two. 'It will be our secret. No one will ever know. Not from me. Not if you do not wish. I give you my word.' He ran a fingertip along her jaw and ended up touching her bottom lip still flushed red from his kiss. 'Please.'

'I cannot risk—'

'No risk. I simply want to talk, that is all. There is a garden at the back of the club. Very quiet. The windows on that side are all nailed shut.' He and his fellow owners had decided early on that they would make very sure the club was inviolable to peeping toms and nosy newspapers. Nor did they wish to upset their more respectable neighbours. 'Meet me there tomorrow evening at seven. I will leave the gate beside the mews open for you.'

She looked adorably confused. 'I shouldn't.'

He reached out to touch her mask. 'You came here and you shouldn't.'

Her shoulders sagged and he felt a little spurt of triumph, tinged with a dash of guilt.

'If I can...'

Again the careful diction. Perhaps a foreigner trying to sound English, but not an accent he recognised. 'If you can't come tomorrow, then I will wait for you the next evening and the next until you do.'

'I don't know.' On those words, she turned and fled.

But she would. He was sure of it. He'd seen the longing in those amazing spring-green eyes.

He followed her at a leisurely pace, not wishing to scare her. By the time he reached the front door and looked out, the carriage was gone.

'Anything I can do for you, Yer Grace?' Snyder asked.

Jake smiled at him. 'Nothing.'

The man's eyes widened in shock.

Feeling just a tiny bit smug, Jake walked away, humming.

Chapter Two

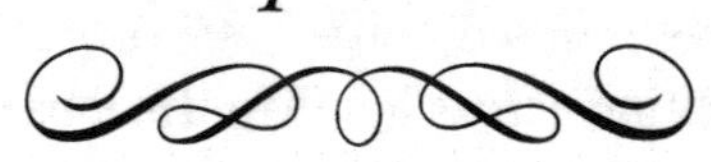

''Ere you are!'

Heart in her throat, Rose swung about, water and suds splashing on the floor. Those were not the deep drugging tones of the man she'd lived in fear would discover her, but Flo's strident angry tones.

She sagged back against rim of the sink. 'Oh, it's you.'

Flo folded her arms across her chest. ''Oo else would it be?' Her expression changed from anger to worry in a heartbeat. 'Wot's wrong?'

'Nothing.' She swallowed the dryness in her throat that had been there since two nights ago. 'I've had extra work,' she mumbled. 'I haven't been able to get away. Perhaps I will see you later.'

Flo narrowed her eyes. 'Oh, no. You'll just go sneaking off again.' She grabbed Rose's wrist and dragged her into the pantry. 'Tell me wot's 'appened. You look like someone died.'

Misery climbed Rose's throat and stuck there in a huge lump at the memory of His Grace the Duke of Westmoor's large hand on the small of her back. The sensation of the tease of his lips danced across her mind and sent chills rushing across her skin. He'd been lovely. So handsome in an unkempt way, his hair a little longer than it should be, his cheeks hazed in stubble, his appearance slightly rumpled. As if he needed someone to care for him.

But, oh, his kisses, they had been truly amazing. Never had she suspected a kiss could be so pleasurable. It was all she'd been able to think about in her bed of a night.

How could she have let him kiss her? Knowing he was one of the owners of the club. Knowing how far above her he was—a duke, no less. How wanton she had been in her enjoyment of his mouth on hers. Worse yet, how she longed to kiss him again.

And she could, if she met him as he'd asked.

She didn't dare, yet the thought of him waiting… She pushed the thought aside. 'Was the dress to your liking?'

'Of course it was. Why do you think I was looking for you?' Flo shoved a handful of coins at her. 'Why haven't you popped in to see us tonight? No one does hair the way you do and the girls have been asking after you.'

She should never have ventured into the Green Room in the first place. If she hadn't, she would never have met His Grace and she wouldn't be walking around with her mind in a whirl and her heart aching.

They'd told her and told her at the orphanage what happened when girls let their emotions and feelings get the better of them. Most of those left there were the product of illicit relationships. As she was. Wanton blood ran through her veins. She'd refused to believe it, until two nights ago. 'I have to go. If Mrs—'

'The sooner you tell me wot's wrong, the sooner you can go back to your dirty dishes.'

She gazed at her friend, at her kind and worried expression. She had to tell someone. Had to. 'You promise you won't tell.'

'Cross my heart and hope to die.'

Rose managed a weak smile at the childish oath. Where to begin? She peeked out of the pantry door. No sign of Cook.

'I met a man.'

Flo squeaked with excitement. 'You are walking out?'

Rose shuddered at the very thought. 'Oh, no.'

Her friend glowered. 'If the bastard took advantage, I'll scratch his eyes out, so I will.'

'Nothing like that,' Rose hissed. 'We danced a bit. He kissed me.' She touched her lips at the recollection. 'He was lovely.'

'So...where's the problem?'

'He's a gentleman. Oh, Flo, I tried on the gown and the mask and he caught me waltzing around in it. I think he thought I was one of the lady guests. He wants to meet me.'

'So meet him. If you like him, that is.'

'How can I?' She gestured to her faded gown. 'He's a gentleman. One of the nobs.' Worse. Far worse. He was a duke, but she did not dare mention that or Flo would guess his identity. 'What would he think if he saw the real me?' The thought of his disgust had her heart sinking to her shoes. All her life she'd been disdained. An unwanted orphan. Child of sin. 'Perhaps he'll think I tricked him on purpose. I can't lose this job.' Or her small room in the boarding house. She was barely able to afford it as it was. She'd have to start all over again and this time with no character. She'd be lucky not to end in the workhouse. Or worse. 'I should never have put on that dress.' She sank on to the hard wooden chair. 'What am I to do?

He'd said he'd wait every night until I met him. What if he really is waiting?'

Flo tilted her head, her blue eyes perceptive. 'You like this man.'

She'd be lying to her friend if she said no and that she did not want to do. 'He was nice.' More than nice. He made her heart do somersaults and her body tingle in wicked places. That last, though, was something she would never admit to anyone.

'Then the real question is…do you want to see him again?'

Dreadfully. The longing in her heart would not be denied. 'I feel horrible every time I think of him waiting.' The back of her throat burned at the idea she would never see him again, except maybe from a distance. 'I should at least let him know meeting him again is impossible. But how could I, dressed like this? I'd be too ashamed. Oh, why, oh, why did I try on the dress?'

Flo ran a glance from her head to her heels. 'You're right. That dress certainly won't do. Leave it to me.' She bustled away.

Rose mopped the water from the floor and she plunged her hands back into the hot soapy water.

Her heart picked up speed at the thought

of seeing His Grace again. She took a deep steadying breath. She couldn't. No matter what Flo said. It was an impossible dream. Hadn't she learned long ago dreams were not for the likes of her?

Of course he would not be waiting.

She'd heard all the rumours about him. How he was before he came into the title. He was a man who loved the ladies. All different sorts of ladies. Never faithful to one particular one. Always out for a good time. There were darker rumours, too. Those she'd ignored.

Oh, he might have shown up once, she supposed, shrugged his shoulders at her non-appearance and moved on.

If only her foolish heart didn't keep wanting to know for certain. And hoping.

Only a fool would spend three nights sitting on a cold stone bench waiting for a woman who had made it pretty clear she wouldn't meet him.

A fool indeed.

Not to mention that the last thing he needed was to become entangled with another man's wife. Dukes didn't do that sort of thing. So what if she'd felt so right in his arms, had eyes the colour of peridots and her kisses tasted of honey and innocence? He had responsibilities now. Duties. The days of dalliance and enjoyment were done.

Besides, he didn't deserve them.

And yet, still he sat here, watching the gate in the wall leading into the garden from the alley. This was the very last time. He'd said it last night, but tonight he meant it.

He got up and paced around the lawn, letting the blood flow back into his backside, rolling his shoulders to ease the tension. Though why he'd be tense he didn't know. All the paperwork he'd ploughed through earlier in the day, no doubt. He needed a drink to relax him, instead of hanging about here like some lovesick swain.

Hell. He didn't even know her name. Had no way of seeking her out. In his mind he called her the lady in red. *His* lady in red, no less, he mocked.

If she didn't come this evening, he'd pin his card to the gate. She could damned well chase after him. He had only come tonight because a gentleman always kept his word. At least, until it was no longer viable. Three nights was more than enough, though he'd likely always regret never seeing her face or getting her name. A feeling he couldn't account for at all. Perhaps it was because of his surprise at seeing her float around in front of the mirror like a goddess come to earth. And the way she'd made him feel something other than numb for those few moments.

Perhaps this was his punishment for all the times he'd missed appointments with his father because he was having such a good time. Just deserts, so to speak. He glanced heavenwards and shook his head. Pure imagination. And wishful thinking.

He returned to the stone bench and eyed it with distaste. Why not simply give up and return to the comforts of the club and a very fine old brandy?

Better yet, he should go home. The thought of the accusing stares of his household slid a dagger between his ribs and into the hollow cavity of his chest. The same guilty pain he felt every time his grandmother looked at him.

He pulled out his pocket watch and flicked open the case with a thumbnail. Twenty minutes past the hour of seven o'clock. Ten minutes and he was leaving.

Once more he paced the edge of lawn and then shot a glance at the garden gate…again.

His jaw dropped. For a moment he thought he might be experiencing a hallucination. Despite the fact that he'd been waiting, he'd been positive she would not come.

Now she was here, he was slack jawed and speechless. Tonight, she was vision in green wearing a far more modest gown than she'd worn the night they'd met, but it also showed off the sumptuousness of her hour-glass figure, the elegant slope of her shoulders and brought out the unusual green of her eyes. Tonight, instead of a river of hair down her back, her tresses were hidden beneath the crown of a straw bonnet, leaving only one ringlet to fall over her shoulder and draw attention to her magnificent cleavage.

Delicious. He almost licked his lips with the desire to taste every inch of her milky skin.

The hesitance in her expression brought him to his senses.

He bowed. 'Madame.' Dash it, couldn't he sound more friendly and less ducal? What had happened to his famous rakish charm?

'I wasn't sure you would still be here.' She sounded breathless. Shy.

He shrugged. 'I gave my word. Though I must say I was about to leave.'

She winced. 'I apologise. I was unable to... come before.'

Was she toying with him? Hoping that by

keeping him in suspense, she could control him? It wouldn't be the first time a woman had tried such ploys. He was too old a hand at the game of flirtation to be caught in such a way. Then why was he staring at her with a besotted grin on his face? *Idiot.*

He took her hand in his and kissed the back of her glove.

She dipped a curtsy.

Another man of his rank might have deemed her courtesy an insult, for it was neither deep enough or held long enough to be deemed anywhere close to correct. Indeed, it was more of a little bob, as if he held a junior rank or no rank at all.

A deliberate snub? Had she heard the rumours and believed them?

He put his hands behind his back, reverting to the posture his father had so often employed to put him in his place.

She glanced up at him from beneath her lashes. A quick shy little glance before she looked at her feet again. 'I did not intend to come at all,' she said in her soft clear voice, the odd little accent once more teasing at his ear. 'But I did not like to think of you waiting.'

She was pitying him? His spine stiffened. 'I can assure you I have not been waiting long.'

She nodded her acceptance of his words, when he had expected her to flirt and tease. Something he would have been perfectly comfortable with. This honesty left him flat-footed. All at sea. 'Since you are here,' he said, more gruffly than he intended, 'perhaps you would care to take a turn about the garden?'

She glanced around nervously and up at the building. 'If you are sure we will not be seen.'

'I am sure.' He held out his arm.

After a slight hesitation that had him on tenterhooks, she rested her hand on his arm.

A tactical error. By walking side by side, the only way he could see her expressions was to bend forward to peer around the brim of her bonnet. And wouldn't that make him look like some callow eager youth. He led her to an arbour where roses grew over a trellis and some thoughtful gardener had set another infernal stone seat. 'Please, sit for a while. I think you will find the view from here to your taste.' He flicked his handkerchief over the stone surface to ensure she would not ruin her gown.

She smiled up at him. 'Thank you.'

Guileless, that smile, and yet it beguiled him none the less.

She perched on the edge of the seat and he

sat beside her, angling his body so he could see her profile while she gazed around.

‘I did not expect so large a garden,’ she said. ‘In London, I mean.’

‘When this house was built large gardens were the fashion. This is one of the few streets where they have not been torn down to make way for a square or a terrace. What is left of the garden is only a small part of what was here before.’

‘It is quiet enough to be miles from the city.’

‘You like the country? What county do you hail from?’

‘I have always lived in London, Your Grace.’

‘So, you do know who I am. Will you honour me with your name?’

She froze.

Another rushed fence. Curse it, what was wrong with him? He lightened his tone. ‘Your first name, if you will.’

‘Rose.’

‘It suits you.’

‘Why? Because my face goes red when I am embarrassed?’

He repressed the desire to chuckle at her defensive tone. It seemed they were both less than at ease. ‘No. Because, as you know, a rose is considered the most beautiful of flowers.’

A cheeky grin lit her face. 'Now that's what you call flattery, Your Grace, and I would prefer we was…were honest in our dealings.'

The slight slip in her vocabulary stunned him. It was not the sort of thing to fall from a gently bred girl's lips. Though a foreigner might make such a mistake, he supposed. 'So exactly where in London do you reside, Rose?'

'I doubt you would know it, even if I told you.'

Or perhaps he was wrong; she certainly sounded haughty enough to be the daughter of a nobleman.

'Are you married?' The question had plagued him from the moment they met.

Surprise filled her expression. 'Mercy, certainly not.'

'So tell me why you were here at the Vitium? Who brought you?'

'I came by myself, on my own two feet.'

He shook his head. She would not win in a war of words. 'Only patrons and their guests are permitted through these hallowed portals.'

She laughed out loud. 'Hallowed. I think not.'

Again, every word was formed with care. Perhaps she was the daughter of some foreign dignitary. Or a very accomplished actress.

He stretched out his legs. 'I am glad you came.'

'Me, too. I wasn't sure you were real. Half the time our dance seemed like a dream.'

He cocked a brow. 'A good dream, I hope?'

Gah, really? He was actually fishing for compliments?

'A lovely dream.'

He found himself tongue-tied by the sweet smile on her pretty lips, the genuine light in her eyes and the blush on her cheek. He wanted to kiss her lips. Badly.

'Shall we walk some more?'

She popped up on her feet. 'I would like that. Do you know the name of all these plants and bushes?'

'Some of them, certainly.'

Rose still could not believe she was doing this. Walking with her hand on the arm of a duke. Conversing as if it was an everyday thing. At any moment he would guess she was an impostor in borrowed clothes and revile her. She'd likely lose her job, too.

What had she done?

She'd let Flo and the other girls talk her into borrowing a gown suitable enough to wear for her gentleman, and helping her with her hair.

After all, they had said, twittering in excitement, she had helped them so many times. Gloves had appeared on her hands and parasol on her arm and all topped off by a straw bonnet they all declared was fetching.

Fine feathers did not make a fine bird or a sow's ear a silk purse, but she had desperately wanted to be convinced. Silly goose.

Or she had until she reached the gate.

If Flo hadn't pushed her through, she would have fled.

Now she wished she had run, because she had the sense he was not all that glad to see her. He seemed more reserved than he had the other night, cooler, more distant.

'I really didn't expect you to be here, you know,' she said, lifting her chin.

'You think I would not keep my word?'

Oh, now he sounded insulted. An angry duke was not a good thing. She straightened her shoulders. 'That is not what I meant, Your Grace. It was I who failed to keep our…' What did one call it?

'Our assignation.' He said it casually as if it meant little of import.

Assignation. She savoured the word and stored it away for future consideration.

'So, you see,' she said, 'I assumed you would

have far more important things to do beside wait for me.'

A brow quirked as if her words surprised him. 'You are here now.'

Blasted man, could he be any more stiff and starchy? The silence grew heavy. It must be her turn to say something. Oh, dear. What did one discuss with a duke? 'I…um…what sort of tree is this?' She gazed up into the leafy branches that cast a gentle dappled shade over the gravel walk.

'Beech.'

Trees were trees. Though she did know there were different kinds, she had no idea how to tell them apart. She'd seen little enough of them as a child and not much more since starting her employment. 'How do you know?'

While he looked a little taken aback, he stopped to poke at a crack in the paving slabs with the toe of his boot. A strange little shell rolled out, brown and prickly and curling away from the centre. 'For one thing, this is its fruit. A beech nut, if you will.' He pointed at the trunk. 'The bark is distinctive, as are its leaves.' He reached up and pulled down a branch so she could see close up. 'Other trees have serrated leaves, but the combination of all three tells me this is a beech.'

'Did you learn that at school?' The orphanage had taught her to read uplifting sermons and her bible, and how to do sums, but most of her education had been about making herself useful to people with money. Plying a needle, making tallow candles and soap. Sometimes one of the guardians had loaned her other things to read, Gothic tales and such, but the matron had stopped it, said it had given her ideas above her station. Improving texts were best for the likes of her.

But those glimpses into other realms had made her realise that if she wanted to get on in the world she needed to improve herself. She'd emulated the speech of the grand ladies who sometimes came to do charity work among the orphans and read everything she could get her hands on whenever she had a spare moment.

'Actually,' the Duke was saying, 'my family estate has acres of trees of all different sorts. We learned about trees almost the way we learned to walk.'

'We?'

His expression darkened. 'My brother and I.'

'You have a brother.'

'Had. He died.'

While he had done his best to sound nonchalant, she heard pain in his voice and when she risked a glance at his face, saw it in his eyes. 'I am sorry.'

He grimaced. 'I also have a sister.'

'She lives with you?'

'She is a…widow. She and her daughter reside mostly in the country.'

'Your parents?' she said tentatively, then winced. He wouldn't be a duke, would he, if his father was alive? There seemed to be a great deal of death in his family. One always imagined the nobs to be immune from such disasters. 'I'm sorry, I do not mean to pry.'

He stopped and gazed down at her with a question on his face.

Blast. Of course, anyone moving in his circles would know these things. Breath held, throat dry, heart thudding in her chest, she waited for his denunciation.

Instead, he once more held out his arm and they continued walking. 'My mother died when my sister was born. My father, little more than six months ago.'

While he sounded calm enough, tension radiated through him as if the words were hard to say. She had the urge to wrap an arm about his waist and give him a hug. Goodness, he'd probably take a fit if she did any such thing. Still, she patted his arm in silent sympathy and his amazingly blue eyes when he glanced down held a smile. 'My grandmother lives with me. A feisty old lady she is, too. Always trying to boss me about.'

She chuckled, because she sensed that was what he wanted—no, needed—and also because the idea of anyone bossing such a fiercely commanding man about was laughable. 'And what is it that she wants you to do?'

His face became inscrutable. 'Marry. Produce the heir.'

'And you do not want to?'

'I'll do my duty.'

He stopped at a flowering shrub. 'This is gentian.'

A deliberate change of subject. She might not be educated, but she wasn't stupid. 'How pretty.'

'And this is a rose bush.'

'Hah. Very funny.' The blossoms were perfect and a lovely pale yellow.

He dropped her hand and removed his fob from his pocket. He detached a small knife and cut off the stem of a blossom a day or so past the bud stage, but not yet in full bloom. With his little knife he cut off the thorns and handed it to her with a bow. 'While not as fair as you, I hope you will accept it as a token of my esteem.'

She giggled.

He cocked a brow. 'You find me amusing, Madame?'

Oh, dear, had she insulted him again? 'I find such flowery nonsense amusing. It does not sound like you at all.'

Again the strange questioning look. 'So it is honesty your prefer.'

She knew she was plain, but did she want him to say it? Better he said what he thought instead of puffing her up only to let her fall. After all, by the light of the candle, in that gown and the mask, he would not have been able to make out her features. Perhaps that accounted for his reserve. He was disappointed.

'I do prefer it.'

The smile he gave her was so sweet, so endearing, it almost took her breath away.

'Then honesty compels me to say I have never in my life met a woman like you.'

Ouch. Clearly her attempt to be ladylike was failing badly. To hide her embarrassment, she brought the rose to her face and inhaled deeply. The delicate scent brought a smile to her lips. 'And I have never smelled a rose so sweet.'

He opened his mouth to say something, then

gave a swift shake of his head as if he thought better of it.

'Tell me about you,' he said, beginning to walk again.

She tucked her hand under his arm. 'There is not much to tell.' Not much of interest to him in any case.

'You have siblings?'

Siblings. Another unfamiliar word. But they had been talking of families. He must be asking about members of hers. She made a stab at the meaning.

'I have no brothers or sisters.' That she knew of. 'My parents are also dead.' Dead to her, for they'd never come to claim their bastard daughter. 'I live with distant relatives.' Liar. But what else could she say? That she lived in London's rookeries? That would certainly spoil his image of her as a lady. Anyway, what difference did another white lie make, when nothing about her was real.

They had come to a wall. The end of the garden, she assumed. She turned back and was surprised to see only the chimneys of the house were visible, through the trees. 'I suppose we must go back.'

'I wanted to show you something.'

The girls had been very free with their advice as they helped her dress. Flo's last warning rang in her ears. 'If he says he wants to show you something, watch out. He might want to show you more than you want to see.'

'Such as what?' she had asked.

The girls had collapsed in laughter. But when they realised she was serious, they had looked worried. 'How did such an innocent come to work in a place like this?' one of them grumbled.

'He might want to show off his manly bits,' one of the others said. She pointed below her waist.

'Not if he's a gentleman,' Flo said severely. 'Not the first time. Still, be careful.'

Rose blushed at the memory.

'I really should go back.'

'Rose,' he said, shaking his head at her. 'It is nothing to fear.'

'The archbishop said to the actress,' Rose mumbled under her breath.

He laughed outright. 'I heard that, you little minx. Where on earth did you hear such a thing? From one of the servants, no doubt. I advise you not to use it in company.' He swept back a tangle of shrub that trailed down to the ground, honeysuckle, she thought, to reveal a swing hanging from the limb of a large tree.

'Oh.' She felt extremely foolish.

'Sit. I will give you a push.' He glanced up at the sky, 'And then you probably should go, before dusk draws in.'

He was right, the sky above was a much deeper blue now and the sky to the west was turning golden and pink.

He held the wooden seat steady by the ropes while she sat. The thing wobbled beneath her bum. She gave a little shriek.

'It is all right. I won't let you fall.' He frowned. 'Hold on to the rope above the knots.'

Right. Of course. She'd seen pictures of this. She could do it.

'Relax.' His grin was infectious and, yes, there was a little dimple in each cheek she hadn't noticed before. Her stomach gave an odd little hop. With a swallow, she eased her death grip on the rope.

He pushed the seat and it swung forward a foot and back a foot. She gasped. He pushed again on the backward swing. This time she went farther and her feet were far off the ground. She felt as if she'd left her stomach somewhere behind her. It caught up to her the moment she started going backwards.

She shut her eyes tight.

He pushed again.

She opened her eyes as the air rushed against her face and tugged at her hair as the ground fell away. This must be how birds felt when they flew.

'Tell me if it's too high,' he said the next time he caught the wooden seat and pushed off again.

Her body relaxed. It wasn't too high. It was wonderful. She laughed, throwing her head back, gazing up into the tree. The rushing air forced the bonnet from her head, the ribbons caught, then let go and it flew away. A strange sense of joy filled her. She couldn't help it. A feeling of…freedom. She smothered the urge to laugh until she was breathless.

Gently, carefully, as if she was precious, he brought the swing to a stop. He came around to face her a smile on his lips, gazing down at her with such a look in his eyes, she felt seared to her very soul. A feeling something like the one when she had when they danced in the Green Room.

Slowly he dipped his head.

She lifted her face to meet his searching gaze, a sense of wonder filling her heart. A feeling so powerful, it felt as if it would burst out of her chest.

Their lips met.

The magic of his kiss swamped her, so light and tender, a brush of his lips, a touch of his tongue that made her insides tighten and her breath leave her lungs in a rush.

His arm went around her, bringing her to her feet, her body flush with his. She twined her arms around his neck, floating on a cloud of hot sensation, her breasts feeling heavy and full, her heart pounding against her ribs, her whole body melting into his.

One large hand cradled her face, warm, strong. When had he removed his gloves? Why did she care? Feeling his skin warm against hers, his strength held under control yet supporting her with a sureness that made her feel weak, was heavenly.

He nipped at her bottom lip, teased with his tongue until on a sigh she opened her mouth and let him taste.

A Florentine Kiss. She'd always thought it sounded nasty, but this was lovely. It created hot shivers across her skin, wicked pulses low in her abdomen, an expanding sensation of joy that made her heart feel too large for her chest.

A groan rumbled up from his throat and his fingers speared into her hair.

One of her hands had, of its own volition, settled on his chest. It trembled in time to the beat of his heart. The sensation seemed to travel all the way from her fingertips until it took up residence deep inside her stomach.

Her head spun with the onslaught of heat and cold and lightning seemingly happening all at once.

His free hand cupped her hip, pulling her close to his lovely lithe body, so firm against hers. The ridge of his arousal pressed against her belly. Her dazed mind sounded a warning. She pushed at his chest, felt resistance, then, to her relief, he eased away, their lips continuing to cling for a fraction longer. He stepped back.

He was breathing hard.

As was she.

What must he think?

Wanton. Just like your mother.

She covered her mouth with her hand before she said something stupid. Like, thank you. Or, again, please.

With horror she realised her hair had come down and was now a mess of lopsided curls. 'I should go.' She looked around for the bonnet. It wasn't hers to lose.

'Rose.' He held out a hand to her, a careful smile on his lips. 'Sweetheart.'

The sound of the endearment made her want to weep. Couldn't he see, she could never be his sweetheart? She wanted a home. A family. A husband. If she didn't leave now, that dream would be over.

While he had been kind and very sweet, that kiss meant he knew she was no lady. Knew she was not his equal in any respect and he had as good as said he would be marrying soon. A lady. A woman of his own class.

There was no sign of the bonnet. Darnation, she would buy Diana a new one. 'I'm sorry. I cannot do this.' She picked up her skirts and ran.

The crunch of his feet on the gravel followed. Got closer.

She spun around. Backed into the gate. Hands pressed flat against rough wood behind her. 'Don't.'

His expression was puzzled. Perhaps a shade angry. And he had her bonnet dangling from his fingers.

She put up a hand to halt him. 'Please. Let me go. This was a mistake. I'm sorry.'

He froze, his body rigid. 'I beg your pardon, Rose.' He bowed.

The hurt in his eyes stopped her breath. The urge to stay wrenched at her heart, perhaps even her soul, she felt such a pang. Staying would make things worse. If he knew what she was, then it would ruin everything. Spoil the memories.

She whirled around. In seconds she was out of the gate and running. At the end of the alley, she collided full tilt with someone. She let out a shriek.

'Rose!' Flo's voice.

She had waited, despite Rose telling her not to. She almost collapsed with relief.

Flo held her by the upper arms, her eyes blazing as they search her face. 'The bastard. Wot did he do?'

'No, no. He didn't do anything. It was me.'

Flo's gaze went back up the alley. 'Blasted toffs.'

'Please, Flo. I want to go. Now.'

Clearly torn between wanting to seek out the man and needing to help Rose, Flo hesitated.

'Flo, I need to go home.'

With a curse, Flo put an arm around her shoulders and turned down the street heading for Cheapside.

Chapter Three

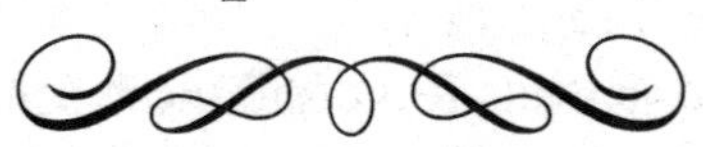

Heavy-eyed and muzzy-headed, Jake lifted his gaze from the numbers dancing across the page of the ledger and stared at the straw bonnet sitting on the corner of the desk.

What had he been thinking? He was the Duke, not the carefree second son any longer. He had responsibilities and, as his father had reminded him with his dying breath, a duty to the Westmoor name. A duke didn't go about importuning ladies in a hidden garden. Surely even he had too much pride to abase himself before an unwilling woman. His brother would never have considered such a thing.

Besides, even if she was not a member of the *ton*, Rose was innately a lady in every respect. The rake in him had recognised her innocence from the first and he had come so close to scaring her to death, she'd had to run from him. It did not bear thinking about.

After swearing to his father to do his duty by the title, at the first temptation to come his way he'd returned to his old careless impetuous ways. Shame flooded him to the core of his being.

Thank heavens Rose had more sense.

And yet something inside him kept urging him to seek her out.

He could do it. He could find her. A widow or wife living on the edges of society in search of a bit of harmless adventure would be known to someone. As a duke, he had unlimited resources. And he could bend her to his will, make her want him if he put his mind to it, too. He'd charmed enough ladybirds and widows in his salad days to know his appeal to the ladies. A charm he'd never given a second's thought. Until now.

Not that he would. It wouldn't be honourable.

He really ought to apologise, though.

Those last moments with his father floated through his mind.

'You swear you will give up your rakish ways and give the title its due? For my sake.'

'No!' he'd yelled. *'You are not going to die.*

You must not. I do not want this—' His voice had broken.

A heavy sigh. *'Do your duty, my son. That is all I ask. Care for Eleanor and my mother.'*

Fingers, clammy and cold, had clenched on his hand.

'Swear it.'

His throat had felt raw. His eyes had burned.

'I swear it, Papa. On my life.'

'I trust you, my son.'

The grey eyes had closed for the last time.

Trust was a heavy burden. Jake squeezed his eyes shut and prayed for respite, for an hour or two of sleep before he returned to the house where his father had placed a life of duty and honour upon shoulders ill-prepared to bear them. Burdens he had never wanted.

How many times during his youth had he rejoiced that the dukedom was his brother's destiny and not his, while he went his merry way.

'You here again, Westmoor?'

He looked up at the impatient tone.

Frederick loomed over him, glaring down. 'Do you not have a home to go to? Oh, wait. You do. A ducal mansion.' He inhaled and curled his lip in distaste. 'God, how much wine have you drunk?' He whisked the decanter off the desk and deposited it back on the tray on the console between the shuttered windows. 'You stink of brandy. Go home. Bathe, for God's sake.'

Frederick's brusque manner hid a caring heart. Jake knew this, but he simply glowered at his friend. 'I have as much right to be here as you do. I am doing something useful.' He glanced down at the ledger. Trying to anyway.

'We employ a bookkeeper for that.'

'Someone has to oversee the bookkeeper.'

What on earth was the matter with him? Fred's advice might not be to his liking, but it wasn't wrong.

Besides, it was a lady's prerogative to choose her protector. A gentleman simply shrugged and moved on if he wasn't picked. He toyed with one of the blue ribbons from the bonnet and twined it around his fingers. Not that he'd suffered such rejections in the past. After all he'd been the second son of a duke, fabulously wealthy in his own right and his reputation for generosity had not gone unnoticed.

Until now. Damn it all, he needed to think about something else. About those in his care. His grandmother, for example.

When had he last seen the old girl? He cast his mind back with effort. Two days ago? Three? She'd be worrying. The thought of her in distress made his stomach roil. Another failure to add to a string of them he dragged behind him like anchors.

Fred peered at the bonnet. 'What is that doing there?'

'Nothing. I found it in the garden. One of the girls must have dropped it. I thought I would ask around.'

'I doubt any of them would want that old thing back.'

'Probably not.' Jake picked it up and dropped it in the rubbish basket.

'Well, I'll leave you to it,' Fred said.

'Not on my account, I hope. I'm leaving.'

'I only came by to check on the state of the cellar, which I have done. See you later, Westmoor.'

Fred left, closing the door behind him.

Jake forced himself to his feet. He was done here. There was no point in pretending to read numbers when he could barely see them. He picked the bonnet out of the bin and hung it on the back of the door. *Just in case.*

He wandered off to the stables. He deliberately did not glance at the garden gate and nor did he utter a word at the reproving glance he received from his coachman for keeping him waiting till some ridiculous hour of the morning. Again. Thank goodness the stables at Vitium et Virtus offered comfort for long-suffering servants.

Once home, he went straight to his room, endured the ministrations of a valet who did nothing but complain about the fit of his coats and the state of his linen, and shut himself in the library, which he now used as his office. Even after all these months, he still couldn't bring himself to use the ducal study.

Instead, he'd had them bring a writing table in here along with the various documents he needed day to day. He'd also had them cover the most recent family portrait. His father, brother, sister and himself. Something about the way his father and brother looked out of that frame made him feel inadequate. And as guilty as hell.

Why had he not done as his father had asked him on that last day?

Such a simple request. For some reason he could no longer fathom, or justify, he had taken umbrage at the implication that he had nothing better to do than dash off to Brighton to curry favour with the Regent.

If only—

He cut the thought off and returned to the

pile of correspondence awaiting his attention. Why had he never realised how much work it was, being a duke? Likely because his father and brother had never involved him in the routine running of the Duchy.

Nor had he wanted them to. Had he?

He shut his eyes, briefly. No. He had not. He'd been having too good a time as he'd so often gloated to an older brother weighed down by responsibilities and paperwork.

Too busy enjoying the charms of the fairer sex, his unbelievable luck at the tables and running Vitium et Virtus with his friends. Running it and enjoying its entertainments. Though he had to admit the sameness of it all had begun to pall some time ago.

The library door opened to admit an elderly lady with her hair powdered and her back ramrod straight, despite needing the support of her cane. A pair of piercing grey eyes fixed on his face. Eyes like his father's. And his brother's. His were blue, like his mother's and Eleanor's.

'Grandmama. Good morning.'

A beauty in her youth, she was still a handsome woman in her seventies.

She snorted. 'Don't "Grandmama" me in that cozening tone. It is mid-afternoon. Where have you been? I having been wanting to speak to you for two days now.'

'Out. What can I do for you?'

She pursed her lips, but plucked a letter from her reticule. 'Eleanor asks if she may come to town next week. She wishes to shop.'

Eleanor. Something else his father hadn't seen fit to tell him about. If ever he discovered who the father of his niece was, who the man was who had abandoned his sister to a life of secrets and loneliness, he was going to roast him on a spit. 'She may come whenever she wishes, as I told her.'

'Your father...'

'In this one thing, Grandmama, my father was an ass.'

The starch went out of his grandmother and all of a sudden she looked old and frail and sad. She sank into a chair. 'It was on my advice that we sent her away,' she admitted, sounding miserable. 'I thought it was for the best. You know your father always took my advice when it came to your sister after your mother died.'

Jake bit back a hard retort about his father needing to think for himself and came around to sit beside his grandmama on the sofa.

She reached out and touched his hand. 'You are a good boy, Jake. You have a kind heart.'

Not always. His mind went back to Rose. He'd upset her very handily, when clearly she did not fancy him the way he had fancied her. It was such a spur-of-the-moment thing, he barely understood it himself.

Dash it. He would find her and make sure she had suffered no ill effects as a result of his reckless behaviour. It was the honourable thing to do. But right now his grandmother needed him. 'Shall I ring for tea?'

'No, thank you. I need to get a reply off to Eleanor in the post. I want to assure her right away that she is welcome. Any delay and she will think we don't want her and these days, with my stiff joints, writing is a slow business.'

'Why do you not let me hire a secretary for you or a companion to help with such things?' It was not the first time he'd made the suggestions since her last lady companion had departed.

She shot him a steely-eyed stare his father would have been proud of. 'Your wife would be companion enough, should you deign to obtain one.'

He masked a wince. 'I have to find a willing lady first, Grandmama.'

Her brows lowered. 'Excuses, excuses. Why,

I have introduced you to a dozen suitable young women over the past few weeks.'

His hackles rose. He was perfectly capable of finding his own wife. When he was ready. 'It is too soon, Grandmama. We are barely out of mourning.'

'Your father would have wanted you to secure the succession as soon as possible. You danced with Mrs Challenger at the ball you threw for her and Challenger. You could have used the opportunity to meet this Season's crop of debutantes. But, no, not one other lady did you ask to dance.'

His scalp tightened. Every muscle in his body felt tight. He now knew how a fox must feel when chased by the hounds. He forced himself to remain polite. 'The ball was a favour to one of my oldest and dearest friends. Right now, the affairs of the Duchy require my complete attention. Let me get those in hand and then I promise you I will do my duty and attend every ball and assembly from John o' Groats to Land's End. I will leave no stone unturned. No maiden left uninspected for her suitability.'

She laughed and shook her head. 'Ridiculous boy. You always did have a way with words. But…' she wagged a finger gnarled by the ravages of rheumatism '…I will keep you to that promise. Or the spirit of it anyway.'

She limped out of the room.

Eight hours later, Jake found himself entering Vitium et Virtus in search of an hour or two of sleep before the sun rose. Again. He'd forced himself to remain at home, to go to bed like a normal person, under his own roof—and lain awake all through the darkest hours. Now, at almost dawn, he needed sleep to the point of desperation.

Snyder greeted him briefly, took his coat and hat and left him in peace.

If there was peace to be had. The servants would soon be bustling about their chores.

He should have come earlier. He strolled past the Green Room and against his will opened the door and looked in.

Naturally no one was twirling about in front of the mirror. No one was there at all. And in the interim he'd come to the conclusion he should forget about Rose. Seeing her again, he had concluded, would only make his restlessness worse. He had a duty to the Duchy as his grandmother had pointed out. He must make a good marriage if he was to secure the future of his name and the dynasty entrusted to his care. Albeit reluctantly, he'd given in and taken up the mantle and the strawberry-leaved coronet. Blast it.

The weight of that mantle and crown had him dragging his steps towards the owners' private quarters. He passed a maid already at her work in the grand hall, the entrance used by paying members.

On her hands and knees polishing the marble floor, she was scrubbing so hard that her bottom moved in counterpoint to the swish of her cloth.

A very attractive, lushly curved bottom it was too. Drawn by some unnamed instinct, he paused to watch, feeling a strange sense of kinship with that sweetly rounded bum. A palm-tingling urge to stroke and squeeze. And she was humming quietly to herself. A familiar refrain that… No. It could not be.

His gut clenched. He felt ill. She was not… He refused to allow it.

Unable to stop himself, he walked stealthily around her, but she must have seen a movement from the corner of her eye, because she jerked upright, still on her knees, and looked up at him, her face pink with exertion—

'Rose!'

She winced at his shout.

* * *

Staring at the Duke, Rose felt horror roll through her in a sickening tide. Another half-hour and she would have been hidden away in the kitchens for the rest of the day.

He was staring at her as if he expected her to say something. She dropped the rag, wiped her hands on her apron and pushed to her feet.

She bobbed a curtsy, keeping her head respectfully lowered, her gaze on the floor, wishing he'd walk away. Or that the floor would crack open and swallow her up. 'Your Grace.'

All she could see were his feet planted squarely on the patch of marble she'd scrubbed clean. She waited for him to move on. She didn't dare look at his face, at the disgust she'd see in his expression.

Or the anger.

'Well?' he said softly, menacingly. 'Are you going to explain?'

'Explain what?' She winced. She hadn't intended to speak out loud. A glance upwards at his implacable expression sent a shiver down her spine. It was far worse than a show of anger. He looked merely curious. Almost cold.

'Explain why you never told me that you work here.' He looked down his ducal nose.

'You do work here? Have been working here for some time?'

And was unlikely to be working here much longer. She nodded miserably. 'As a scullery maid.'

He folded his arms across his chest. 'So what were you doing in the Green Room the other evening?'

She shrugged. 'I had been mending the gown. I tried it on to see...' Dash it, if she was going to be let go, it might as well be for the true reason. 'I wanted to see what I would look like in such a lovely gown.'

His frown deepened.

She held her breath, waiting for the full force of his wrath.

'You made me think you were gently bred. A lady.' Not angry, disappointed.

What right did he have to be disappointed? 'If you'd thought me a lady, you would not have met me in private or kissed me without permission.' She winced at her scolding tone. What was the point of feeling embarrassed? She was what she was and she cared nothing for his opinion, good or bad.

Only she did. Heat rushed to her face and she let her gaze fall away. 'I apologise, Your Grace. I—I did not set out to trick you. It simply happened. I should never have met you in the garden, however. For that I am sorry.'

His feet did move away then. A few steps and then silence. She looked up, expecting him to be gone, not to find him perched on the second step of the stairs up to the great subscription room.

He gestured for her to come closer and she found it odd when she approached that she was in fact looking down on him by an inch or two.

It made him seem less imposing, less of a threat and more like the man she had met in the garden. As if they were somehow equals. They were not. A fact she would do well to remember.

'This time you will tell me the truth, if you please.'

She clenched her hands at her waist. 'What is it you want to know?'

He narrowed his eyes at her obvious defensiveness.

What did it matter? She was going to lose her job anyway. She shrugged.

'Very well. What is your real name?'

'Rose Nightingale.'

He made a face of disbelief.

'Is too,' she said.

'Very well, Miss Nightingale. How long have you worked at Vitium et Virtus?'

'Four months or so.'

'Do you live in or out?'

She hissed in a breath. Why did he want to know that? Only a few of the employees here lived in. He must know that, being an owner and all.

'Out.'

The answer was received with a heavy silence.

'I will collect my things and leave.' What else could she say? Clearly she had lost any regard he might have held for the woman he thought she was. An ache scoured the inside of her chest. She was wrong to have let herself be swept up in what was really was no more than a foolish dream.

'You want to leave?' he asked.

She frowned at him. A horrid suspicion entered her mind. Did he want to continue where they had left off only…? Now he knew who she was…what she was, would he treat her differently? With less respect?

'I think it is for the best.'

He regarded her for a long moment. 'You are going home?'

'Yes.'

'To your family.'

Truth. She had to tell him the truth. She had said she would. And then he really would despise her utterly. 'I have no family left that I know of.' She lifted her chin.

'Oh, Rose,' he said, shaking his head, sorrowfully.

'I have done nothing to be ashamed of.' Her face flushed again. 'Nothing that has brought harm to anyone else.' Even if she was a bastard. Born on the wrong side of the blanket, the nobs called it. She called it irresponsible.

To her surprise, he looked startled, as if her declaration surprised him. What? Did he think because she had no family, *she* was some sort of undesirable? Or worse yet, a woman of low moral character? She closed her eyes briefly. That was it, most likely. And now, like a lackwit, she had as good as told him there was no one in the world who cared what happened to her. 'Besides, it is none of your business where I go from here.' She turned away.

'Rose, wait.'

She swung back to face him.

He rose to his feet. 'You don't need to go.'

'Are you saying I haven't lost my position?'

He approached her warily, as if she might

bite him if he got too close. 'No, I mean. Well, obviously I would find it difficult when…'

She narrowed her eyes at him. 'When?'

He rubbed a palm over his jaw in an odd upward motion. 'I mean, I do not like to think of you…well, scrubbing the floors.' He gestured at the rag and bucket in the middle of the floor.

She frowned. 'There is nothing wrong with scrubbing floors.'

'You could be so much more.'

Anger bubbled up at the disdain in his tone. More? Such as being his mistress, perhaps? What else could he mean? 'I am perfectly content, thank you. I certainly don't need to make my living…' She stopped before she said something really rude.

'I intended no insult, Rose.'

He was the one who sounded insulted. He had gone all ducal, looking down that lordly nose of his.

She was a fool for letting herself be swept up by a dream. Really, she was. 'I wouldn't like Your Grace to feel uncomfortable with my presence. So I will remove it.'

He reached out as if to stop her. She jerked away, and a look of chagrin passed over his face. Followed swiftly by a haughty stare. 'Very well. If you insist. Go.'

She breathed a sigh of relief, tempered by a large dose of despair.

She had liked working here. And the rules had protected her from unwanted attentions, as they had not in the residences where she had worked. Until she'd gone and broken those rules. She was going to miss her friends, too. Especially Flo.

Inwardly she groaned as the full implications of her stupidity landed in the pit of her stomach like a rock. Once her landlord learned she had lost her job, she'd be out on the street, unless she found another one quickly. She would certainly never find another employer as generous as the V&V.

She picked up her bucket and rag. Perhaps if she apologised properly he would let her stay?

When she turned back to ask him, he had gone. For a big man, he moved very quietly. The reason she hadn't heard him when she had been foolishly prancing around in the Green Room and again today when she'd been washing the floor.

Sadly, she shook her head and walked to the lower reaches of the house. If one of the owners of the club wanted her gone, what could be done?

She almost fell over when he stepped in front of her as she was about to enter the kitchen. She backed up hastily. 'I thought you went.'

'I came back.'

She tried not to roll her eyes. 'Was there something else?'

'I—' He huffed out a breath. 'You don't have to go. Keep your job. Just—just keep out of my way. All right?'

It took a moment to process the words. She nodded stiffly. 'Then please be aware, Your Grace, I am required to wash the floor in the front hall every day at five-thirty in the morning and it takes me half an hour.'

'I take note, Miss Nightingale.'

She gritted her teeth. 'It's Rose, Your Grace. Just Rose.' A duke did not offer courtesy to a servant, not if he didn't want to cause talk.

'Rose. Good day.'

Good? What was good about today? This wasn't finished. She could feel it in her bones and down her spine. But the reprieve would give her a chance to find a new position before he changed his mind and she was let go without a character.

As the day progressed she became less worried about him changing his mind. All seemed just as usual. No calls by Mrs Parker to see her in her office. As a precaution, she stayed close to the kitchen, never being tempted into visiting her friends in case she ran into the Duke. When, at the end of the work day there was still no threat of dismissal, she heaved a sigh of relief. It seemed all was well. She scuttled out of the side door as quick as a wink, not wanting to tempt fate by lingering in the Green Room.

'Rose.'

A tall lean shadow detached itself from the darkness in the alley outside the back door.

She swallowed the dryness in her throat. Her heart sank. 'Why are you here, Your Grace?'

'I want to talk to you.'

Here it came then, after all. Her notice.

'Allow me to escort you home. We can talk while we walk.'

'I'm not taking you to where I live. I am a decent girl, I am.' Her landlord would be scandalised. Well, perhaps not. He didn't seem to care about that sort of thing, given what his other tenants were up to. But she didn't want anyone getting the wrong impression about her. It wouldn't take much and coming home on the arm of a toff like him would do it.

The Duke frowned and looked about him. 'You can't surely be intending to walk the streets alone.'

'Today is no different to any other day, Your Grace.'

He looked nonplussed. 'You will, however, permit me to walk you, if not all the way, then at least to the end of your street.'

The firmness in his voice said he was not to be denied.

'As you wish,' she muttered. She'd find a way to be rid of him long before then. She knew the neighbourhood like the back of her hand, whereas he surely did not.

They walked some distance in silence and she kept waiting for him to tell her she was dismissed. Finally she could not stand it any longer. 'What is it you wished to talk about?'

He gave her a look askance. 'I have a request to make of you. Well, more of a proposition, I suppose.'

Her heart stilled. Did she really want this? She gripped her basket tight.

Jake could not figure out what was the matter with him. He was usually so articulate, so charming around women. With Rose, he kept stumbling over his words like an adolescent stumbling over feet too large for a gangly body. And heaven knew, every time he opened his mouth he seemed to put one of those very large feet right in it.

He also noticed that while Rose seemed willing to let him walk beside her, she deliberately kept her small basket over the arm closest to him. Effectively keeping him at a distance.

Well, perhaps that wasn't such a surprise. He'd been so horrified to see her on her hands and knees that morning he'd been unable to think straight. A nap had sorted him out, somewhat. After all, finding her, knowing where she was, had enabled him to relax enough to actually close his eyes without being haunted by images— He cut the thought off. Nonsense.

He had been able to relax merely because loose ends drove him to distraction. Rose was no longer a loose end. That was all.

'What is this...proposition?' she asked, clearly irritated by his continuing silence.

'It is a matter of some delicacy,' he said, trying to frame what he wanted to say in a way she would not take amiss. He'd rehearsed it a couple of different ways in his mind, but as her responses to him in the past were always such a surprise they threw him off stride, he wasn't quite sure how to put it.

'Are you asking me to keep your confidence in this matter, Your Grace?'

There, that was what had intrigued him about her. Her quick understanding. Her sharpness of mind.

'I am. More than one matter, actually, but we will take them one at a time.'

She nodded firmly. 'I am no gossipmonger.'

He tried to squash his scepticism, given his intimate knowledge of the female gender, and was conscious of squaring his shoulders. 'It is with regard to my current living arrangements.'

She looked at him sharply. 'Go on.'

They turned on to Cheapside. He gritted his teeth. The idea that Rose walked these streets alone had his anger building again, as it had when he'd learned of her address from the housekeeper. The woman had frowned at him mightily when he'd asked for it. Worse yet, she'd more or less told him to leave the girl alone, as if he had the reputation for being some sort of lecherous beast who preyed on servant girls.

A look of the sort his father used to give *him* when he was a lad had put her in her place. An incivility for which no doubt an apology would be required at some time in the future. The woman had told him all he needed to know without further demure.

'To be honest the house has seemed empty since my—' he forced the words past his lips '—since my father and brother died. It needs a feminine touch. My grandmother is rather elderly and cannot cope.' He grimaced. 'With anything really. She keeps mostly to her rooms.' Only emerging to nag him about getting married. About the need for a legal grandchild to inherit. But that was not Rose's business. That was his problem to solve in the future when he had mastered his ducal duties.

He plunged on, surprisingly anxious to have her answer. 'I wanted to offer you the position.'

A small silence ensued. His throat tightened. He risked a peek at her face. Her lovely mouth was set in a thin straight line. 'You want me to live in your house.'

'It wouldn't work any other way. You will be well paid, of course. Far more than your wage as a scullery maid.'

For a moment she looked torn, then her chin firmed. 'I cannot.'

Cannot? He didn't understand. 'I will, of

course, provide you with a suitable wardrobe. You do not have to worry about—'

'This is my street. I bid you good day, Your Grace.'

And before he could say another word she took her heels and ran into the nearest alley.

Not her street.

A long way from her street.

In one of the worst neighbourhoods in London.

Damn it all. Why had she run, when he'd likely made the best offer of a job she had ever received in her life or was ever likely to receive?

I cannot.

A strange feeling entered his chest, sharp, ugly. Did she have a husband? A child? Such impediments would account for her reaction.

Face it, man. She didn't want the job. There were lots of women who would be thrilled to get such an offer. Find someone else and leave Rose to it.

Yet what had he said to make her upset enough to dash off down a street nowhere near where she lived? At the very least he ought to ensure she had arrived home safely and that she understood her current position at Vitium et Virtus was secure.

Did he really want to know what was stopping her from taking what had been an outstandingly generous offer?

He sighed. He really had no choice if he wanted to sleep tonight, though why that was the case when he barely knew the girl, he could not fathom.

Chapter Four

Rose perched on the edge of the small truckle bed tucked beneath the eaves in her rented chamber.

Pressure built behind her cheekbones. A lump formed in her throat while the backs of her eyes scalded. She clenched her hands together trying to breathe. She would not cry.

A sob escaped.

She swallowed it down and glanced around the shabby room. At the brave flutter of floral fabric covering the window. At the scrap of carpet beside the bed she'd bargained for at the market. At the worn-out broom she'd salvaged from the rubbish bin at the V&V. She could not help comparing what she had to what the Duke of Westmoor had offered.

She didn't know if she was upset because he

had made such a dreadful offer, or because she had turned him down.

A bitter smile pulled at her lips. Likely a bit of both.

He was such a handsome, charming man. Sometimes. When he wasn't making tempting offers that undermined her efforts to maintain the standards she'd set for herself so many years ago.

She dashed a tear from her cheek that seemed to have escaped without her knowledge.

What was she to do? Her stomach pitched. This time he would see her dismissed. She was sure of it. She shouldn't have run. She should have thanked him before refusing.

The thought hit her like a blow.

She should have explained why she did not want to be his mistress. He wasn't a bad man. He was simply man who expected to get his way in all things. She had met enough of those in her time and he was, after all, a duke. But she did not think him deliberately cruel. If she had explained, he might have understood.

Or not. But at least she would have had her say instead of running away like a coward.

Truth be told, if she had stayed, she might well have said yes. The thought of his kisses and the tender way he'd held her in his arms when they danced had tempted her sorely.

That same temptation had led her into the mistake of meeting him in the garden, of seeing him one last time to tell him they should not meet again. Clearly he now thought her a low sort of creature, given the way she earned a living.

The rosy dreams she'd been clutching to her heart since the hours spent in the garden turned to ashes before her closed eyes.

Not that she'd expected to see him again. She really hadn't. She'd simply enjoyed the dream. It made the day pass faster and the drudgery of her life seem less hard.

This offer made a mockery of those innocent imaginings. Didn't she know better than to have dreams? Had she not learned to live day to day? To survive by hard work and keeping herself to herself? She'd let herself be lured into the pitfall of wanting more and look what he'd offered. Hope. It was such a stupid thing.

A cacophony, louder than usual, drifted up from the street below. An argument. Someone run afoul of her landlord, no doubt. Someone unable to pay their rent.

She shivered. She'd seen more than one family evicted from this house for that crime.

Heavy footsteps thumped their way up the stairs. She expected them to stop on the floor below. More than one set, she thought. No one ever came all the way up to her little garret. And yet something about the determination in those steps brought her to her feet.

They did not stop until they arrived at her landing. A fist thumped on her door.

'Who is it?' Her voice was not as firm as she would have liked.

'It is I, Miss Nightingale.'

The cultured accents were unmistakable. Westmoor. How on earth had he found her?

''E says 'e's a friends of yourn,' the belligerent tones of her landlord added. 'Shall I throw 'im down the stairs?'

'I'd like to see you try, my good man.'

'Would yer? Put 'em up, I says.'

Goodness, they were going to come to fisticuffs on her landing.

She rushed to slide the bolt and open the door.

The Duke, with nary a hair out of place, was grinning conspiratorially at her landlord. Money went from a ducal fist to a grimy grasping hand. Blast the man.

'Miss Nightingale.' The Duke removed his hat and bowed.

'You tricked me.'

'As you tricked me. May I come in?'

'I did not trick you.'

A movement on the staircase caught her eye. Old Mrs Carter was at the forefront of a growing group of spectators. Oh, this really was too much. Her reputation was going to be ruined.

She opened the door wider. 'Please come in.' She certainly did not want her neighbours listening to the conversation that was about to ensue.

The Duke ducked his head beneath the lintel and entered. The ceiling was too low for him to stand fully upright. Wincing, she gestured to the only chair in the room. 'Please, be seated.'

He eased his large frame on to the rickety chair as if fearing it would splinter beneath him and looked around.

Shame filled her.

Followed by anger.

She'd been proud of her little room. Her own place, rented with the money she'd earned. 'What are you doing here?'

He started to rise. 'A gentleman may not sit in the presence of a standing lady.'

They couldn't? There was nowhere for her to sit but on the edge of the bed. She perched there and clasped her hands in her lap to stop herself from throwing something at him. Or perhaps to hold herself together from flying into a thousand miserable pieces now he knew the full extent of her poverty.

'I came to make sure you arrived home safely.'

She stared at him. 'I manage to arrive home safely every day without any help. What you have done is made every occupant of this house wonder about my respectability.'

He gave an impatient sigh. 'This is not where you should be living, Rose. You deserve better.'

'What would be better about being your mistress?' The words were out before she thought about them. Heat scalded her cheeks. Her stomach twisted in a knot. She fixed her gaze on the patch in her carpet. 'Please. Go. You can let Mrs Parker know I won't be working at the V&V any longer. I have found another job.'

She clenched her hands harder and prayed she would be able to do so.

'Rose.' His voice sounded grim.

What now? Would he strike out? Like the first gentleman whose advances she'd refused. She'd left that position. And several more after it.

She risked a glance at his face, ready to run or to defend her honour. Not easy when one was already sitting on the bed.

The stern, aloof Duke stared back at her. 'I beg your pardon,' he said stiffly. 'My behaviour led you to misconstrue my intentions.'

Misconstrue? She frowned. Not a familiar word.

'Misunderstand,' he said as if realising the source of her puzzlement, 'from the Latin *construere*.'

'What is to misunderstand?' she asked, quelling her interest in his explanation.

He tugged at his neckcloth. 'The position I was offering in my house was not as my…' He pursed his lips as if he had a bad taste in his mouth. 'It was as something else.'

An odd feeling pierced her chest. A feeling of hurt. Because she wasn't good enough or pretty enough or something to be his mistress?

'You want to hire me as a servant in your house?' She felt queasy at the thought of making up the fire in his room as he slept, possibly not alone. Of cleaning and polishing his floors as he walked passed her, unseeing with his friends. Of said friends pinching her bottom. They were the sorts of things that had kept her moving from one job to another. It was also the reason why the V&V with its rules and regulations for servants and customers alike had been so perfect.

She shook her head. 'I—'

'I want to offer you the position of companion to my grandmother.'

As the words began to make sense, she couldn't help a bitter laugh. 'A companion to your grandmother? Is this some sort of jest?'

Even she knew such a position was well above her station. She wasn't even good enough to be his mistress, for heaven's sake.

'She's lonely. She doesn't go out much. Normally such a position would fall to an indigent relative.' He shuddered. 'The only such females available are not those I would wish under my roof. You won't find it onerous. Grandmama rarely leaves the house, but she needs someone to help write her letters, fetch and carry and make sure she eats. That sort of thing. My duties mean she is frequently without any company at all. Or any…supervision. My sister is busy with her young daughter, or I would ask her. I honestly think Grandmama would take to you. You are honest, kind and, Mrs Parker informs me, one of the few under her supervision who can read and write well.'

Mrs Parker. Of course, that was how he had discovered her whereabouts. Why hadn't she thought of that? Still, she couldn't help but approve of a man who so obviously cared about his grandmother. Cared about his family. How could she not? It was all she had ever longed for in the deepest regions of her heart. A home. A family who loved her.

For one blissful moment acceptance hovered on her tongue, then the enormity of what he was asking struck her. Yes, she could read and write, but she was nowhere near well enough educated to mix with her betters. 'I'm sorry, it wouldn't work. I wouldn't know how.'

He gazed at her from beneath lowered brows, his jaw a determined jut.

This was a man to whom people did not usually say no. She steeled herself for an argument. 'Truly, I cannot. Your grandmother needs a proper lady. I couldn't possibly—'

'Rose,' he said, his voice deep and dark and delicious as he interrupted her speech. 'You are every bit as much a lady as one who bears the title. You speak as well as any lady I know, act like a lady and no one would think otherwise unless they knew. I certainly didn't.'

'I don't always speak like a lady. I don't understand all those long words you use. And what if your grandmother learns I am one big fat lie. Wouldn't she be angry?'

He shook his head. 'Who will tell her? We

shall say you were previously employed by a distant relative on my mother's side.'

'And what of your friends? Will you tell them that, too?'

'What I do, who I employ, is no one's business but mine.'

'How arrogant,' she muttered. Inwardly, she smiled at finding a use for the word she'd read in the newspaper that morning. When he pressed his lips together, she thought she might finally have annoyed him enough to make him leave her in peace.

But, no, he continued to view her with that intense gaze of his, as if he saw right through her. A look seemed to melt her from the inside out.

'At least speak with my grandmama before turning it down. Who knows, she may not offer you the position. She can certainly be a bit difficult at times.'

The poor man looked…worried. She almost felt sorry for him. Fortunately, his grandmother would have more sense than he had and she would not look at Rose with such hopefulness, either. 'And when she turns me away, you'll leave me in peace? Never speak to me again?'

He inhaled a quick breath. 'I will never

speak to you first. However, should you speak to me, I will respond.'

Like that would ever happen. 'And I will keep my position at the V&V if she does not decide in my favour?'

'Naturally.'

Strangely, she had every faith he would keep his word. Which was odd, because she rarely trusted anyone. 'Very well, then. Let us go and meet your grandmother.'

He gave her a startled glance. Clearly he had not expected her to give in so quickly. She smiled sweetly. 'Is something wrong?' Like the drab gown she was wearing? Or her rough work-reddened hands?

'Not a thing,' he said more cheerfully than she expected. 'While we walk, I will explain a few of the niceties of meeting a duchess, if I may.' He gave her a piercing blue stare. 'You do plan to give this a good shot, I hope.'

Fair was fair. 'I will do my best.'

'That is all I ask.'

As he escorted her down the stairs and out into the street, she had the feeling he was smirking as if he thought he had won, though his face showed nothing. Hah. One look at her servant's garb and his grandmother would show her the door. And that would be that. Life would go back to the way it was before.

The thought gave her a queer little pang in the centre of her chest.

At the sight of his own front door, Jake breathed a sigh of relief. All during their long walk, he'd half-expected Rose to bolt again. If she had, he had no doubt she'd do everything in her power to make sure he didn't find her a second time. And then how would he ever be free of his irrational worry for her safety.

He still couldn't stop thinking about what might have happened to her if some other man had caught her waltzing around in that particular dress with that particular look on her face.

It was a sight no red-blooded male could have resisted. He certainly hadn't had the strength of will. He couldn't help thinking about what had almost happened to her at *his* hands because he had completely misread who and what she was. He'd not had a clue she was an employee.

It had been pounded into his head by his father from an early age that a gentleman never exploited a servant beneath his roof. It wasn't done. Yet he'd come far closer to breaking that rule than he liked to think.

Of course, he could have ignored her once he did know and simply thanked his stars for a lucky escape. He would have, too, if she hadn't seemed so damnably vulnerable.

Simply watching the sensual movement of her body while she was washing the floor had heated his blood to boiling. Sooner or later one of the coxcombs who haunted Vitium et Virtus would have spotted her and, rules or no rules, taken advantage.

Jake could not abide the thought. The tightness the idea caused in his gut was not jealousy, could not possibly be jealousy. It was merely the need to protect a good but naive young woman from harm.

When he'd gone to her lodging, he hadn't quite known what he intended, but the moment he'd seen the bright scrap of fabric fluttering at the window of her shabby room, along with the worn bit of rug so neatly patched on the floor, every instinct within him rebelled at leaving her there.

He'd felt so strongly he'd ridden roughshod over her objections. Was still riding roughshod, truth to tell.

When a footman opened the door at the ducal mansion, Jake stifled a grin at the way the man hid his surprise at the sight of Rose who was also in for a surprise.

While his grandmother could be starchy, she had never considered herself above her fellow man—or woman. She was the direct descendent of a yeoman long-bowman who fought at Crécy, as she would tell anyone who cared to listen.

He waved the butler away when he stepped forward to take his hat and gloves and instead deposited them on the hall table. The less intimidating things seemed, the more likely he was to win this round.

Rose, who had no outer raiment to remove, kept her gaze fixed straight ahead, her chin up in brave defiance.

Yet tension stiffened her shoulders and a twinge of guilt at her discomfort assaulted Jake's conscience. He pushed the notion aside. After all, she was the one who had issued the final challenge.

'Her Grace?' Jake enquired of the butler.

'In her withdrawing room, Your Grace,' the butler said.

Jake winged an elbow at Rose. 'Shall we, Miss Nightingale?'

'We shall,' she said, her voice little more than a whisper and tinged with dread.

Damn it all. She was far more nervous than she appeared on the outside. 'She doesn't bite, you know.'

She didn't relax.

They climbed the stairs up to the first floor and into the east wing. His rooms were in the west wing. Or rather that was where he still kept his things. The ducal chambers were also located here in the east wing. He never used them.

The first time he had entered his father's bedroom he had felt like an intruder. Or an impostor. Or perhaps a very bad actor. The underserving villain in a play.

He opened the door to his grandmother's suite and ushered Rose in with a light touch to the small of her back.

'Grandmama, I would like you to meet a young lady introduced to me by a distant relative of my mother's. Your Grace, Miss Rose Nightingale. Miss Nightingale, Her Grace, the Dowager Duchess of Westmoor.'

Rose sank into a curtsy fit for royalty, but since his grandmother was related to some of those, it was not completely out of place.

Startlement appeared in those ancient grey eyes for the merest moment, then Grandmother smiled. 'Miss Nightingale. What a pleasure. How delightful. Are you visiting in town?'

'Miss Nightingale is seeking employment,' Jacob said, as he informed Rose he would during their walk to his house. 'Her present position is unsuitable.' It was the truth. He ignored Rose's gasp of shock.

Rose blushed, but her gaze held anger when she shot him a glance.

'My dear Miss Nightingale,' Grandmama said, 'anyone instrumental in bringing my grandson to see me is welcome in this house.' She frowned at Jake. 'I so rarely see him these days.'

'Grandmama,' Jake scolded, with an apologetic smile. 'Miss Nightingale will think I neglect my duty.'

'You neglect your pleasures, my boy, you are so busy fulfilling your duties. Ring the bell for tea, do. Miss Nightingale, please, be seated.' She patted the sofa cushion on her right.

A good sign. If she had been dismayed or displeased she would have pointed to the chair at the end of the tea table. A chair known for its discomfort. No visitor stayed long seated upon that chair.

As long as Rose didn't decide to reveal exactly where she had been employed all should be well.

He tugged at the bell pull and reclined in his usual armchair.

'Grandmama, I believe Miss Nightingale would make you an excellent companion. I am sorry we did not give you any advance notice, but it did not occur to me until this very morning.'

His grandmother looked intrigued. 'What sort of employment have you undertaken in the past, Miss Nightingale?'

Rose lifted that stubborn little chin and Jake had the urge to nip at it. And then to kiss her luscious lips even though he knew by the martial look in her eye she planned to foil his plan.

'I have been working as a scullery maid.' She sounded as if she expected to be thrown out on her ear. Extraordinary bravery.

His grandmother stiffened. His stomach dipped. It seemed he did not know her as well as he thought.

The elderly lady narrowed her gaze on Rose, but there was a gleam of amusement in those faded eyes Jake hadn't seen for many months. 'A scullery maid.'

Rose nodded firmly.

'Good honest labour, Miss Nightingale, but

beneath you, I think. My grandson was right to bring you to me.'

Rose's jaw dropped. 'But—'

The butler entered with his usual troop of footmen who glided about until the tea tray was properly presented before departing on silent feet.

'Please, Miss Nightingale,' Grandmama said, 'do pour. My hands are a little shaky at times and it makes it all such a chore.'

With a startled glance directed at Jake, Rose did as directed, making an exceedingly creditable job of it, too.

'Where did you learn such skills, Miss Nightingale?' Grandmama asked gently.

'I trained as a housekeeper,' Rose said. Her expression held surprise as she set the teapot back in its place. 'My age has precluded my obtaining such a position as yet.'

'Trained where?'

'The Foundling Hospital.'

'I see.'

It was his grandmother's turn to shoot him a look that spoke volumes, or it would have were he able to translate its meaning.

'Do you know anything about your parents, Miss Nightingale?' Grandmama asked.

Rose stiffened. Looked uncomfortable.

Jake had the urge to stand between her and his grandmother's probing questions, but it would not do. If she could not stand up for herself, then her grandmother would dismiss her as missish.

Grandmama's eyes narrowed. 'I beg your pardon, my dear. I do not wish to pry. I was merely curious.'

Rose drew in a breath. 'I know nothing at all.' From her pocket she drew out a little pouch. A needle case that looked as if it had been stitched by a child. She unfolded it and brought forth a broken mother-of-pearl button. 'I have this half-token. But no one returned to claim me.'

Grandmama's eyes swam with tears for a brief instant. So brief, Jake thought he might have been mistaken and Rose did not see it at all, since she was busy tucking away her treasures. At the thought of her always being alone in the world his throat felt deucedly tight.

Grandmama sipped at her tea, her expression thoughtful.

Rose handed him his cup. Nothing ventured, nothing gained. He took a mouthful. Perfect. He glanced at his grandmother over the rim. 'Well, Your Grace. What do you think? Will you accept Miss Nightingale as a companion? Knowing someone is keeping an eye on you will relieve my mind of a worry while I toil away at the mountain of paperwork on my desk.'

Rose kept her gaze firmly fixed on her hands in her lap. She had not touched her tea. Clearly she expected rejection.

Grandmama shot him a glance. 'Highly recommended I think you said, Jacob.'

'Very highly recommended.'

'By a relative of your mother's? One you have confidence in?'

'Indeed.'

Grandmama smiled. 'Miss Nightingale, do you think you can bear the company of a crotchety old lady day after day?'

Jakes shoulders felt suddenly a great deal lighter.

Rose's jaw dropped. 'You actually want me to be your companion? Surely some lady of rank would be better suited—'

'A lady of rank would likely drive me to distraction within a week,' Grandmother said. 'Sniffing about each request. Complaining about lost advantages. Tippling at the brandy when she thinks I am not looking.'

Jaw dropping, Rose looked at him for confirmation.

'Her Grace is right,' he said lazily, casually.

'Cousin Susan, before she went home to her mother, was always half-seas over. It was why Grandmama sent her packing.'

'That wasn't the half of it,' Grandmama said. 'I caught her snooping about in my correspondence. Not something Miss Nightingale would be about, I am sure.'

Rose shook her head.

'And you won't be stealing the silverware either, I'll be bound.'

'Grandmama!'

'Well, that nurse you hired certainly did.' She adjusted the shawl over her shoulders with a little twitch at the fabric. 'I'm missing one of your grandfather's snuffboxes. His favourite, to boot.'

'Perhaps it is simply misplaced,' Rose said with a placating smile.

'Perhaps,' Grandmama admitted. 'And perhaps you will help me find it. That is, if you will accept the position?'

Rose's eyes widened.

Jake watched with bated breath as she considered the offer. Finally she nodded slowly. 'Yes. I will, Thank you. Thank you both. I will do my very best to please.' Rose smiled. It was bright and happy and hopeful. It came from within and seemed to shove warmth at the cold empty feeling in Jake's chest.

'Excellent,' Grandmama said, beaming. 'Jake, you will inform the staff and have Miss Nightingale taken up to her room. The same one Cousin Susan used. Once she is settled, she and I will go through Eleanor's wardrobe and see what clothes are suitable for making over.'

It seemed Grandmama had found a project. She already looked brighter than she had for weeks.

Rose glanced self-consciously at her drab skirts. 'Really, I couldn't impose on your generosity.'

'Nonsense. You must and you will, for I cannot have my companion looking as if she is underpaid. People will think me a nip-farthing and that I cannot allow.'

'People?'

'Well, there are bound to be callers now we have put off black gloves. And morning calls when you are up to snuff.'

The look on Rose's face said she thought that would never happen. He wanted to grin at her, or chuck her under the chin; instead he simply nodded his agreement.

Grandmama turned on him with a sly smile and a gleam in her eye. 'It is certainly time the new Duke took up that side of his duties. He needs to find a bride.'

Jacob's stomach sank to his shoes. Blast the woman. He'd been hoist by his own petard. But he could see from his grandmother's determined expression that if he wanted to haul Rose out of that dreadful slum, he was going to have to bow to his grandmother's wishes in this matter. He should have guessed she'd turn matters to her own advantage.

He became aware of Rose watching him with an air of hope. Hope he would turn his grandmother down, no doubt.

'I shall look forward to it.'

Warily Rose edged into the stables at the back of the house and passed the first stall. The beast with its head hanging over the halfdoor was enormous. Terrifying. It rolled its brown eyes and blew a hay-scented breath in her direction. Where was the blasted man?

These past few days had moved far too fast for Rose's comprehension. Her Grace had swept her along on a tide of dressmakers, milliners and hairdressers, not to mention shoemakers and assorted other tradesmen indispensable to the companion of a duchess. The worst part of it all was not understanding why Westmoor, as she was now to call him, really wanted her to take this position. Nor why a footman followed her all the while like a lost puppy, making privacy impossible.

When she had tried to send the young man about his business, he had looked anxious. Her Grace's orders, he had said. In case she became lost.

Only until she knew her way about, Her Grace had informed her, when she had asked. For example, did she know she was not to visit a gentleman alone? Should a lady ever, even by chance, you understand, be alone with a gentleman, then the door was to remain open at all times with a footman hovering a few feet away.

As if *she* was some sort of lady.

Finally, she had tracked the Duke down. After seeing him from her chamber window return from his morning ride, she had slipped out of the house by the side door and made her way to the stables.

She inched past the hind end of another large animal, this one nosing around in its manger. To her relief, the next stall contained the man she sought. She blinked. Busy grooming a horse, he had not noticed her presence and she paused, not sure if she dared interrupt. She'd heard much about the eccentricities of the nobility, but this menial work seemed a little odd, even for a duke who owned the most disreputable gentleman's club in London.

Coatless, with his shirtsleeves rolled up to the elbows displaying strong forearms dusted with dark hair, she had an excellent perspective of a pair of broad shoulders displayed to advantage. And a delicious view of a muscular rear end as he brushed the horse's glossy brown coat with long sweeping motions. Her insides clenched. Warmth suffused her skin.

She ought to close her eyes or turn away, she really ought, but she stood silently burning up inside, watching the elegant strength of him. Longing crept through her, as it did every time she encountered this man, despite the way he kept his distance.

The way she felt around him did not seem to lessen with familiarity, either. The more she saw of him, the more attractive she found him. Never before had she been so tempted by a man. It was the reason for her need to speak with him. To hand in her notice. She had to leave before she was overcome by desire.

Thank heavens he was not the least affected by her presence. When he noticed her at all, he seemed coolly amused.

The thought gave her courage.

'Your Grace?' It came out more of a whisper than actual words. She swallowed the dryness and tried again. Louder. 'Your Grace.'

He swung around, his eyebrows climbing to hide beneath the lock of dark hair that had fallen forward over his forehead. Something flashed in his eyes, gone too fast for her to be sure what it meant. The sweat trickling from his temple and trailing down his cheek riveted her attention. A sudden urge to taste that trail with her tongue stole her breath and left her speechless.

'Miss Nightingale.' His dark brows crashed down. 'What are you doing out here?' He seemed to be looking around for someone else. 'You should not be out here alone.'

The horse stamped an enormous hoof and she leapt backwards.

He patted the animal. 'Steady, boy,' he said gently, soothingly. 'You'll get your turn. Right now we have a guest.'

He gave her an encouraging smile, causing dimples to appear each side of his mouth, and her stomach to flutter. 'Old Sev, here, thinks I should be paying attention to him, instead of talking to you.'

She steeled herself against his charm. 'If you

hide from him, the way you hide from me, it is no wonder.'

The frown returned. 'I do not hide from you, Miss Nightingale. I see you at dinner when I am home. And in the drawing room afterwards. I very much enjoyed your reading from Gray's "Elegy" the other evening.'

Right. He'd enjoyed it so much he'd bid them goodnight after half an hour. 'I mean, we have not had an opportunity to speak privately.'

His lips thinned. 'Nor should we. As my grandmother's companion—'

'That is precisely what I wanted to talk to you about.'

He looked puzzled and perhaps even a little angry, or was it something else she saw reflected in his gaze? 'Is there a problem? The servants lacking in respect? If so—'

'No, no. Everyone has been most kind.' Extraordinarily respectful, in fact. As if she was some sort of duchess. Honestly? The only thing making her uncomfortable was him. Knowing he was there in the house, sensing his presence and feeling the disturbing need to seek him out as if there was more between them than employee and employer.

There wasn't. There could not be. Yet no matter how often she told herself not to think about him, her mind kept going back to his kiss until she could barely sleep of a night. Taking this position had been a very bad idea indeed. The last thing she needed was to be led astray by a nobleman. She knew where that would lead.

He grimaced, put the brush down on the top of the rail and wiped off his hands on a rag. 'Something is troubling you, Miss Nightingale, for you to seek me out here.'

He left the stall to loom over her. A half-step back and she was up against the central pillar. A snuffling from behind her made her jump and look around at yet another great beast observing her over the top of a half-door.

Westmoor put out steadying hand. A brief warm clasp on her elbow that sent hot shivers racing over her skin. She tried to ignore the reaction.

'Steady on.' He spoke in much the same tones as he had used on his horse. 'They wouldn't hurt you even if they weren't all safely gated and barred.'

She inhaled a deep breath. Tried for calm. All she succeeded in doing was breathing in the scent of horses and him. The spicy scent of his cologne overlaid with the clean sweat scent of a male engaged in hard physical labour. A man who bathed regularly, ran a dukedom, yet took pleasure in grooming his own horse.

She gripped her hands together. 'I want my old job back.'

Please let me go back.

Normally, Jake would have been far from pleased at being interrupted. The stable was one of the few places people left him alone. Gave him space to himself and his thoughts. His initial delight at seeing Rose in what he considered his domain had taken him aback. He'd been certain the distance he had created between them had solved the problem of his fascination. After all, a gentleman did not importune the females living under his roof.

He stared at her face, at the determination reflected in her eyes and her hands clasped tightly at her waist. He had no wish to keep her here against her will, but nor could he abide the thought of her returning to Vitium et Virtus or her old lodgings. 'You would really prefer to go back to scrubbing floors and living in that dreadful building rife with rats and dirt and surrounded by thieves and vagabonds than work for my grandmother?'

She stiffened as if insulted. 'There were no rats in my room.'

She had avoided his question. He moved a step closer. She had nowhere to go given the horse behind her. A suspicion arose in his breast. 'Is it my grandmother? Has she been too outspoken? Too testy? She's not the most patient person. Too used to getting her own way. Shall I speak to her for you?'

'Your grandmother is the soul of patience.' She gazed at him with pain in her eyes. 'But I feel like such a fraud. She has to explain the simplest things. A real lady would know these things.'

This was reason for her anxiety? 'I am sure she is only trying to be helpful.' He saw from the way she recoiled this had not helped. He shrugged. 'You catch on very quickly.' That did not seem to help, either.

He reined in his anger at the idea she wanted to leave and called upon reason. 'My dear girl, your fears are unfounded. A woman does not need a title to be considered a lady. I promise you no one would mistake you for anything else.'

She did not look in the slightest convinced.

'And besides, you can't leave, not when, for the first time in months, Grandmother is acting more like her old self. It is you who has wrought this change. It is not only your help she needs, I realise now, it is your company. She was lonely.'

Her eyes widened a fraction and for a second he saw a crack in her determination. She shook her head. 'Surely when your sister arrives—'

If only it were so. 'Eleanor will stay for a short time only and then Grandmama will be alone again.'

Rose gave him a look filled with suspicion. 'Could you not prevail upon her—?'

'No.' He stiffened, realising he was about to be rude when he wanted to be conciliatory. He knew he was overly defensive where his sister was concerned, but he feared he had said more than he should. 'I beg your pardon. Eleanor would not brook my interference in her life. Nor could I lay my duty on her shoulders. She has enough—' He shook his head at the urge to unburden himself about his sister. These were his concerns and not to be shared. 'My sister's business is—' Damn it all, now he was being rude.

'None of mine,' she finished. 'You don't have to mince words with me, Your Grace. But what will she think about the likes of me currying favour with your grandma when she arrives?'

'I can assure you Eleanor will be as glad to

see Grandmama come out of the doldrums as I am.'

She shook her head. 'It isn't right. Just look at this gown.'

'You look...' He stumbled over his choice of words. She looked divine in primrose yellow. The gown skimmed her lovely figure, emphasising her curves, without being immodest, and brought out the amazing light green of her eyes. They had a gold sunburst in the centre, he realised. Her blonde hair, professionally cut and coiffed, framed her face, enhancing her beauty. 'You look perfectly acceptable to me,' he temporised, not wishing her to take umbrage. He might as well have not bothered judging by her glower.

'Fine feathers do not fine birds make and it will take every bit of my wages to pay for it.' Her eyes glistened with moisture. She blinked it away.

His heart sank at the sight of her misery. 'Rose.' He wanted to hit something. 'The gown is a gift from my grandmama. Would you hurt her feelings and throw it back in her face?'

She shook her head. 'No,' she whispered. 'I just want to go back to the life I know.'

He leaned his forearm on the pillar, gazing into those worried green eyes, certain she was keeping something back. 'Tell me what is really troubling you.'

She swallowed the lump in her throat. 'Your grandma is talking about taking me with her to call on proper ladies. I am sure to put her to shame and then what?'

'Nonsense. You are making a mountain of a molehill. Nothing could be simpler.'

'To you, maybe. You were born into it.' Panic threaded through her voice.

A feeling of triumph went through him. Finally he had discovered the source of her worry. For this he had the perfect answer. 'Then I will go with you and make sure you do not make any fatal mistakes.' Though it would be a risky business spending too much time in Rose's company, for she offered far too much temptation. Hopefully his presence nearby would be enough to steady her, for it would not do to pay her too much attention with the old biddies looking on.

'She accepted an invitation to a Venetian Breakfast at Greenwich.'

He flinched.

Her expression turned to one of satisfaction. As if she knew she'd played a trump and won the trick. Well, he would not allow it. 'All the more reason for you to accompany her. If Eleanor were here, she would not go. It will be the first gathering Grandmama has attended since—' He took a deep breath. 'Since I came into the title. I must certainly go along and both she and I would be most grateful if you would agree to bear her company.'

She stared at him as if nonplussed. 'Grateful?'

'It will be hard on Grandmama, Rose. There will be condolences and sympathy. She will need your support as well as mine, for I cannot be at her side at all times.'

Her shoulders slumped. The urge to kiss away her fears was overwhelming. Especially since there was no one about to see.

'It is nothing to worry about, I assure you,' he said instead. 'A few old dowds and their menfolk having a picnic beside the river. I'll see you through it.'

'You promise?' she said grudgingly. She grimaced. 'It would please your grandma to have your escort, for sure. She worries that you are becoming reclusive.'

He felt distinctly disappointed that she had not said it would please *her* to have him along. 'It is my duty to escort you both.'

Her gaze slid away. 'Very well, I will stay, but only until she finds someone better. More suitable.' She narrowed her eyes. 'And you must promise me you will look for such a person.'

She really didn't trust him. Or was it men in general she didn't trust? Trust was something a man had to earn. He certainly hadn't earned his father's. Yet he was not prepared to give in on this. Not yet. 'Let me offer you a compromise. If you are still of the same mind in four weeks, I shall not put forth another objection to your departure. I will guarantee you your old job back and will pay you everything I promised. But please, for my grandmother's sake, give this opportunity a fair chance.'

She swallowed.

The salary he had offered her as a companion was more than she could earn in five years at the V&V and had been out-and-out bribery, but he didn't care. One of the few privileges of being a duke was getting what you wanted.

'Well?' he said.

Slowly she nodded. 'Three weeks more then, since I have already almost completed the first week.'

He stopped himself from laughing at her audacity. Damn, but he liked her spirit. 'It is not exactly a prison sentence, you know.' He put up a hand to prevent her from saying another word. 'All right. Three more weeks.'

He stuck out a hand. She clasped it, as if intending to shake on their agreement. Instead, he brought it to his lips and pressed a fleeting kiss to her knuckles. Her little shiver heated his blood. She was not as indifferent to him as she pretended. A heady blood-stirring thought he did not need.

Yet, unable to resist, he flashed her a charming grin. 'I will see you at dinner, Miss Nightingale, where we shall discuss which invitations we shall answer in the affirmative.'

'Affirmative?'

'Those to which we shall say yes.'

Her eyes widened for a second, but nodded. 'At dinner.' With wary glances at the horses, and a less-than-happy expression, she left as quietly as she had arrived.

He frowned. Was he being purely selfish in encouraging her to stay? Hardly. Being constantly in Rose's company and unable to do more than be polite would be hellish.

This was for his grandmother's sake. Nothing more.

So why was he now looking forward to the dinner hour more than he had in weeks?

Chapter Five

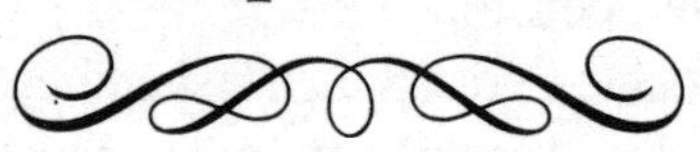

Chin pointed ceilingwards to permit the placing of an emerald in his cravat, an emerald much darker than the colour of Rose's light green eyes, Jake became aware of a strange sound issuing from his valet.

'Are you humming, Clacket?'

The sound stopped. 'I believe I am, Your Grace. I beg your pardon.' Clacket stepped back to admire his handiwork, his brown eyes bright in his round baby face.

'And what has you lifting your voice in joy, may I ask?'

Jake felt a bit like humming himself, which was odd. It was only dinner, but the prospect of sharing a meal with Rose always lifted his spirits and without the aid of brandy.

'Joy, Your Grace?' Creases formed between sandy brows. 'I supposed I am somewhat pleased. After all, it is the very heart and soul of a gentleman's gentleman to see his gentleman departing from his care well turned out. It has been a while since Your Grace has taken much of an interest in his appearance.'

And tonight he had permitted the man to trim his hair and shave him clean before dinner. 'So you deem me well turned out?'

Clacket pursed his lips and brushed a hand across Jacob's shoulder as if to smooth the material. 'Reasonably, Your Grace. Perhaps we might ask for a slightly better fit of the coat, but it would be nothing to take a seam in here or there, the coat being a little less snug than was your wont in the past, but otherwise...'

The coat was a little loose. Before the accident, Clacket would have struggled to get the coat on him. It had fitted like a second skin, as fashion demanded. Now, he slipped it on with ease. He must have lost weight. He frowned at himself in the pier glass. He'd dropped a stone at least. And he looked paler than normal. When and how had that occurred?

He was also hungry. It seemed his appetite had returned with a vengeance. Or was it simply that he was looking forward to crossing verbal swords with Rose? He had no doubt she would fight him every step of the way, when she realised just how many invitations he planned his grandmother would accept.

Invitations that six months ago he would have scorned as being a bore, given as how they tended to be small family affairs for those left in town over the summer. Card parties, the odd musical evening, or picnic, as well as the obligatory morning visits his grandmother deemed essential to a man seeking a wife.

Not that he was. Not yet. He wasn't ready to tread the path to the altar. But he was ready to get back on the social horse. To show his face in polite society on a regular basis. He'd not been to a single event since he'd thrown the ball for Fred and Georgiana. And curse any of them who muttered behind his back about his culpability. Or about Rose.

Indeed, the best part of it all would be escorting Rose to those events. He could not help but wonder what she would make of it all and was secretly looking forward to hearing her candid opinions.

Perhaps all the gadding about would also help him sleep. Clacket finished inserting his diamond shirt buttons and began the task of tidying up.

Humming under his breath, Jake went down

to the drawing room to await the ladies of the house.

Oliver joined him a few minutes later. His friend eyed him up and down. 'You are looking better than the last time I saw you.'

'You are not.' His friend looked rather harried.

'Why the urgent note to come to dinner?'

'I need your help.'

Oliver eyed him askance. 'Spit it out, man.'

'I have a young cousin up from the country. She's agreed to act as companion to my grandmother, but she needs a bit of town bronze. A formal dinner will bolster her confidence before we set out into the shark-infested waters of the *ton*.'

'Trying to pass a country bumpkin off on to the *ton*? Can't be done, old fellow. Sorry. They will spot her a mile off.'

He hadn't. 'I'll trust your judgement on that after you have met her, but I am sure Grandmama or I can help her over any rough spots.'

'Like a horse? Of all the queer starts you've ever had, Westmoor, this takes the cake, I must say, but I'm happy to spend an hour or so with Her Grace. She's a good old stick and has always been cordial.' His eyes gleamed. 'Besides, if you are going to poke a stick in the *ton's* eye, I don't mind being part of the action.'

Not everyone was forgiving of Oliver's background. As a boy he had taken great pains to never give them an opportunity to criticise him by maintaining the highest standards of good breeding. He would know if Rose was ready to face the *ton* and would not hesitate to say if she was not. 'I will abide by your opinion.' He poured them each a glass of sherry.

Oliver sipped his and nodded his approval. 'Nice vintage.' He turned as the door opened to admit the ladies and bowed. 'Your Grace.'

'Oliver. How lovely of you to join us,' Grandmama said. 'Miss Nightingale, let me make Mr Oliver Gregory known to you. He is a good friend of my grandson's.'

Rose curtsied the perfect depth for a non-titled gentleman. Grandmama had obviously started the task of moulding Rose into shape. She didn't want Rose to suffer embarrassment any more than he did.

'Can I pour you a sherry, Grandmama? Rose?' Jake asked.

'Miss Nightingale does not imbibe, Jake. But I will take a glass.'

'Perhaps some ratafia, or orgeat, Miss Nightingale,' Oliver said. While his expression was bland, Jake had no doubt he was inspecting her from her head to her heels and his tone indicated he was not displeased with what he saw.

'Thank you,' Rose said. Her smile was a little too warm for Jacob's taste. He forbore from saying so, but once she had her drink in hand he drew her towards the window and left Oliver catching up on gossip with his grandmother.

'When you reply yes to a gentleman you can be a little more haughty,' he said. 'No need to look as if he has offered you a special gift when he is simply doing his gentlemanly duty.'

'Sorry.'

'And no need to apologise for anything. A lady is always right. About most things anyway. Under the right circumstances.'

She frowned. 'I have no idea what you mean.'

And no wonder. He scarcely understood himself. Blast it. He had to stop thinking of her as his lady in red. She was now a female under his protection. Out of bounds. Was that not half the reason he had offered her the position in the first place? The other half, the need to protect her, was an aberration he must ignore. 'Never mind. You'll get the hang of it.'

The butler announced dinner and Oliver went ahead with his grandmother, while Jake brought Rose in on his arm.

Arm in arm they watched while Oliver demonstrated how to seat a lady and Grandmother demonstrated how a lady took her seat. Standing there with her on his arm, a strange sense of comfort filled him. Mentally he shook his head and held out Rose's chair. She accomplished the whole sitting down in skirts to the manner born. He felt an odd sense of pride at her elegance and style. As if he'd had something to do with it. It was all Rose herself. He had been foolish to worry about such a simple thing.

The rest of the meal was taken up with polite conversation and Jake desperately trying not to bash Oliver on the nose when he flirted with Rose—all in the cause of helping her get some polish, damn him.

By the time they partook of dessert, Rose was flagging. Her eyes were shadowed by effort and her smile strained.

'And now we ladies will retire for tea,' Grandmother said with a kind smile for her charge. 'We will leave these gentleman to their port. Will you be joining us in the drawing room later, Oliver?'

'I greatly beg your indulgence, Your Grace, but I have a previous engagement elsewhere for the rest of the evening.' He rose and came around to help Grandmama rise. Jake did the same for Rose.

Oliver bowed over Rose's hand. 'A pleasure to meet you, Miss Nightingale. I hope I have the felicitation of meeting you again.'

Rose frowned for a second as if puzzling out his meaning, then smiled her sweet lovely smile that had Jake once more wanting to shove the far-too-handsome Oliver out of the room.

Rose dipped a little curtsy. 'If you are going to Lady Dearbourne's Venetian Breakfast you will indeed be felicitated.'

Oliver's eyes danced. 'I would not miss it for the world.'

Rose followed his grandmother out of the room.

When the door closed behind them, Jake turned to Oliver. 'Well, what do you think?'

Oliver gave him a hard look. 'I think she is a delightful young woman. I have only one doubt.'

Jake tensed, concerned she had not passed muster in his friend's eyes. 'And that is?'

'Your intentions. Are you toying with that sweet *innocent* female?'

He bridled. 'Certainly not.'

'Good,' Oliver grunted. 'I saw the way she looked at you. Don't break her heart.'

Jake bristled.

Oliver cut him off. 'I really must go, old chap. By the way, my visit to the Club Plaisirs Nocturnes in Paris provided some novel ideas.'

'Thinking of bringing them to Vitium et Virtus?'

'I am. We are losing custom.'

'Boredom setting in. I'm bored with it myself. Not to mention up to my ears in work for the Duchy. Perhaps we should divest ourselves of it.

Oliver grimaced. 'I'd hate for Nicholas to come back expecting it to be here and...'

It always came back to the same thing. Their hope, forlorn though it was, that Nicholas would return. 'You are right. We should probably wait.'

A bit of a pall descended on them as Nicholas's ghost intruded. They'd kept it going in his memory after all.

Jake saw Oliver out and climbed the stairs to the drawing room. Only when he reached the top step did he realise he had left his port untouched in his eagerness to join the ladies. Or one particularly lady.

Damn it.

Rose lay in bed, looking up at the canopy. Blue silk, no less. How on earth had this happened? When would she wake up and discover it was all a dream?

Nightmare more like. Women like her did not end up under the roof of a gentleman for no good reason. Though his stated reason was for the sake of his grandmother, how could she believe him?

A strange uncomfortable feeling in the pit of her stomach made her roll over on to her side.

Moonlight poked fingers of light through the gaps in the curtain, casting strange shadows in unexpected places and forming bars of brightness across the counterpane.

Sleep seemed further away than ever. She should have brought the book of sermons she'd been reading to Her Grace. She'd been desperately trying not to yawn then, and Her Grace had actually dropped off for a minute or two. Bless the poor old dear, she'd had a very busy day.

Perhaps she should go and fetch the book from the drawing room. Another dose of that would surely have her eyes closing in no time.

Better yet would be a book she would actually enjoy reading. The house boasted a library. Her Grace had pointed it out, but they had never gone in there. Since Her Grace had a store of books in her chambers, there was no need to seek out more. Yet all of them were exceedingly dull.

Feeling too warm for comfort, Rose clambered out of bed and poured a glass of water from the jug on the nightstand. As she sipped she walked to the window and looked out.

The last time she had looked out she had seen the Duke heading out, probably to the V&V in pursuit of more manly entertainments than listening to her read to a sleepy grandmother.

She hated the idea of him going to the club.

There were girls there who would—she pushed the thought aside as an image of Flo came into her mind. She had sent Flo a note saying she'd found employment elsewhere, but little more by way of an explanation, which made her feel guilty and sad. Flo would miss her, she was sure, when no one else gave a fig for what became of her.

Somehow she would find a way to meet her friend and tell her the full story. One day.

She headed back for the bed, then changed her mind. There was no point in tossing and turning for hours. She'd get a book or two from the library and read until she fell asleep.

Another wonderful indulgence of this new life of hers. Books. Hundreds of them.

She pulled on her dressing gown, lit her bedside candle from the one in the sconces outside her door and headed downstairs.

The library was in the other wing. Passing through the dimly lit grand entrance hall, she was surprised at the lack of a footman on duty at the front door since His Grace had gone out.

Perhaps he had his own key.

The corridor to the rooms on the west wing's ground floor ended at the library, if she recalled correctly. She pushed open one of the great double doors and was delighted to see shelf upon shelf of books lining the walls in highly polished glass-fronted shelves. She lifted her candle to better see the titles.

At a sound her heart gave a hard thump. Her breath caught in her throat. She whirled around.

'Your Grace,' she gasped.

Chin resting on his palm, he stared at her from behind a table piled high with ledgers. His shirtsleeves glowed a startling white in the light of the moon coming through the window as he rose to his feet. 'Rose.'

So intent on her task, she hadn't seen him on the other side of the room. 'Why are you sitting in the dark?'

He made a soft sound and arched his back in

a stretch. 'The candle must have gone out.' He sounded surprised. 'I must have nodded off.'

She drew closer. 'You were working? I thought you left the house after dinner.'

'Keeping track of my movements, Miss Nightingale?' Now his voice sounded frosty.

'Not especially. You do pass right beneath my window on your way to the stables. I happened to be looking out when you headed that way.'

'I beg your pardon. You did indeed see me. I had intended to go…to go…well, out, but I changed my mind.'

She couldn't stop the glad little feeling that lifted her heart a fraction. 'What are you working on?'

He dragged his gaze from her face to the papers and account books. 'This month's reports from various properties and tenancies the Duchy owns.'

'Do you not have employees to do that sort of thing?'

He nodded and a small smile curved his lips. 'I do, but they are employees. It is important to check their work from time to time.'

As the housekeeper always checked the maid's work once a day to make sure no one was shirking their duties.

'And what brings you to my office in the middle of the night?'

His office? 'I was told this was the library.'

He shrugged and glanced around. 'It is more comfortable than the estate office where my man of business and my secretary are in and out all the time. Here, I can work without interruption.'

Unless someone like her started prowling around at night. He didn't say it, but she could imagine the words coming from his mouth without any difficulty.

'I should go.'

'Please don't. You came for a book. Perhaps I can help you find one.'

She gazed longingly at the lovely full shelves. 'I didn't expect quite so many to choose from. I am not even sure where to start. I'll come back another time.'

'I insist you take something with you.' He came around to her side of the desk. He lit his candle from hers. 'What did you have in mind?'

He was so tall.

And his shadow danced across the books, stretching up to the ceiling the closer he came. The scent of his cologne filled her nostrils. The warmth of his body penetrated her flimsy robe.

A small shiver passed down her spine. Not fear, but something altogether different. Pleasurable. She forced her mind to focus on their conversation. 'Something other than the books of sermons your grandmother enjoys.'

He smiled slightly. 'We have all kinds of books. Travelogues. Atlases. Flora and fauna. *The Farmer's Almanac. La Belle Assemblée.* Or if you would like something a little more entertaining, there are novels by Walter Scott or Fielding.'

She forced herself to listen to his words, rather than the dark and delicious cadence of his voice that seemed to beckon her closer. With some effort she kept her distance as he wandered the shelves naming the various works. So many books. She had no idea where to start.

'Of course there is always dear old Hannah More, if you feel in need of a bit of moral uplifting.'

'"*Forgiveness is the economy of the heart... forgiveness saves the expense of anger, the cost of hatred, the waste of spirits,*"' she quoted and chuckled ruefully. 'I have read lots of her work,' she said. 'They provided them at the—' She cut herself off. Her Grace had told her never again to mention the Foundling Hospital.

'It's all right, Rose. You don't have to pretend with me.'

'I shouldn't have to pretend at all.'

Jake did his absolute best not to look at Rose's sumptuous figure wrapped about in a lace so sheer he was sure as she entered the room he had seen… No, he was not going to think about it. He was a gentleman. She'd given him her trust.

Even as he quelled the urge to stroke a finger down the rope of plaited hair lying over her left shoulder and breast, he could not prevent himself from inhaling the scent of lavender from her evening ablutions rising from the warmth of her body,

That was too much to ask of any man. Especially with a woman as attractive as Rose. In the light of their candles, her skin had a translucent quality. Like very fine china with a light behind it, yet the glow was all her own.

He would not give in to his urges.

He hoped.

For that would be a betrayal.

'Are you in the mood for entertainment or sleep?' he asked, forcing himself to focus.

'Oh, something of each, I think.' She smiled. The pretty curve of her lips took her face from merely lovely to beautiful, the gold in her eyes seeming to reflect candlelight. 'I am not being very helpful. And I certainly do not wish to disturb you at your work. I really did think you were out.'

'No matter.' He had gone to the stables, found all there asleep including his horse and come back again. Restless, he had decided to work on some of the paperwork he had not got to during the day.

For a moment he thought he was dreaming when Rose floated in, for he had dreamed of her more than once. Dreamed of kissing her.

But a gentleman did not kiss a lady companion.

'I decided my time would be better employed going through one more ledger before I retired.'

She glanced at the desk. At the brandy decanter and the empty glass. Her gaze skittered away. 'Your grandmother worries about the hours you spend working.'

He grimaced, putting distance between them, as much for his own sake as hers. 'I have a great deal to learn and not much time to do it.' If the Duchy wasn't to end up in a great deal of debt. His father had worked equally hard, but Jake was fast coming to realise that his father did not have much of a head for business. He had simply followed the methods his own father had employed.

Methods that were no longer working as well as they had once done.

Each year the income had declined and each year it had declined more than the year before. There were improvements that needed making, in farming, in buildings, in husbandry. All of which took money. And the coffers, while not empty, were not up to the task, either.

Rose wandered the shelves, cocking her head from time to time to read a spine that caught her eye. The wall opposite the windows did not contain any cabinets, because of the fireplace. As she walked past it, she glanced up at the portrait covered in black crepe above the mantel and then over at him with sympathy in her gaze.

'Another picture of your family?'

Grandmother must have told her about the one in the drawing room. 'My mother. My father couldn't bear to look at it.'

Understanding filled her face. 'Your father and brother were killed in an accident, your grandmother said.'

He stiffened. So Grandmother had gone into detail. He wondered what more she had said. Whether she had spoken of who should really have been in the carriage with Father that night.

The coldness he'd felt when he learned of the accident rose up like a fog. Surrounding him. Chilling him to the bone. Guilt pressed down on his shoulders. He turned away, headed for his desk. Pushed papers around. Aware of her watching him. Aware of her sympathy.

'You miss them,' she said. Not a question.

Yet for some reason he could not quite fathom, he answered, 'Like the very devil.' He closed his eyes. 'I beg your pardon.'

'It is all right, Your Grace,' she said, her voice soft but clear in the silence. 'You don't have to pretend around me, either.'

He shouldn't have to pretend at all.

A moment later she was by his side, slipping her arm around his waist, leaning a cheek against his shoulder and giving him a squeeze. Never in his life had he felt such comfort. He brushed his lips against her temple, felt the beat of her heart against his ribs and knew without a doubt this was a supremely bad idea.

As they turned towards each other she tipped up her face. She was a petite woman, barely coming up to his shoulder, and while robust, there was a fragility about her. Perhaps that was the reason he felt such a need to protect her from her world.

A heartbeat later, their lips met and he wasn't thinking at all.

He was feeling. Relishing the soft curves pressed against his chest. Enjoying the way her waist dipped beneath her ribs as his hand roamed her back. Tasting the honeyed sweetness of her mouth as their tongues tangled and danced.

A sweet sigh brushed against his cheek and she moved closer into his embrace until they melded into one.

He'd missed her kisses like the very devil, too. He just hadn't let himself realise it. 'Rose,' he said, drawing back to look down into her face. 'This is a bad idea.'

'Yes,' she agreed softly, moving not one inch and gazing at his mouth with a hunger that drove claws into his own need.

And when she lifted up on her toes to press her lips to his, he took what she offered.

To Rose, the sensation of being held remained a novel experience. Few people in her life had put their arms around her as far as she recalled. And only this man had ever embraced her with such gentle care. His touch seemed to reach into her very soul. And the way his kisses made her feel was heaven on earth.

A heaven she hadn't known existed, or that it could be shared with another. Her body trembled and yearned and her heart seemed to want to pound itself free of her chest. She twined her arms around his neck, for support and because she wanted to touch him, too. The feel of his silky hair against her fingers was enchanting and wicked.

Pressed against his chest, her breasts felt full, heavy, sensitive, and the only thing between them was her night attire and his shirt. The heat of him through the fabric was lovely. His hands on her buttocks as he drew her close were firm yet gentle. No rough pawing and scrabbling, simply a closing of the distance between them in a way that made her melt helplessly against him, submitting to his strength.

The way he nibbled at her bottom lip sent a piercing sensation arrowing deep into her body. And when his tongue swept her mouth, hot shivers raced across her skin and between her thighs flutters and tiny pulses made her moan.

This was the delight between a man and a woman that the wardens at the Foundling Hospital had warned against. And that the girls at the V&V had whispered and giggled about. Why had she never understood?

Could anything so heart-stoppingly beautiful be evil? But this was only the beginning. The start. Against her belly, she felt the hard ridge of his arousal. The male flesh that, when joined with the female, made babies.

Something that ought only to happen between wife and husband, if those babies were not to be cast out unwanted and alone.

Before, when she'd thought he was going to ask her to be his mistress, she'd fled. Now held in his embrace, his kisses made her weak, needy and full of a longing she was not sure she had the strength to resist after all.

For long moments she let herself whirl in the maelstrom of sensations, heat, jolts of tension and tingles in nameless places. But this man was a duke who needed to marry and get himself sons. Over and over his grandmother had talked of his wedding with such wistfulness it pained Rose to hear it.

While he might enjoy dallying with her—indeed, it was clear the enjoyment was mutual—he could never marry a foundling. A bastard without a name. He would marry someone of his own class. A noble girl with noble connections.

And if she let this thing happen now, between them, he would eventually cast her off, as he had cast off many before her according to her friends at the V&V. She'd paid close attention to the gossip after their dance. She'd learned about his mistresses and what he gave them when he bid them farewell.

None of his women had ever complained about his generosity, according to the girls, and none had ever lasted more than a year. She might not be worldly, but she knew what happened to those women. Ultimately they ended up in places like the V&V, plying their *trade*.

She'd sworn she would never tread that particular road even if she was starving. Yet here she was very close to…

She broke their kiss. 'Your Grace,' she pleaded.

The haziness in his gaze dissipated in a flash of understanding. He straightened, his lovely blue eyes full of regret. Gently, reluctantly, he held her arms firmly in his hands, as if he sensed her weakness, and stepped back with a grave smile. 'Choose as many books as you like. I will see you in the morning.' He left without a backward glance.

Rose watched him leave with a heavy heart. Knowing he had more sense than she did, more control, did not help settle the unsteady beating of her heart, or the sense of loss as he left. Not in the least.

Nor the embarrassment curdling in her stomach.

By her boldness, her wantonness, she had ruined what should have been the simple offer of sympathy for a man who felt the loss of his family keenly.

Women in his class of society did not do things like comfort a man with a kiss. Nor did they wander the halls in the middle of the night dressed in their nightclothes. She had taken pride in having standards and yet she had succumbed to the first handsome man who had shown interest. She had let herself down. Flooded by the heat of mortification, she picked a book at random and returned to her room. She didn't bother to open it, but simply blew out her candle and huddled beneath the covers.

Why, oh, why had she kissed him? Had what she had seen in his expression been regret or disgust? A painful certainty curled up in a tight hard ball in her chest. Whatever it was, an impetuous kiss had likely ruined her one chance to make more of her life.

Chapter Six

The next morning there was no sign of the Duke at breakfast or when they entered the carriage to leave for Lady Spear's At Home, despite his promise to go with them. Clearly he had been disgusted by her wanton behaviour. Misery rested heavily in her chest. She hadn't realised how important she found his good opinion. And now she had lost it.

They were admitted to Lady Spear's house by a very lordly-looking butler, who announced them to the company assembled in the drawing room in sonorous tones.

'Lend me your arm, dear Miss Nightingale,' Her Grace murmured as they lingered on the threshold. 'I am feeling less than steady on my feet.'

Thus she and Rose swept into Lady Spear's

drawing room together instead of Rose following at a discreet distance and remaining unnoticed. She'd been outmanoeuvred by a frail old lady with a will of iron. As she looked about her, she realised there were far more people in attendance than she had been given to expect.

A large-bosomed woman in deep purple hurried forward to greet them. 'Your Grace.' The woman curtsied. 'You honour us.'

The Dowager Duchess accepted the homage without blinking an eye. 'Dear Lady Spear, I would like to introduce my companion, Miss Nightingale. Rose, this is Lady Spear, our hostess. Miss Nightingale has kindly consented to join my household.' She smiled fondly at Rose. 'She is most helpful.'

In other words, she was held in esteem by Her Grace, so don't be treating her badly.

Rose stilled. Apparently she was becoming adept at deciphering the politics of society manners, after all. But then she had good teachers in the Dowager Duchess and the Duke. If only she hadn't messed it all up. She pushed off the feeling of impending doom. There was no sense in worrying about what could not be changed, she'd decided in the wakeful early hours of the morning. Practical advice she was having trouble following.

'And how is His Grace?' Lady Spear asked.

While her voice held sympathy there was a gleam of something less kind in her hazel eyes as she peered at the Dowager Duchess, who released Rose's arm to make a careless gesture with her hand. 'He'll be along shortly, so you may ask him for yourself. He would have come with us, but urgent business delayed him.'

Rose swallowed her surprise. It was the first she'd heard of urgent business. Or was the old lady telling a fib?

Lady Spear's eyes widened. 'Oh, I—' She visibly pulled herself together and beamed. 'That is wonderful news. I will be honoured.' Her tone turned a little sly. 'It has been such an age since anyone has seen him.'

Rose found herself clenching her fist at the woman's insincerity. Forcibly, she relaxed her fingers and once more took Her Grace's arm. It trembled a little beneath her hand. Worry replaced irritation. 'Perhaps you could find Her Grace a chair, Lady Spear,' she said quietly but firmly.

'Yes, Eloisa, do find me a chair,' the old lady added imperiously and gave Rose a conspiratorial smile.

'Oh, pardon me, Your Grace. Please, come

this way.' She led them to a group of other elderly ladies seated around a low table.

Having seen Her Grace settled, Rose took the wooden chair placed by a footman off to the side and a little behind Her Grace. She breathed a sigh of relief. Here in the corner, she could observe without being noticed, just as Her Grace had promised.

A dark-haired gentleman approached Her Grace and bowed. With a start, Rose recognised him. Mr Oliver Gregory.

Such a handsome man with his dark skin and startling green eyes. But nowhere near as handsome as Westmoor. Not in her eyes. Her heart gave a funny little skip.

Mr Gregory bowed with elegance when he reached their group, his brief smile encompassing all the ladies in the circle and somehow included Rose, too. How did he do that? 'Ladies. I bid you all a pleasant day.'

The ladies murmured their greetings with much fluttering of fans and adjusting shawls. There was something odd about their reaction. As if they would prefer he had stayed away. All except Her Grace, who greeted him with a warm smile and an outstretched hand. He bowed over it. 'Your Grace. How delightful to meet you here and with Miss Nightingale, too. A great pleasure.'

The other ladies turned to look at her. Exactly what she had hoped to avoid. Heat flashed to Rose's cheeks. She stammered something in reply.

He bowed as befitting her station. 'Are you quite well, Miss Nightingale?' His eyes held concern.

Dash it all, her sleepless night must be showing. 'Perfectly, I thank you, sir.' She spoke a little more stiffly than she had intended, but once more he had drawn other gazes to her little corner.

He gazed down at her, with a slight frown. He leaned a little closer. 'You know, it is the strangest thing. I keep thinking I have met you somewhere before our dinner the other evening, but it isn't possible.'

Of course he'd seen her before. He'd often been in the room when she'd cleaned out the fireplace in the owners' private parlour. All the owners had. Once, this man had kindly opened the door for her when she was struggling with her buckets and brushes. Guilt swept through her. How would he react if he knew who she really was? She clenched her hands in her lap.

'The first time we were introduced was at dinner with Her Grace.'

His lips tightened as if he had noticed the subtle change in her answer, but to her relief he turned back to Her Grace. 'It really is good to see you out and about again, Your Grace, isn't it, ladies?'

The other ladies nodded and twittered their agreement. 'I thought Westmoor was to accompany you? It was part of my reason for being here. I needed a word.'

'He will be along shortly, I am sure,' Her Grace said, sounding more haughty than was her usual wont with this gentleman.

Mr Oliver's eyes narrowed a fraction, hinting at displeasure. 'Unfortunately, I am unable to await his arrival. I have another appointment.'

'It seems that you are fortunate, young man,' Her Grace said, nodding at the door. 'Here he is now.'

A gasp rippled around the room as the butler announced the Duke of Westmoor. Rose's heart lifted and, as his gaze caught hers, she couldn't help but smile.

'Careful, Miss Nightingale,' Mr Gregory said in a low voice right by her ear. 'Smiles like that will start the gossips wondering.'

She blushed and looked up at him. His green eyes were dancing with amusement, but there was also a question there and that shadow of puzzlement.

Her heart sank. He was a clever man. He was going to remember. And then what?

The Duke's arrival triggered a great deal more rushing forward and curtsying by Lady Spear and various other women, while the men bowed their greetings. Outwardly, the Duke seemed to take it all in his stride, but Rose saw the shadows in his eyes and the faint lines of strain around his mouth.

She wanted to go to him to offer her support, but how could she? She was merely his grandmother's companion. Which reminded her, she was neglecting her duty. Rose tucked the shawl she was holding around the Dowager Duchess's shoulders. 'In case you feel a draught,' she murmured.

'Such a kind, thoughtful girl you are,' Her Grace said with a smile. 'I am very fortunate to have found you.' She turned to the woman at her side. 'Finally, I have found a companion worthy of her hire.'

The other lady's glance skimmed over Rose. 'Who is her family?'

Rose held her breath.

'Distant relatives of my son's wife,' the old lady said.

A gasp almost escaped Rose's lips. That was an out-and-out bouncer. She opened her mouth to deny it, then closed it again. What would it serve? She would only embarrass the old lady by revealing the lie.

She inched her chair back a little farther into the shadows of the corner.

While Her Grace exchanged gossip with her companions, Rose sat as still as possible, her hands folded neatly in her lap, and tried to disappear into the background. Yet over and over her gaze was drawn to the Duke holding court with a group of young ladies. Her heart squeezed painfully. She forced herself to look away, yet somehow she could not stop herself from being aware of his every movement, every expression on his face, no matter how brief.

He wasn't happy.

Also, though his gaze never strayed her way once, she had the oddest feeling she had his undivided attention. But it wasn't possible. Not for a moment.

A footman arrived with a dish of bohea for Her Grace, added cream and sugar, according to the old lady's likes, and placed it in front of her. By the time he had served Her Grace, the footman, clearly aware of her lowly status, had moved off, though no doubt he would come back around when everyone else was served.

Indeed. His next stop was the Duke, whose expression was now a picture of grim dissatisfaction. Another footman arrived with fancy little cakes and Rose filled a plate for her employer who was deep in conversation. She placed the plate at Her Grace's elbow and retired to her seat.

A moment later, the footman returned with a cup of tea for her. Surprised, she stared at him. His face was bland, as was the face of the footman behind him waiting to offer her a plate of cakes.

Something made her glance in the direction of the Duke and for a moment their gazes met. With a slight nod of satisfaction, he turned to speak to the lady at his side and Rose wondered if she had imagined their exchange of glances, so attentive did he seem to be to the lovely young lady.

She glanced at the clock. A mere twenty minutes had passed. Her Grace had promised they would not stay long and wondered how she could possibly manage with a plate of cakes in one hand and a cup of tea in the other. Fortunately, a fair-haired gentleman standing nearby seemed to realise her dilemma. He came over with a smile and bowed. 'I fear we have not been introduced. I'm Faxford—Spear's eldest. Perhaps I may be of assistance.' He signalled to a footman. 'Fetch a table, would you, John?'

The footman scurried off, returning a few moments later with a piecrust table, which he set within arm's reach of her chair.

'Sorry about that. Stupid fellow should have seen you needed somewhere to set your cup down,' the young man said, taking her plate and setting it down.

She smiled her gratitude.

Her Grace turned around. 'Faxford, Miss Nightingale is my companion and you will cease your flirting immediately.'

'Miss Nightingale,' Faxford said with a cheeky grin and a bow. 'A pleasure to meet you. I knew I'd winkle an introduction eventually.'

Heat flooded Rose's face.

Jake cursed under his breath at the sight of Faxford hovering over an embarrassed Rose. He hadn't asked the footman to provide her with a cup of tea in order to give the blasted fellow an opportunity to show off his gentlemanly manners.

He shouldn't have done it at all. Servants gossiped.

He resisted the urge to join his grandmother and give Faxford a set down. A kindly employer ensuring his mother's companion got a cup of tea was understandable, just. The same employer acting like a jealous fool would be quite another.

And now she was smiling at the fellow, albeit shyly. He clenched his jaw so hard, his back teeth ached. He turned away, only to see a matron with her marriageable daughter in tow striding in his direction.

Avoiding catching the woman's eye, he sauntered to his grandmother's side and bowed to the ladies. 'You will let me know when you are ready to leave, Your Grace?'

His grandmother hid her surprise. 'I will, dear boy. Thank you.' She turned back to the lady with whom she was conversing.

Faxford, blast him, grinned cheerfully. 'The ladies love their gossip.'

'Indeed,' he said repressively.

The young man shifted from foot to foot. 'What do you think about this business in the north?' he blurted out, clearly trying for another topic of conversation. 'This riot.'

'I read about that,' Rose said. 'Some are calling it a massacre. It warrants some sort of official investigation, I should think.'

Faxford blinked his surprise. 'By Gad, Miss Nightingale, are you a bluestocking?'

Jake raised a haughty brow. 'You raised the topic, Faxford. Hardly fitting in mixed company.'

The young man visibly wilted. 'Oh, right. I beg pardon. My mistake. If you will excuse me, my mother is trying to catch my attention.' He bowed and to Jake's satisfaction scurried off.

Rose frowned at him. 'Surely such an important event is everyone's concern?'

Jake's jaw dropped at her challenging tone. He gave her the same haughty look he had given Faxford. 'I have no intention of engaging in rumour-mongering, Miss Nightingale and that is what it would be since I do not as yet have all the facts.'

She frowned, clearly undeterred. 'Hardly a rumour. Troops called out to quell a riot, if you believe the government. A massacre of citizens, if you believe those present. The real question is how is the truth to be discovered, Your Grace?'

Rose was right of course. Her argument was the same as that he had presented to Prinny that very morning. Not something he could bruit abroad, however. Discussions with the Prince Regent were confidential. 'You suggest some sort of impartial enquiry, I assume?'

She wrinkled her brow thoughtfully. 'Is it even possible?'

'It certainly ought to be.'

She glanced up at him. 'What did he mean by calling me a…a stocking, was it?'

Jake lowered his voice. 'We can discuss it later.'

Anger rose in Jakes's throat at the worry on her face. He wanted to march over to Faxford and make him apologise. Yet with the old biddies looking on, they would find themselves the subject of gossip in a heartbeat should he do so. He set his jaw and said nothing.

'Why, we have been here half an hour already,' Grandmama said, smiling up at him and filling the awkward pause in their conversation. 'Jacob, would you have the carriage brought around?'

Jake bowed. 'It will be my pleasure.' He tried not to notice Rose's anxious expression. He would explain it later.

Westmoor joined his grandmother and Rose in the drawing room after dinner, though he had not joined them for the meal itself.

'Will you explain what is meant by bluestocking, Your Grace?' Rose asked once the servants had withdrawn. She hadn't found the word in the dictionary she had borrowed.

Her Grace looked up, her mouth wrinkling as if she'd tasted a quince. 'Did someone call you that, Rose?'

'Faxford,' Jake answered. 'The idiot.'

'I gather, then, being a bluestocking is not a good thing,' Rose said, her stomach falling away. Oh, why, oh, why had she said anything at all? And just when she'd begun to feel more comfortable in her new position.

'It means a young woman who is more interested in politics and education than she is in gowns and dancing,' the Dowager said.

'A lady is not supposed to be interested in the events of the day?' It hardly seemed right. 'Shouldn't soldiers attacking women and children concern everyone? Not to mention the unrest it has caused. There is talk of revolution.'

The old lady's chin trembled. She looked at her grandson. 'Jake, is this true? Are the peasants rising against us?' She shuddered. 'One cannot but help think of France.'

Rose's stomach pitched. 'I am sorry, Your Grace. I did not mean to scare you.'

The Duke's lips thinned. 'We do not have

peasants in England, Grandmama. And let us not jump to conclusions. That was your advice, was it not, Rose?'

Rose wished she'd never opened her mouth. Anyone of nobility would be scared witless after what had happened in France.

The old lady fixed her grandson with an intense stare. 'Cooler heads must prevail, Jacob. I am relying on you to speak to the Prince. To make him see reason. This is England. Our soldiers do not run roughshod over the populace. Now, if we have quite exhausted this topic, I find I am tired. Ring the bell, Jake. I wish to retire.'

Her heart sank. How could she have been so thoughtless as to upset the old lady? 'I am sure it will all be resolved satisfactorily in the end. I am sorry if my careless words caused you worry.'

'Nonsense, child. My weariness has nothing to do with politics. I need my sleep after all our gadding about today.'

Jake rang the bell, then went to help his grandmother to rise. 'I will escort you up, Grandmama.'

'No need. Previs is here now. Finish your tea, Jake. Entertain Miss Nightingale. Perhaps you would read to her for a change.'

The elderly butler had indeed arrived and was handing the old lady her cane and offering an arm. They staggered out, closing the door behind them. An unusual mistake. Should she get up and open it? Would it not seem distrustful? She glanced at Westmoor for his reaction and was surprised at his strained expression.

'I am so sorry, Your Grace. I would not upset your grandmother for the world. She has been so very kind.'

When he said nothing, she felt compelled to continue. 'I told you I'd muck things up. Me pretending to be a lady is such a…' she waved a hand to encompass everything around her '…farce.'

She had never seen a farce at the theatre, but she'd read them. Shakespeare's *A Midsummer Night's Dream* and *As You Like It*. People dressing up as what they were not. While as funny as all get out, things often ended badly.

'Rose,' Jake said.

There was something in his voice that made her look at him more closely. He was laughing? She bridled. 'What? Do you find me amusing?'

'Not at all,' he said, laughter dancing in the depths of his eyes. 'Poor young Faxford. The brainless idiot didn't have a clue what you were talking about. That is why he called you a blue-stocking.'

'How mean. I promise to be more careful.' Something inside her shrivelled a little.

'You certainly don't want people to think you have any sort of brain,' His Grace said, agreeably.

She glared at him. 'Why must women act like foolish creatures without a sensible thought in their heads?'

He must have realised her distress, for he reached over and patted her hand. The touch of his bare skin on hers sent tingles rushing across her skin.

'I'm teasing, Rose. I like you just as you are. Unfortunately, one derogatory remark can be picked up and passed from person to person until one's reputation is in tatters. Men love to deride intelligent women. It makes them feel superior.'

'Derog…' She frowned as she tried to get her tongue around the unfamiliar word. 'De-rogatory. I assume it was something intended to hurt.'

'From the Latin, *derogatorius*, meaning impairing in force or effect, criticising.'

Her head whirled. 'You speak Latin?'

'I learned Latin. No one speaks it any more.

But that is beside the point. Faxford is a twit, whereas you are eminently sensible.'

A feeling of pride at his praise swelled her heart. 'Which account do you believe?'

'The prognosis is not good.' He winced. 'I apologise, I forget you have not had the same opportunity to—'

'Oh, I know what that means. It is a medical term for the course of a disease.' She had heard the doctors at the orphanage use it. 'You think there is cause for concern?'

'I do. I ran into Tonbridge, a military man with friends in the army. He believes the press has the right of it, for a change. Resentment among the people is building.'

She gasped. 'Revolution?'

'No need to look so hopeful, my dear.'

They both burst out laughing.

When their laughter died away, once more Rose looked so adorably serious, Jake wanted to kiss her.

'You really think it will come to that?' she asked.

'Let us hope not, though there is talk of Acts which will not be popular with the people.'

'You will speak against them in the Lords?'

He ignored the pang of guilt. 'I have no seat.'

She frowned at him. 'You are a duke, are you not? A peer?'

'I am. But there are customs and processes to be observed. I haven't bothered.' He hadn't felt he had the right or the need. Against his will his gaze flicked to the swath of black crepe covering the picture over mantel. 'I have been otherwise occupied since gaining the title.' If one could call it a gain. He frequently felt he had been much better off as plain Lord Jake.

'Did your father take an active role in politics?' she asked casually.

'He did.' A memory made him want to smile. 'He and I were not always in accord with how the country should be run, but he was...assiduous in voting his seat.'

She glanced down at her hands. 'Assiduous.' She rolled the word around her mouth. 'I see.'

What did she see? Guilt pricked his conscience. A feeling he resented. 'What are you thinking, Miss Nightingale? That I should take up the cause of our northern citizens, perhaps? Insist that any soldier who used his sword on a member of the public be tried for murder?'

'Not the soldiers,' she said quickly, softly. 'Those who gave the orders.'

'Men like me.'

She stiffened. 'You are offended. I do not

agree with those who call for an uprising, you know. Too many people will be hurt, most of them women and children. I do, however, believe the way the country is run must change. Ordinary people must have more say.'

'By Jove, you really are a bluestocking, Miss Nightingale.' At the sight of her hurt, he touched a finger to her nose. 'I mean that as a compliment.'

'And you will…vote your seat, is it called? On this matter?'

'I do not know.' A very shameful truth. 'I really do need more information.' But he would speak to Tonbridge again. The man seemed to have more knowledge and intellect than most and he was also a ducal heir. 'I will think about it, certainly.' But to sit in his father's place in the Lords, the very idea made him nauseous.

'You still grieve for them,' she said softly. 'Your father and your brother.'

Shock rippled through him. At the words. At the look of understanding rather than sympathy that somehow made their deaths all the more real, when most days he still did not fully believe it. He forced his gaze away from the black crepe that hid nothing of their faces from his mind's eye. 'Shall we read that poetry as Grandmama suggested?' He reached for the book.

'No, thank you, Your Grace.' She was already rising to her feet with a small smile. 'It has been a very long day, with more than its share of excitement. I think I, too, will retire.'

Frowning, he shot to his feet. Had he said something wrong? Now he looked at her, he realised she was a little pale and drawn. Naturally she would have found her first foray into society daunting. Yet she'd still had the wit and the energy to debate politics with him. 'Very well, I shall escort you up.'

'No need.'

'It will be my pleasure.'

Without further demur she placed her hand on his arm. He walked her sedately up the stairs to the door of her chamber.

She stopped and he opened it. About to step inside, she hesitated, looking up at him. 'You do not think my error today is irredeemable, then? I would hate to give Her Grace cause for embarrassment. I—I have come to like my position here.'

Wonder of wonders. 'I think your little *faux pas* will scarce make a ripple.'

'Foh-pah?'

'It is French for error. A minor mistake.' He spelled it out.

She shook her head. 'How will I ever learn all of this?'

'You have made great strides, Miss Nightingale, do not doubt your ability.'

She swung around to face him, a smile on her face. 'You know I don't think I ever thanked you properly for this opportunity. Indeed, I came most unwillingly, I believe.'

'You did. Believe me, no thanks are required. Your presence is a boon of the highest magnitude. I haven't see Grandmama in such good spirits for a long while.'

'You are good man, Jacob Huntingdon, despite your attempts to hide it.'

Surprised, he stared at her. 'Why would you think I—?'

She touched a fingertip to his lips. 'You hated that event today, yet you came to please your grandmother.'

Not only his grandmother, but he wasn't about to admit that to Rose. 'It was my duty.' He sounded stilted. Uncomfortable. But what was new about that? Nothing in his life was comfortable. Except perhaps his private moments with Rose, when he could be himself.

She shook her head at him. 'You really deserve more than duty, Your Grace.'

His breathing quickened at her teasing tone.

The urge to smile back pulled at his lips. He closed the distance between them. 'What would you suggest?'

The delicious scent of her body filled his nostrils, her warm smile was an unexpected welcome. He wanted to bask in that warmth. To drink his fill of her sweetness. He should not. Must not.

As she placed her hand flat on his chest, he found himself wanting to hold it. He clenched his fists behind his back instead. He would not treat her as if she was anything less than a lady, even if she could never be his lady, in red or any other colour. He steeled himself to step back. 'I beg your pardon. A gentleman should not importune a lady under his roof. I—'

'If I was truly a lady,' she interrupted softly, 'you would not have kissed me last night.'

Regret speared him. An apology leapt to his tongue. But that little hand gripped his lapel tight enough for her knuckles to show white through her skin. 'And if I was any sort of real lady I would not have kissed you back. I don't want you to go.'

She rose up on her toes and pressed her mouth to his.

Unable to stop himself, he swept her into the circle of one arm, deepening the kiss, while opening her door with the other. He edged her inside and closed it behind them. A long moment later, he lifted his head, breathing hard.

'Rose. That is what I call an ambush. And it is not the first time I have been ambushed by a lady. So don't think it.'

She was panting and staring at his mouth with the kind of raw hunger that called to him on a very basic level. 'You really do kiss beautifully, Your Grace. I have missed those kisses.'

'Call me, Jake, sweetheart, please.'

'Jake, right now, I would love it if you would kiss me again.'

He had never been propositioned so sweetly or so devastatingly. He fought to find some rational thought, some reason why he should walk away and…found nothing but the desire to kiss her again.

A groan rumbled up from his chest. Where Rose was concerned when it came to kissing, he had almost no willpower. A kiss, that was all it would be, and then he would leave.

He touched his lips to hers.

Chapter Seven

Rose wasn't quite sure when she had decided she could give up her long-held principles and take this daring step with a man who could never really be hers.

Perhaps the sight of him in such delicious and tempting undress as he groomed his horse, or the way he treated her like part of his family, or patiently explained the meaning of a word she had never heard before, had made her feel this overwhelming fondness.

Or perhaps it was the terrible loneliness she had sensed in him in that drawing room this afternoon when, despite the crowds around him, he had seemed to stand alone. Surely the man deserved someone to care about him, the way he cared for his family. While she could not stand at his side, in private she could offer him affection.

And, yes, gain something for herself. A feeling of being needed.

Truth to tell, she really had missed his kisses.

Clearly, he was far too much a gentleman to press for what she had indicated was unwelcome so it was up to her to take the first step. Another thing to be grateful for in a life where so few decisions had been her own.

And Jake's kisses were blissful. Intoxicating. A word she now understood, though she had never imbibed strong drink.

She opened her lips to his tongue's gentle request along the seam of her lips, sighed as their mouths melded. Aching deep in her heart, she let her fingers wander through the silk of his hair, absorbing every whisper of sensation against her skin. The hard bulk of his broad chest pressing against her breasts. The hand caressing her back as he drew her close, the feel of his arousal against her belly.

Each breath she took was not enough. Dizziness made her head swim and her knees feel weak, yet she had no fear of him letting her fall. His heat and his strength surrounded her like a barrier against the world. Nothing and no one would harm her when she was in his arms. Safe as she had never been safe before.

What wonderful memories they would make

and for a while, he could forget his duty and be himself. A good kind man. She cupped his face in her hands and he broke the kiss, looking down at her, breathing almost as hard as she was. That he wanted her, she had no doubt.

His hazy gaze sharpened. His expression became enquiring. 'Rose?'

'Jake,' she whispered.

He shut his eyes for a moment. When he opened them, they were clear, his emotions bare. He looked tortured. 'Do you know how rarely anyone calls me by my own name?'

She brushed back the lock of dark hair that liked to fall on to his forehead. 'Jake, I...' How to say this without sounding forward?

He stepped back. 'I should go.'

She caught at his hand. He glanced down at where their fingers intertwined, then lifted his gaze to her face. The muscles in his jaw flickered. 'I am not made of stone, Rose.'

'Nor am I.' The thunder of her heart made it impossible to speak, so she smiled at him. Swallowed. 'Stay. Please?'

His eyes widened.

She'd been too forward. Or had she? The heat flaring in his gaze said otherwise.

He put his hands on her waist. 'Do not say it, if you do not mean it.'

Relief flooded through her. She could not stop the chuckle of delight that bubbled up in her throat. 'I never say things I do not mean.'

A small smile curved his lips. 'Never pretend, was what you said.'

She nodded slowly. 'Never.'

He shook his head slightly, but his smile broadened. 'You are lovely. Delicious. Gorgeous. Delightful.'

All words she recognised. Words that made her heart swell with an odd kind of pride that he would use them to describe her. She felt almost...precious. As if this moment was as important to him as it was to her. She twined her arms around his neck, gazing at his lovely mouth that formed such lovely words and her body tightened in anticipation of his kiss. 'Jake, I...'

'Mmm?' he murmured, nuzzling against her neck, tasting a spot beneath her ear that sent strange surges of that same tight feeling rushing between her thighs. She rolled her hips against him, pressed closer.

'I forget everything when you kiss me.'

'Me, too.' He drew in a breath. 'You are sure you want this?'

She chuckled. 'I have never been more certain of anything in my life.'

A shudder rippled through him. 'A gentleman really does not take advantage of the women in his household. I do rather pride myself on being a gentleman, you know.'

Only too well. It was one of the things about him she found so endearing. Irresistible. But not when it held him back. 'Can't we just be Jake and Rose tonight? No titles. Not employer and employee. No rules. Merely two ordinary people enjoying each other's company.'

He stilled as if considering the idea. So cautious, her Jake. So very thoughtful. 'I would like that, Rose. Very much. You have no idea how much.' He chuckled. 'Jake the footman. I think it sounds well, don't you? A devil of a fellow I am below stairs, too. But you...' he rubbed his nose against hers in a gesture of affection '...are the only one I want.'

Want in the carnal sense. She understood his meaning and could not help but smile at his rascally grin. He could not know how her heart ached to hear that she was the only one he wanted. She'd had so few friends in her life, she would treasure his declaration even knowing he was being his usual flirtatious self. He had a family who loved him and could not possibly understand how lonely her life had been until now.

She was starting to feel as if she belonged somewhere.

She instilled laughter into her voice. 'Lawks, now. Wouldn't that be something? You a footman and me the upstairs maid.'

'Who have ducked into the upstairs linen closet while everyone is at breakfast.' Now he sounded mischievous.

'We must be very quiet,' she murmured, stroking her fingers through his hair. 'We wouldn't want the housekeeper catching us. We'd cuddle in the dark and you would whisper about your dream of becoming a butler, while I talked grandly of being the housekeeper.'

'And in between, I would steal a quick kiss.' He pecked at her cheek and she turned her face to catch it on her lips. The kiss was not in the least quick.

She melted against him, wanting to burrow into his skin, to feel him close.

He groaned, lifting his lips from hers and letting his mouth cruise her cheeks, her nose, her forehead, their bodies limpet tight.

'You will have to kick me out, Rose,' he muttered. 'I swear I do not have the will to leave of my own volition.'

Volition. He did say such funny things. But she knew what he meant. 'Then stay, Jake. I am not one of your noble misses with a reputation to guard.' Though she had guarded herself for years. But then no man had offered her the least temptation.

She could see from the expression on his face that he was torn between doing the honourable thing and fulfilling her request. And while this was not what she had ever intended—indeed, was against the rules she had set for herself—it would hurt if he turned her down. She would not give him the chance. Not now that she had made the decision.

This might well be her only chance to be with him. His sister could arrive at any moment and likely her presence in the house would preclude her and Jake from finding time to be alone.

She worked down the buttons of his coat and then his shirt, longing to reveal that wonderful expanse of chest. It did not take long for her to lay his torso bare, for he helped her pull the shirt over his head between plundering kisses that never seemed to end.

He was a beautifully constructed man. All lean muscle and lithe sinew. His arms were as defined as any sculpture she'd seen in a book. From grooming horses, no doubt. And his chest and stomach above his waistband made her mouth water with the desire to run her tongue along each ridge and shadowed dip. To see if he tasted as good as he smelled.

She eyed the buttons holding his falls at his waistband, but he spun her around, holding one arm about her waist while plying her nape with whisper-soft kisses.

'Let me take your hair down.' He barely waited for her nod before pins went flying about her feet and the curls she had spent an hour or more to fix in place were spilling around her shoulders in mere seconds.

Fair was fair.

God, Jake couldn't believe how much he desired Rose, when he hadn't wanted a woman for weeks or maybe months. Unable to resist, he bent and buried his nose in her golden tresses, breathing in the scent of lily of the valley. Sweet and innocent like her, but also incredibly alluring.

He swept her hair aside and gently sank his teeth into the tender skin where her shoulder joined her neck, loving the taste of her on his tongue and caught up by a primal urge to leave his mark. Though he would never do it in truth, the idea sent what little blood remained in his brain rushing south.

'Have you known many saucy footmen, Rose?'

She gave a low sensual chuckle 'Enough, Jakey-boy.' Her low husky voice sent tingles down his spine.

Relief. He'd had the suspicion—but ordinary people did not need to worry about such things as lineage and family blood. Saints preserve him, what he wouldn't give for just a few hours to be Rose's ordinary footman, without responsibility or duty to anyone but himself. Free to choose.

Not six months ago he'd been ordinary as far as the *ton* were concerned. The second son of a duke who led an idle life mostly unnoticed on the marriage mart. Safely hidden in his brother's shadow, he'd even kept the wealth derived from Vitium et Virtus and other investments a carefully guarded secret. Neither his father nor his brother had known how large he'd grown his personal fortune.

He would have been able to make Rose an honourable offer, had he been so disposed. Would he have been disposed? Unlikely. He'd never been one with marriage on his mind. He liked his independence too much. A pang twisted in his chest. He'd gone through life pleasing himself. Utterly selfish and thoughtless. Ultimately others had paid the price for his rottenness and would continue to do so.

He pitied any woman who became his wife. He simply wasn't cut out for marriage and yet he'd do as required by duty. He'd promised.

He didn't deserve Rose, but nor could he refuse her what she wanted. He wouldn't refuse her anything if it would make her smile, for if he was good for anything, it was bringing a woman pleasure. More pleasure than any footman ever had or ever would, of that he was certain.

She sighed at the touch of his lips and bent her head forward in a submissive posture that had nothing meek about it. This was a demand.

He could not help the smile the small gesture brought to his lips, any more than he could help kissing the lovely tender flesh at her nape one more time.

Slowly, he undid the buttons of her gown and the tapes of her stays, exposing the filmy fabric of her chemise, through which he could see the delicate nobs of her spine and the sharp-angled shoulder blades. Rose had not always eaten well.

The thought caused a stir of anger in his gut.

Gently he turned her to face him. She tipped her face up, a teasing smile on her lips and a softness in her expression that made him ache with need.

But this was not about him and his desires, it was about Rose. He took her lush lips, carefully, tenderly, as he pushed the gown and stays down over her arms and the lovely swell of her bottom, to slide to the floor with a little sigh. Echoed by Rose against his cheek.

Her arms went about his neck and he plundered the dark heat of her mouth, tasting her, feeling her melt against him, moving her hips against his erection in an erotic dance that practically had him coming apart. He broke the kiss on a groan. 'Let us at least make use of the bed.' He kept his voice light, but it was a heartfelt plea none the less.

She patted a cheek. A gesture of affection he couldn't recall anyone ever doing before. It was comforting. Familiar. Kind. Friendly. When were his lovers ever friendly or kind? Or anyone else for that matter.

'I'll be back in a moment,' she said and whisked herself behind the screen. 'You can finish undressing if you like.'

He did like, very much, and he guessed much of the reason for her disappearance was modesty. The thought of Rose being shy was almost too erotic for his sanity.

It didn't take him long to strip down and hop into bed, discarding all the covers but the sheet. Several moments passed. 'Rose, what—?'

'Precautions,' she said from behind the screen. 'No unwanted mistakes—' A small sound of triumph. 'Sponges and what not.'

Heaven have mercy on him, she was taking charge of the whole business. And what a relief it was to know she thought as he did and her preparedness eased some of his doubts about taking advantage. 'What a competent woman you are, Rose.' But responsibility was not hers alone. 'You know there is no guarantee.' He almost kicked himself for his honesty. His lust almost kicked him, too. He ignored those selfish male urges. 'I, too, will take precautions.'

She appeared from behind the screen looking adorably flushed with embarrassment. 'Then we should be doubly sure.'

He lifted the sheet with a welcoming grin and she skipped up the steps and on to the bed and into his arms.

'Now,' she said, sounding very pleased with herself, 'where were we?'

He gazed up into her sparkling eyes, so full of mischief, the glossy strands of her hair falling around them trailing across his chest like tormenting fairy fingers. 'You were kissing me.'

She ran a fingertip along his eyebrow and then patted the end of his nose, the admonishment startlingly novel. 'Was I, now?'

He couldn't resist, he flipped her on her back and leaned over her, grinning like a fool. 'Or perhaps I was kissing you.' He nipped at her earlobe. 'What do you think?'

She shivered. 'I think,' she said solemnly, 'we were kissing each other.'

She wrapped her arms around his neck and pulled his head down, even as she rose up to meet him.

Such sweetness. He gave himself over to the pleasure of her lips and her tongue and the feel of her tiny fingers wandering his back, tracing his spine, exploring the shape of his buttocks beneath the sheet wrapped around his hips. He wanted those fingers on another part of him, but this wasn't one of the many bold lovers he'd had over the years. Ladies knowledgeable in the art of *amour*.

Her modest blushes were a testimony to hurried couplings in the dark of an evening off. The housekeeper at the ducal estate where he had lived as a boy had explained this to him and his brother when they reached thirteen.

She had warned them off all the maids in the house with threats of dire consequences. Something he'd taken to heart, until his brother had introduced him to a local widow who knew all the tricks required to keep a lusty boy happy.

He'd never bothered the maids in the house. But here he was bothering his grandmother's lovely, adorable and terribly sweet companion.

Which was worse. She was under his protection.

He broke the kiss. 'Rose, are you really sure you want this?'

The dreamy smile on her lips as she gazed up at him was enough to drive a man mad. 'I am really, really sure.'

The words drove his conscience into a deep dark corner even as it noticed there was a touch of sadness in her voice his desire refused to examine in detail.

Learning how to please Rose, when likely she did not yet know the answers, was going to be a pleasure and a delight.

He pressed a swift kiss to her lips, her chin, her jaw, then swirled his tongue around the rim of her ear.

She squirmed, her hip nudging against his painfully hard erection, making his head swim. He sucked in a breath and she stilled.

'You liked that,' he managed to ask.

'It tickled.' She sounded bemused. 'Everywhere.'

'Including here?' He laid his palm over her breast, slowly letting her take the weight of his hand, feeling the tightly furled nub against his palm with a smile.

'There, too,' she said, arching up into his hand, encouraging him to stroke. He paid careful attention to that breast, teasing the nipple lightly through the sheer fabric of her shift, while watching the reactions flutter over her face. Surprise, pleasure, desire. Never had he seen anything quite so erotic as a woman learning her pleasures.

Having patience was going to kill him before he was through.

He moved to her other breast, performing the same gentle motions with hand and fingers while he lowered his mouth to taste the tightly furled nub of the first.

Then he suckled. Her thighs parted, her hips rolled into him and he pushed one knee between her legs, giving her the pressure she sought at the apex to her thighs. She moaned her pleasure.

He came up on his knees and gradually eased her shift upward until he could get his lips and tongue on her naked breasts. Beneath him, her hips arched towards what instinctively she knew she wanted, but he refused to be rushed, no matter how much delayed gratification pained him. He gritted his teeth and with his hands still playing with her breasts, he kissed his way down her ribs to lay his cheek upon her flat stomach.

She flattened her hands over his still cupping her breasts, as if she feared they would wander off elsewhere. They wanted to. He eased one out from beneath her clutching fingers and showed her how to stroke her own breast, while he continued to tease the other. He combed his fingers through the golden little triangle of curls and her hips came up in response.

The sensuality in that simple little twitch had him wanting to drive deep within her heat. Soon. He promised it would be soon as he gently parted her folds and felt her heat and the damp on his fingers.

She froze for a second, then lifted her head to see what he was about. He pressed a kiss to her stomach, swirled his tongue in her navel and she sank back against the pillows, parting her thighs wider in an invitation he had no hope of refusing.

Not if he wasn't to disgrace himself entirely this first time.

And there would be many other times when he could take it more slowly, no matter what she thought.

He rose up on one hand, took her hand and guided it to his shaft. 'Tell me where you want me, sweetheart.' Let there be no mistake about who was in charge. He had been robbed of what he had thought were his choices; he would take none from anyone else.

Her small hand closed around him.

He watched the delight in her face with puzzlement, for not only was she delighted, she was also surprised. And curious. She rose up on one elbow to look at him, rapping him on his nose in the process. He ignored his pain and watering eyes, because he was entranced by her look of wonder.

'I'm supposed to do that, too?' she asked, letting go of his shaft and cupping him, exploring the texture. Hadn't she ever been given the chance to feel her partners?

He swallowed at the pleasurable sensations rippling up through his body as she caressed him, her gaze focused on what her hand was doing.

'Only if you wish,' he said, hoping she did

with a longing that caught him off guard. As if the memory would be something to treasure for years to come.

Grasping him again, she frowned in concentration and guided him in the right direction. He nudged forward into her folds and, as he slid forward another fraction, she made a small sound, a cross between a sigh and a squeak of fear.

He froze.

She reclined back on to the pillow. 'More,' she demanded.

He gritted his teeth against the urge to drive into her and eased forward another fraction, into the heat and the wet. It snugged around him, so hot, so tight, it was so unbearably delicious his head spun with pleasure. His hips jerked a little more than he'd intended and she gasped.

Pain?

He lifted his gaze. She was biting her bottom lip. Her eyes were squeezed tight shut.

'Did I hurt you?'

He wasn't a small man, but he had never encountered a woman so small and tight and—'Rose!' He wanted to curse.

She flexed her hips experimentally. 'My. That is nice. I think I am getting the hang of it.'

Well, damn it all, not for one moment had he expected this. To be her first. 'Rose, we shouldn't—'

She wrapped her legs around his thighs, effectively holding him in place. He shouldn't. He really should not.

'You cannot stop now,' she said, flexing again.

Even if he wanted to, with her holding him fast, he could not. And he really did not want to.

Slowly, gently, he eased deeper into her body, too slowly for her it seemed at times, but he refused to let her hurry him, he was not going to cause her pain. To distract her, he kissed the lovely mouth that would urge him to go faster. He teased her breasts to keep her focused elsewhere. Finally he was seated fully. Only then did he rise up to look into her face.

What he saw in her expression almost undid him. The haze of desire, the pleasure, the sensuality of her smile—all were so much more than he could ever deserve.

He started rocking against her and she quickly picked up the rhythm, lifting her legs up around his waist to bring him closer and harder against her, and there was no longer any hope of doing anything but taking her into bliss. To do anything else would be a crime.

He suckled at her breast while she met him stroke for stroke and he heard by her cries and soft moans that she was so close, yet she did not know what her body sought.

He reached between them, sought out the place he'd found on his earlier exploration and circled it with his thumb. She writhed against his hand with a sound a protest.

'Let it go, my sweet,' he crooned. 'Let it happen.'

A second later she fell apart.

He held off long enough for her to spasm tightly around him, to draw on him and then somehow his brain managed to wrest back a measure of control. He withdrew and spilled on her belly.

He collapsed. Wrecked. Overcome. And feeling for the first time in a long time that he wasn't completely alone.

Whatever that meant.

Languid in a haze of warmth, her body lax, Rose became aware of a heavy weight pushing her into the mattress. Jake. Lovely Jake. Who had just—

Heaven help her, she'd gone and done it. Something she had always said she would not. And she'd enjoyed it, too.

Without a smidgeon of regret. Indeed, there was a whole lot of joy bubbling strangely inside her, trying to escape. Not that she'd ever dare express how she felt in such terms. He'd likely think her foolish or some such, mock her for being silly, and then she'd be mortified.

Mortified. Such an interesting word. She'd read it in a book and looked it up in *Johnson's Volume II*, an enormous set of tomes Jake had placed on tables in the library for her use. She stretched, luxuriating in the strange new feelings coursing through her veins.

Jake threw the sheet back and went to wash himself off. He shot a considering glance from across the room, rinsed out the cloth and came stalking back. 'Your turn.'

Tenderly he washed her belly and her thighs with his mouth set in a thin grim line. He had more smiles while brushing his horse. 'What is wrong?'

'If I had known, I would have been more careful.'

More careful? Everything had been too lovely for any sort of words she could think of.

'You will likely be sore come the morning.' He tossed the washcloth across the room and it landed with a *thunk* in the basin. 'Why did you leave me to believe this was not your first time?'

She must have looked as blank as her mind felt, because he tapped her nose with a finger, much as she had done to him earlier. It was as if they had their own private language. The thought pleased her.

'Rose, this is no smiling matter,' he said sternly. 'You have never been intimate with a man before.'

'Not like that I haven't. Had the odd kiss and a cuddle, but that was all. Never met anyone I liked well enough. Besides, live-in servants can't marry and…' She bit her lip.

His expression became thoughtful. 'Is that what you want?'

'I haven't given it much thought.' Not quite the truth, but really a husband and family had been little more than a dream.

'You deliberately misrepresented matters.' He sounded bemused.

'Mispre— What?'

'Misrepresented. Made me think you were something you weren't.'

She pulled the sheets up to her chin. 'Are you accusing me of lying?'

He pulled her close and kissed her forehead.

'Misleading me. You said you'd known a great many footmen.'

'I was a housemaid. Houses are full of footmen.'

'Then it is my mistake.' He petted her hair where it lay across her shoulder. 'I should have been more direct. When I asked you if you knew them, I meant in the biblical sense.'

'The biblical…' She shot upright. 'You meant had I swived them?'

'Yes. I'm afraid I did.'

'Then you should have said so.'

'Indeed.'

She frowned at him and realised he was smiling, but not in a mean way. He looked pleased.

'Come here, sweetling. Cuddle up. I find I am too tired to think, right at this moment. I want to hold you.'

She snuggled into his embrace. 'I didn't mean to misrepresent,' she whispered against his chest.

He stroked her back. 'I know. Are you comfortable?' He shifted his arm.

She moved so that one leg draped across his thigh. 'I am now. Are you?'

'Very.' His head moved as if he was trying to see her face. 'Rose, you would tell me if you weren't happy here, wouldn't you?'

Would she? They had promised to be truthful. 'I will.'

'I worry that I might have been a little high-handed.' He gave her a little squeeze. 'I would not like to think of you feeling trapped.'

'I like it here. I just fear making a terrible mistake and putting you all to shame.'

'You couldn't.'

If only she could be as confident.

'Rose?'

'Yes.'

'Was it your dream to become a housekeeper?'

She recalled her playful words of earlier. Clearly he had been listening. 'Once it was. More recently I have been thinking of becoming a dressmaker.'

'A seamstress,' he said with a yawn he tried to disguise.

'No. A proper dressmaker. To the fashionables. Like Mrs Gill of Cork Street. The girls at the V&V said I do wonders with their gowns.'

'Would you rather—?'

'I am fine where I am at the moment. What about you? Did you dream of becoming a duke?'

He stiffened. 'It was the very last thing I dreamed of, I can assure you.' He sounded offended. Cold.

'But—' She bit the words off as she recalled it was his older brother who should have inherited. 'I am sorry, Jake. I did not mean—'

'Forget it. I had better leave now. We don't want anyone finding me here.' He threw the sheet back and pulled on his breeches and shirt.

She winced. Somehow she had ruined the moment. Gone was the easy camaraderie of moments before. The autocratic Duke was back—cold, efficient and displeased.

'I did not mean—'

'I don't wish to discuss it further.'

In moments, he was dressed and walking out of the door. 'Goodnight, Rose.'

He didn't even kiss her.

'Goodnight,' she whispered, but he was already out of the door and would not have heard.

It seemed it was all right for him to ask her questions, but not all right for her to do the same.

Well, they had promised to be honest with each other, and if she had trespassed somewhere he did not want her to go, then it was right he should let her know.

Still, his refusal to talk about himself hurt. A great deal.

Jake slowly came to his senses, taking more than a moment to recognise the unfamiliar feeling of well-being spreading throughout his body. And then he did.

The sense of loss at the realisation that he wasn't still with Rose was surprising and none too welcome. He'd always been a rolling-stone sort of chap when it came to women, making good his escape at the earliest opportunity, and had been true to form last night. He could still recall the hurt in her eyes when he'd left.

Her question had touched him on the raw. Now he wished he'd stayed. Not that he could or would explain. Thinking about it made him feel ill. He certainly wasn't going to tell anyone else.

He stared at the light coming through the window. By Jove. It was morning. He'd slept all night, once he'd crawled into his own bed. He couldn't remember the last time he had awoken in his own bed, let alone slept there for several hours on the trot.

Or when he'd last awoken feeling remarkably at peace rather than desolate. It would have been even better if Rose had been here to share his good mood. He stilled. Not something he should want. Not now. Not ever. Good lord, he'd been wrong to let lust carry him away in the first place. It would never happen again.

He wished he believed that, truly he did, but

he knew beyond a doubt that things had not yet come to their natural conclusion. Unless after his rudeness, Rose decided to turn him away.

He shrugged. She wouldn't be the first one and likely not the last. It meant nothing. But he couldn't help hoping that she would forgive his lapse in manners.

His valet entered and started. 'Your Grace!'

Jake sat up. 'That is me.'

And for the first time the very idea of it didn't make him want to hit something.

'Shall I fetch a tray, Your Grace?'

'No. I'll go down for breakfast. Fetch some hot water. would you? There's a good fellow.'

It didn't take him long to shave and dress, though he was held up by his valet, who insisted on trimming his nails. When he entered the dining room he was surprised to discover his grandmother and Rose already eating.

'You are rather early this morning, are you not, Grandmama?' He leaned forward to kiss the papery wrinkled cheek she presented.

'Have you forgotten the Dearbournes' Venetian Breakfast is today? You were to escort us.' She swivelled in her chair and looked up at him. 'You look different. What have you done?'

'Nothing.'

'Rose, does he look different to you?'

Rose cast him a swift glance, then looked down at her plate, a rush of colour across her cheekbones. 'He looks the same as always, Your Grace.'

'Hmmph.' His grandmother went back to her eggs. 'You hadn't forgotten you promised to escort us, have you, Westmoor?'

'I had not.' He just hadn't recalled it was today. He'd been too busy feeling good about beginning the day feeling so cheerful and well rested. 'We leave at eleven, do we not?'

'We do. Which is why Rose and I are eating now. It might be three in the afternoon before Lady Dearbourne puts out a morsel of food.'

He groaned. 'Truly?' He'd gone last year with a couple of friends while his grandmother had gone with his father and brother. Jake had only stayed an hour or so before heading off for more enjoyable pursuits. This year there would be no departing early.

He filled his plate and sat down at the head of the table. Something that usually made him feel like a usurper. This morning it gave him the chance to sit between his grandmother and Rose and charm himself back into both ladies' good graces. 'Are you well, Grandmama?'

'As well as can be expected at my age, my boy,' she said, narrowing her eyes at him.

'Glad to hear it.'

'And how are you this fine morning, Miss Nightingale?'

Again he received only the briefest glance. 'Very well, thank you, Your Grace.'

'I do wish you would call me Jake, or at least Westmoor, or people will think it strange.'

The pink in her cheeks turned a darker shade. She pushed her eggs around on her plate. 'I prefer to maintain the proprieties, Your Grace. May I pour you some tea?'

Grandmama looked from Rose to him. Her gaze sharpened. She raised a brow. 'You seem very cheerful this morning, Jacob.'

'I am.' He glanced at Rose, couldn't stop himself, but she kept her gaze fixed on her plate.

'I'm glad to see it,' Grandmama said, looking pleased. 'Very glad. Aren't you pleased, Rose?'

Rose jumped. Her gaze flew to his and back to his grandmother. 'I am sure it is not my place to offer an opinion, Your Grace.'

Jake felt nervousness like a kick to the gut. Clearly she was not feeling the same *joie de vivre* he was this morning. At least, not with him. Women were such sensitive creatures.

She continued to poke at the food, barely eating a mouthful.

'Hmmph,' Her Grace said. 'And here I was thinking you and my grandson were getting on so well.'

Rose looked ready to hide under the table. 'His Grace is very kind, Your Grace.'

Kind. Was that what she was calling it? He realised his grandmother was watching him and forced his frown away.

'Young people,' Grandmama said with a snort.

'What about young people, Grandmama?' he asked.

'They cannot see what is beneath their noses, that is what. Jacob, you will have the carriage brought around at eleven, if you please. Are you finished, Miss Nightingale?'

'Quite finished, Your Grace,' Rose replied, putting down her knife and fork.

She'd barely eaten a thing. Blast it. But what could he say? He got up and held his grandmother's chair. Rose did not wait for his assistance, but came around the table to take his grandmother's arm and support her progress out of the room.

Devil take it. So much for feeling better than he had in days. Now he had a sense of impending doom.

And then there was Eleanor and Lucy's arrival to be considered. He wasn't sure if having them here would make things better or worse for Rose. But he did know one thing—last night must not happen again if it was going to make Rose unhappy.

Suddenly the day did not seem quite so bright.

Chapter Eight

To Rose's relief, Jake had seen her and his grandmother into the town coach and had ridden on ahead. She wasn't quite sure how she would have managed if he had travelled with them in the carriage. Awkward did not begin to describe the way she felt. It wasn't that she regretted their lovemaking, exactly. It had been something beyond her girlish imaginations. Quite wonderful, in truth. But she did feel as if she had let herself down. She had always assumed she was far too smart to let her attraction for a man overcome her good sense. That she was no better than the mother she had blamed for her situation came as a disappointment.

In addition, she did not like the feeling of keeping secrets from his grandmother, who was regarding her intently. Not in an unfriendly way, more a sort of knowing glance, as if at any moment she might wink. Imagination, surely? Or a guilty conscience. Her Grace would probably toss her out on her ear if she so much as guessed what Rose and Jake had been up to.

Not Jake. His Grace. Using his name would be a terrible slip in public. Besides, it had all ended rather badly, so it wasn't as if it would continue. If only she hadn't made such a stupid comment. Of course he hadn't dreamed of being a duke. Still, there was no reason for him to get so stuffy about it. She hadn't meant anything by it. She could only hope he wasn't regretting offering her this position.

A feeling of excitement took up residence in her stomach as the carriage turned into the drive. Her Grace had tried to explain what a Venetian Breakfast entailed and it sounded like it might be fun. She would just have to be careful what she said and did and not make any more silly mistakes where Jake was concerned.

He was waiting to greet them when the carriage set them down at the front door and escorted them around the side of the house. The Marquis and Marchioness of Dearbourne met them on the terrace and directed them to lawns that sloped down to the River Thames at the back of the house where the guests were assembling.

The scent of late-summer roses swirled around them. Bunting fluttered from bushes and poles in the light breeze on what had turned out to be a day of blue skies and a few puffy clouds.

The drive had been a scant five miles from the ducal town house to Dearbourne Villa, but Rose, despite her misgivings, had enjoyed every moment. It was the first time in her life she had been what she thought of as *out in the country*, though Her Grace had assured her this was, by most, considered as an extension of London. Why, the old lady had exclaimed, they were going nowhere near as far as Windsor.

The villa was not as grand as the Duke's mansion, but it was no paltry affair, either. It had the look of a fairy castle, in fact. Pennants flew at the top of turrets and one could almost imagine armed knights standing on the tops of walls decorated with crenulations.

Since Jake had very properly taken his grandmother's arm, Rose was free to wander along behind them taking in the sights. There were tables set out in the shade of trees that clustered at the edge of a field that the Marchioness had called the lawn. There were also open-sided tents in bright colours, providing shade and seats as well as blankets for those who liked to sit on the ground.

Some of the tents shaded tables full of bottles and glasses, while footmen and maids strolled among the guests, looking dreadfully hot, offering trays of full glasses or carting away the empty ones.

Rose could not help feeling sorry for those servants and their heavy clothing in the summer heat, while the ladies were in the lightest of muslins. Some of the gentlemen lounging on the blankets had stripped down to their shirts and waistcoats.

Al fresco. Rose savoured the exotic Italian words.

Jake organised a chair for his grandmother beneath one of the canopies and offered Rose the one beside her. Instead, she took one to the rear and shook her head when he looked as if he might argue with her choice. She leaned forward to murmur in the Dowager Duchess's ear, 'Is there anything you need, Your Grace?'

'A glass of champagne wouldn't go amiss.'

Jake grinned. 'Leave that to me.'

He strode off, looking every inch the nobleman. Utterly gorgeous. Rose hoped her face didn't betray her thoughts. She fixed her gaze on her hands. The last thing she wanted to do was draw attention to her feelings about him. 'Do you need your shawl, Your Grace? Out of the sun, you might find the breeze a little cool.'

'Not at the moment, my dear, but thank you for your kind thought.' She gestured with her cane at some ladies and gentlemen wandering around with what looked like mallets. 'Have you ever played pall mall?'

'I have not, Your Grace.'

'You should try it. It is all kinds of fun.'

Rose frowned as one of the gentlemen put his hands around a lady to help guide her mallet as she swiped at the ball. Games. When did a maid have time for such games? Or an orphan for that matter?

The Duke returned with a waiter bearing several glasses. He handed one to Her Grace, then attempted to offer one to her. 'No, thank you.'

'Try it,' Her Grace said with an encouraging smile. 'You will find it refreshing.'

'I prefer not,' she said, surprised at the old lady's warmth of tone.

'Persuade her, Jacob,' the old lady said.

Jake frowned. 'Miss Nightingale must decide for herself.' He sounded so aloof the chill of his voice sent a shiver down Rose's back.

His grandmother frowned. 'Jacob, really—'

He waved the waiter off as if he hadn't heard. Of course he wouldn't encourage his grandmother's companion to indulge in strong spirits. It had been something they had complained about with regard to her predecessor. And as for his coldness in front of his grandmother, she was glad of it. The old lady saw too much. More than once she had asked Rose if she didn't think her grandson a most handsome fellow.

He sipped at his drink, arranging himself beside his grandmother's chair. Rose could not see his expression, but she could well imagine the aloof look on his face.

A few minutes later, the Marchioness bore down on them. With her was a young lady in a white sprig muslin. Glossy chestnut locks framed the girl's oval-shaped face shaded by a wide-brimmed straw hat decorated with flowers. She looked lovely and fashionable. The trim on the hem of her gown, a festoon of lace held in scallops by pink silk roses, was gorgeous. The gown must have cost a fortune.

'Your Grace, allow me to present my niece, Lady Alicia Pettigrew.'

The young lady curtsied deeply and batted her eyelashes at the Duke as she rose.

'My lady,' Jake said coolly.

Her lips curved in a friendly smile. 'How lovely to meet you, again, Your Grace.'

She had a slight lisp and spoke in little more than a whisper.

He blinked as if trying to recall her. 'Indeed. Delightful.'

'This is my companion, Miss Rose Nightingale,' Her Grace said into the uncomfortable pause.

The young lady nodded and Rose inclined her head in acknowledgement of the other's superior status.

'Lady Alicia is seeking a partner for a game of pall mall, Your Grace,' the Marchioness said pointedly.

'It would be my pleasure,' the Duke said, looking anything but pleased. He hesitated, glancing briefly at her, then set down his glass and held out his arm to Lady Alicia. 'Shall we?'

It took great effort not to show any emotion. Indeed, she was not sure what emotion it was that made it hard to breathe and had her stomach twisting. Gladness that he had not asked her to join them?

'Don't they make a lovely couple?' the Marchioness cooed.

Her Grace pursed her lips. 'You might say that.'

The Marchioness looked affronted. 'I do indeed. And she is very well connected, you know. I hope you will excuse me, Your Grace, more guests are arriving.' She bustled off.

'Do you think they make a lovely couple?' Her Grace asked, watching her grandson with narrowed eyes. 'I suppose he could do worse. The Pettigrews are a family almost as old as ours. Not to mention the gal has a considerable dowry.'

Was that hope in her voice? Rose gritted her teeth and ignored the clench of pain around her heart. Was Her Grace making a point? 'She is lovely.'

'Lovely.' The old lady turned slightly in her seat with a strange smile on her face. 'They do say beauty is in the eye of the beholder. There's no accounting for people's tastes.'

Did she like the match or did she not? Rose couldn't make up her mind. Not that it was any of her concern. Except it was, because if Jake did decide on a lady to marry, Rose would not be remaining under his roof. She clenched her hands in her lap. She just couldn't.

An elderly lady of enormous proportions wearing a turquoise dress and a wide-brimmed hat tottered over, waving her fan. 'My word, Your Grace, it is warm today. How are you? I heard you were out in company again. About time, too.'

'Sit, Elizabeth, and tell me your news,' the Dowager Duchess said.

The woman collapsed on to the empty chair and dived into a discussion of people Rose had never heard of. Her gaze drifted off to the game of pall mall.

They did make a lovely couple. Rose wanted to take the mallet and bash Lady Alicia over the head with it.

The girl stumbled over what could not have been more than a pebble, or perhaps a worm cast. Rose glowered as Jake caught her before she fell to her knees and set her back on her feet. A trill of laughter wafted across the lawn to grate against Rose's ear.

She could not bear to watch them, yet try as she might her gaze still wandered in that direction. He was her lover and while she accepted the fact that they could never be more…she certainly did not want to watch him flirt with another. It hurt.

She stared at her gloved hands gripped in her lap until there was a lull in the ladies' conversation. 'Is there anything I can get for you, Your Grace?'

'Nothing at all, thank you, Miss Nightingale.'

'Would you mind if I went for a short walk? I feel the need of some exercise.' She needed to be as far from Jake and Lady Alicia as possible. At least until she got her emotions under control.

'I do not see why not.' The expression on the Duchess's face held concern. Rose had the feeling the old lady knew why she needed to get away. Surely not? 'Young people, always so restless,' Her Grace said to her friend. 'Stay within sight of the house, Rose,' she added in a low voice. 'And do not be gone too long. They are sure to serve food at any moment.' Her Grace spoke louder. 'Take your parasol. The sun is very bright today.'

Parasols and gloves and delicate little slippers not at all suited to walking conspired against anything but the daintiest steps, when she wanted to march off at great speed. As far away as possible if the truth were told. But she did not want to cause Her Grace any embarrassment, so she strolled towards the river. Fortunately the grass was dry and would not mire the hem of this very expensive gown. She shuddered every time she thought about the cost.

She wandered towards the bank. The Thames here was very different to the busy river running through the city. Here, there were boats, but none of the tall ships that docked south of London Bridge and none of the ferrymen shouting for custom. It smelled a great deal better, too. It was quiet and it was peaceful.

Slowly she began to calm. Seeing Jake with that other woman had been a painful tug on her heart, even though she had known it would happen. Perhaps she simply needed time to get used to the idea. After all, she was merely an employee. They could certainly never be more than lovers.

It wasn't as if he'd made any promises. As someone abandoned as a baby, she knew better than to expect loyalty from anyone in her life, least of all a man. After all, only a woman lacking the support of a man would give up her child as her own mother had done. And while she might not be all that different to her mother when it came to Jake, she certainly was going to do her very best to ensure no unwanted children would result.

The day was too lovely for such dark thoughts. She took a deep breath. Tried to focus on her surroundings. The air here in the country smelled fresh, like a bouquet of flowers, and if this was not exactly the countryside, it was as close to it as she was ever likely to get.

And yet she couldn't quite shake off her unhappiness or the need to avoid the company of those clearly enjoying the day.

When Jacob returned to his grandmother, after a very tedious forty-seven minutes with the vapid Lady Alicia, he was pleased to find her surrounded by a group of her cronies and having a grand conversation. Of Rose, however, there was no sign.

When his grandmother caught sight of him she waved him over. 'Are you looking for Miss Nightingale?'

He smiled at the assembled grande dames and bowed. 'Good afternoon, ladies. I see you are looking in fine fettle. Our debutantes should beware.'

They smiled with girlish pleasure and there were even a couple of giggles. 'You always were a charmer, Lord Jake,' one of them said, flailing her fan.

Her grandmother gasped. The lady who had spoken flushed. 'I beg your pardon, Westmoor. I haven't seen you since…the accident. My condolences.'

She lowered her voice on her last words. Was

she another who doubted his honour? 'Where is our dear Miss Nightingale?' he asked cheerfully, as if he had not noticed the inflection in her voice.

'She went for a walk.' His grandmother frowned, looking around. 'Quite some time ago, now. Not long after you left. I asked her not to wander too far, but I no longer see her.'

Jake's heart gave an uncomfortable thump. She should not have wandered off alone. Nor should Grandmother have allowed it. 'I'll find her and bring her back to you safe and sound.'

Grandmother's face paled. 'She walked towards the river. I did not think to warn her about the current.'

'Please, Grandmama, do not concern yourself. I am sure Miss Nightingale simply went a little farther afield than she intended.' He bowed and strode down the sloping green sward towards the jetty where several young men lounged about, no doubt hoping to encourage some unwary female to board one of the punts.

Was that where Rose had gone? This urgent need to find her surprised him. In all his relationships with women, he had always been the one in control. With Rose he felt like a ship lost at sea.

How easily she'd abandoned him to Lady Alicia, while she went off having fun. Disgruntlement stirred in his chest. And worry.

Rose was too much the innocent to be safe around these young rakes. Rakes not unlike himself only a few months ago. He had no trouble imagining the sort of things they might get up to.

'Westmoor. How fortunate to meet you here.'

Inwardly, Jake groaned as he realised the source of the hail-fellow-well-met voice with its distinctive lisp. This was a man he'd prefer not to meet anywhere, though he wouldn't give the fellow the cut direct since he was also one of the Marquis's guests. Nor did he wish to appear overly anxious about Rose. Damn the gossipmongers.

He tamped down his impatience and gave a sharp nod to the thickset fellow. 'Bowles.' He'd known Nash Bowles since university. The man lived on the fringes of society. His reputation was, if not tarnished, then not highly polished. He was rumoured not to have paid his debts. Worse yet, he had attempted to entrap Fred's wife into marriage and Nicholas had held him in low esteem. All of which put him beyond the pale as far as Jake was concerned.

Now the blasted man was eyeing him with a

narrowed gaze. Like a predator spotting prey? Damn his impudence.

'I have a business proposition for you,' Bowles said sotto voce, glancing around as if he was imparting some great secret.

'Really, Bowles? At a party?' The man was an idiot. He moved them a couple of steps away from anyone who might be within earshot. 'Send a note to my man of business, why don't you?'

Bowles smiled with the great bonhomie that some ladies found charming. It set Jacob's teeth on edge. 'I want to talk to you about Vitium et Virtus.'

Here? The man wanted to discuss the club in a public place, with ladies present. He glared. 'I have no idea what you are talking about.'

The man bridled a little, then caught himself and flashed another of his oily insincere smiles. 'With Bartlett gone, you have need of another partner, I should think. What if I told you I learned things in Europe that would bring in fabulous wealth? Special offerings for those with unusual tastes.'

Jake kept his hands loose at his sides. He would not let this jackanapes make him lose his temper. He curled his lip in a perfect imitation of his father when disgusted. 'Not interested.'

Bowles shifted from foot to foot, glancing about him. 'Think about it. That is all I ask.' He bowed. 'Good talking to you, Your Grace.' He sauntered away, with a strangely graceful gait for so thickset a man. He flourished his cane as if he wasn't the most irritating man in London.

Jaw clenched, Jake watched him make his way across the lawns, bowing here, and pausing to exchange a word there. Gall. The man certainly had gall. Jake shook his head. He wasn't going to let an idiot like that ruin his day. What was ruining his day was not finding any sign of Rose.

She was nowhere near the jetty. Nor was she one of the ladies lounging beneath parasols in the little flat-bottomed boats being wooed by eager young gentlemen in straw hats.

Rose would not have got into a boat with a stranger.

His stomach settled at that certainty. He looked along the bank. Upstream the edge of the river became reedy and the path petered out. Downstream the path meandered into a small stand of trees intended to look natural, but carefully planted to provide dappled shade. He chose that direction and set off with a lengthened stride.

Around a bend in the path he found her seated on a wooden bench looking out over the river to the fields on the other side. Though she sat with shoulders straight with her hands in her lap, she looked so forlorn his heart wrenched.

And the relief he felt was out of all proportion to discovering her whereabouts.

She did not turn her head when he sat down beside her, but he had no doubt she knew that it was he.

'Rose,' he said softly.

'Your Grace,' she replied, her voice calm.

'Jake when we are alone, remember?' he said in teasing tones, unsure of her mood.

'Are we alone?'

'It would appear so, unless you are hiding some other fellow in the bushes hereabouts.' He gave her a gentle shove with his shoulder.

She cast him a glance of disdain. '*I'm* not hiding anyone.'

'Nor am I.'

'You and Lady Alicia make a very striking couple.'

He winced. 'I would much rather have played pall mall with you, you know, but—' Curse it, how did he put this without making things worse?

She lifted her little chin and looked him in

the eye. 'But we both know she is the sort of girl you are expected to marry.'

Thank God she understood. Even so, her understanding didn't provide any sort of relief. It made him sad. 'At the moment I have far too much to do learning how to manage the Duchy without adding a wife to my list of duties.' At least that was what he kept telling himself, despite his grandmother's urgings.

She stared down at the white linen. 'Your grandmother wouldn't agree.' She took a deep breath. 'I suppose her anxiety is natural after what happened.'

He froze as guilt rose in his gullet, making it hard to breathe. 'Are you saying you agree with her?' Damn it, did he have to sound quite so defensive?

'I beg your pardon. I should not have said anything. I know you do not like to speak of it. I understand how dreadful you must feel.'

'I doubt that you do, actually.' And now he sounded harsh. How the devil had they ever got on to this topic?

She stiffened. 'I, too, lost my family.'

He gazed at her, shocked for the moment. It simply hadn't occurred to him she would see her orphaned state as that sort of loss. Not when she'd never known her parents. 'Rose. I am sorry.'

She gave a brave little smile. 'Of course, they may still be living. I sometimes wonder.'

He had the urge to find out for her. 'Do you know their names? Does the Foundling Hospital have records?'

She shook her head. 'Only my last name. There is no other information. It must have been a difficult thing to do, give up a child.' She glanced up at him, doubt in her eyes.

'Of course it must have been difficult.' He honestly couldn't imagine it. 'There has to be some way to find them.'

She shook her head sadly. 'It is not the way it works. If the mother wants you, she comes back. Otherwise…'

Surely not? Perhaps a man in his position could do what another could not. But he certainly didn't want to make a promise he could not keep.

She gave him a smile. 'So you see, I do understand a little of what you feel.'

He winced. They were back to him. And it wasn't the same at all. Unlike him, she had no reason to blame herself for their loss. They had abandoned her. 'I really prefer not to discuss my family, Rose. It is not the same case at all.'

Her wide eyes and startled gasp said he had hurt her.

'I beg your pardon. I did not mean to pry.' The coolness in her voice made him want to curse, as did the little sniff that made him think she might be trying to hold back her tears. The last thing he wanted was to hurt her.

What he wanted was to hold her, pull her into his arms and kiss her silly. Yet while there was nothing risqué about sitting side by side on a bench in so public a place, anything more would land them both in trouble. And there was nothing he could do about the future.

The most comfort he could offer was a promise. 'I swear I will not make an offer of marriage without letting you know first. Not that I intend marriage in the near future. I scarcely have time for the work of the Duchy as it is.' He handed her his handkerchief. When she did not refuse it, or throw it back at him, he could only assume she was satisfied.

He breathed a sigh of relief. 'I am glad that is settled.' He risked a brief kiss to her temple.

She shivered and leaned into his shoulder. The slightest movement unlikely anyone else would notice. 'Lady Alicia is pretty.'

He hated hearing the sadness in her voice. 'Rose, at this sort of event, a gentleman must do his duty unless he wishes to be thought the worst sort of cur. Her aunt made it impossible for me to refuse. Honestly? I was bored nigh unto tears.' A thought occurred to him. 'How old are you?'

'Twenty.'

Barely a couple of years older than Lady Alicia. 'You have more sense in your little finger than she has in the whole of her body.'

'She's never had to do for herself.' For all that she defended the other girl, she sounded pleased.

Rose would never have to do for herself ever again. When it was time to let her go, he'd make sure she would want for nothing. Not that he would say anything of the sort. Instinct told him that Rose would see such an offer as a bribe. He would have to find a way to accomplish it without hurting her pride.

Since he wasn't marrying any time soon, there would be lots of time to figure it out. 'Shall we go back? We don't want to start tongues wagging.'

She blew her nose and offered him his handkerchief.

'Keep it,' he said, smiling down into her face, seeing her courage in the lift of her chin.

She tucked it into her reticule, picked up her

parasol and put her hand on his arm, the way any perfect young lady would, and while he desperately wanted to kiss her, Jake knew that any sign of disarray would be noted and commented upon and he would not have Rose embarrassed for any number of kisses, though the temptation be nigh irresistible.

They strolled back along the path and out into the open.

Rose nodded at the house where flags and turrets and crenulations abounded. 'It is almost as grand as the Tower of London, isn't it? It must be very old.'

Bless the girl for not making a scene and for trying to make the best of it.

Now he had to decide if he should destroy her image or... Rose was always honest with him. It was one of the many things he adored about her. 'The Marquis had it built scant five years ago.'

Her jaw dropped. 'Really?'

'A sort of Gothic-revival design.'

She frowned. 'He wanted to live in a castle?'

'Like a knight of old. Luckily we weren't asked to dress up in medieval costume and masks.'

She frowned. 'Why would they do that?'

'Why do the very rich do anything? For amusement.'

They were approaching the riverbank where punts and rowboats hung with bunting bobbed merrily against the jetty. Several gentlemen and ladies milled about, waiting their turn to board. One of them waved. 'Your Grace. We are having a race—will you join us?'

Curiosity was rampant on Rose's face. For one wild moment he thought about asking her to take part with him. He grinned at the young man and shook his head. 'Sorry, lads. My grandmother requires Miss Nightingale's services.'

She glanced up at him with regret in her eyes. 'Thank you for your discretion,' she said softly. A bell rang off in the distance. She smiled. 'It seems food is about to be served.'

Damn. He would make up for it later. When they were alone.

Exhausted by her day by the river, Her Grace had retired the moment she arrived home, taking her dinner on a tray. So Rose and Jake had dined alone in ducal splendour. Or as alone as anyone could be attended by several footmen and the butler. The servants had hovered around them like the flies that had hovered over their picnic, darting in every now and then to remove a dish or add a new one. She and Jake had spoken very little.

With the prospect of the night before her, Rose had barely been able to eat a mouthful. Jake hadn't fared much better. Then, when he'd bid her goodnight, he'd leaned forward and whispered in her ear. 'Leave your hair down for me.'

Now Rose sat on the edge of her bed in her dressing gown, transfixed by indecision. Did she go to him? Or would he come here? Her heart pounded in her chest. Her mouth was so dry she might have swallowed coal dust. Questions buzzed around and around in her brain. Had her fit of the megrims beside the river made him regret taking up with her? How could she have as good as admitted to jealousy when she knew very well they would never be more than lovers? Why did he never want to talk about his family?

Should she apologise for bringing it up? Or should she try harder to get him to speak of what troubled him?

Her door creaked open.

Jake sauntered in, a bottle of wine and two glasses dangling from one hand. He wore only his shirt tucked into his pantaloons, but his hair was damp, as if he'd come from his bath.

She had also bathed, but had not washed

her hair, since it had been washed first thing this morning.

He lifted the bottle. 'Care for some champagne?' He set the bottle and the two glasses on the table by window, where two armchairs made a cosy little nook. When she was not waiting on his grandmother, she liked to sit there and read, since Jake had commandeered the library for his office.

She perched on the edge of one of the chairs.

He gave her a charmingly boyish grin. 'Don't worry, my sweet, I am not going to descend upon you like a ravening wolf.'

'That's a relief, I must say.'

He laughed. 'Did I hear a note of regret, my dear? It really isn't my style, I'm afraid, but I can always give it a go.'

She grinned and eased back into the chair, relaxed by his teasing. Now she knew the answer to one question. He would come to her. Obviously. Of course, no one would take notice of the Duke wandering around his own house. Or if they did, they would say nothing if they valued their positions. And since, as his grandmother had complained from time to time, they ran on a skeleton staff with many of the rooms shut up and the furniture under holland covers, he was unlikely to run into anyone at all.

He popped the cork and poured them each a glass and raised his in a toast. 'To us.'

'To us.' She sipped. Tart and a tickle on her tongue. 'So that is what champagne tastes like.' She made a face.

'The more you drink, the better it gets.'

She wrinkled her nose. 'Are you trying to get me tipsy?'

'Not at all.' He pulled her to her feet and sat down in her chair, lifting her on to his lap. 'Well, perhaps a little. You looked nervous when I came in.' His fingers cradled her jaw and he gazed down into her eyes. 'You aren't afraid of me, are you, Rose? I would not hurt you for the world.'

Not physically, at least. Though she had no doubt she'd be devastated when he married. But if this was all she would ever have of him, shouldn't she take it? 'Not in the least bit afraid.' She inhaled a shaky breath and wondered if that was what her mother had thought, too? Well, at least she wasn't leaving the issue of conception to chance. Or to him.

Then there was no more room for doubts, for he was kissing her, tenderly at first, gently, but when she parted her lips his tongue went questing and tasting and the sensations inside her were almost more than she could bear.

She twined her arms around his neck and went questing on her own account, inhaling the clean scent of him, soap and something earthy. His cologne. Stroking the inside of his mouth with her tongue, she was entranced by the slide of their mutual tasting.

Sensations rippled through her body, heat, tingles, shivers. Her skin felt alive and aching for his touch. Her palms wandered the breadth of his shoulders, her fingers slid through the tendrils of his hair at his nape. His heart slammed a beat against her breasts and made them feel full. She pressed hard against him.

Breathing heavily, he eased away from her, brushing her hair back from her face, gazing into her eyes with a slumberous heat that she felt all the way to the place deep between her thighs.

Even if she had wanted to resist him, she couldn't. And not because of the attraction, the primal desire she felt for him, but because she sensed he needed her help to forget his duty and responsibilities for a short time.

It made her feel important. To him.

Something she had never felt before. She'd been useful, yes, but never had she felt as if it was *she* who was needed, not just because of what she could do with her two hands, but because of who she was as a person.

This was how it must feel to be part of a family. To mean something to another person. And she was going to make the most of it while it lasted. She would not think about the future.

She brushed the errant lock of hair back from his forehead and kissed the tip of his nose.

He grinned and gave her an affectionate squeeze. 'That's more like my Rose.'

His Rose. It sounded wonderful. Heart-wrenchingly so.

She pushed the thought aside. She would enjoy the moment. And if that was what her mother had done, then so be it. For if she had not, Rose would not exist at all, now would she?

He reached around her, picked up her glass and handed it to her. She took another sip. Fewer bubbles, less tart on her tongue. 'You are right, it is quite pleasant when you get used to it.'

'Like many things.' He nuzzled into her neck, kissing and nibbling until shivers raced this way and that all over her skin. 'I want to lick you all over, you smell so good,' he said against her skin.

The idea sounded intriguing. Her insides fluttered alarmingly. 'You wouldn't!'

He groaned. 'I would. In a heartbeat, were

you ready for such games. The very idea of it makes me—' He choked off what he had been going to say.

She pushed away from him. 'Makes you?'

'It arouses me to the point where I can no longer think.'

There was no mistaking the bulge of his erection beneath her. She burrowed a hand between them and shaped his length with her fingers. He arched into her hand, eyes closing, his expression intense as if he would savour every touch.

Recalling some of the talk she'd heard among the girls at the V&V, she set her glass down and slid one knee between the outside of his thigh and the chair and then twisted to straddle him, holding his face between her hands and kissing his lips. She shifted forward to seat herself on his lap.

His hips lifted and the contact of his hardness against that particular spot was startling, and so delicious, she wiggled herself more firmly against him.

He groaned and cupped her nape and deepened the kiss, while rocking his hips in a rhythm that had her moaning into his mouth and trying to get closer. In a surge of movement that took her by surprise and made her squeak, he rose from the chair. She clung on for dear life.

He took the two steps between the chair and the bed and, leaning forward, lowered her on to the counterpane. Reluctantly, she released him and lay back. With a smouldering glance at the way she lay sprawled before him, he toed off his shoes, and stripped out of his clothes.

She let her gaze wander over his magnificent body. A virile healthy male who was rampantly aroused. 'I want to lick you all over, too,' she whispered.

His member jerked.

Her gaze whipped up to his face.

He nodded. 'Your words caused that.'

And if she suited the deed to the words? She reached out to trace a fingertip down the hard length until she encountered the soft springy hair at the base. Then she cupped him beneath, wondering at the softness and vulnerability. He must trust her to let her handle him in this way.

He put his hand over hers and showed her how to caress him firmly, curling her fingers around his shaft and sliding them up and down. He released her hand and she tried it for herself, keeping her grip firm, revelling in the hard shape of him beneath the surprisingly silky skin.

He grabbed her hand and raised it to his lips. 'Enough or this will be over too soon.' He climbed up beside her and pressed one thigh between hers while his hands buried themselves in her hair.

Her eyes reminded him of the soft green that heralded spring. Alive and lively, but mysteriously opaque. He'd done his best to stay away from her, to be honourable, but one crook of her finger and here he was. No other woman had ever had him dancing on a string the way this one did. Though there was no triumph in her expression. Or greed. Only affection.

She asked for nothing, when others would have bargained for the moon. Had she done so, he might have tried to get it for her, too.

He shook his head at the astonishing thought. If he ran true to past form, now that she wanted him the way he had wanted her, he would grow bored very quickly and be ready to move on.

Not that he'd ever really encountered another woman like Rose. She was innocent, but wise beyond her years, intelligent, but ill schooled, lovely but without artifice. And she was his.

For now.

Most humbling of all was that she had chosen him to be her first lover.

Guilt racked him. He'd been selfish the last time. Presuming and unthinking when he should have known better. This time he would make it perfect.

She reached up and stroked her small hands over his shoulders. Down his back. His skin shivered at her touch.

He bent his head and took her lips, kissing her until neither of them had breath. His heart pounded against his ribs. His body fought for control, but this time it was all about her. About Rose. He shifted his attention from her lips to her ear, his tongue tracing the delving deep. On a soft cry, she arched up, pressing her lovely soft breasts with their hardened peaks against his chest.

He cruised down her throat, tasting her collarbone, licking at the pulse points on his way, until he nuzzled into her lovely cleavage, intent on gifting her with every bit of his skill. She deserved that and more after he'd been so careless the first time, thinking her experienced.

It still made his stomach knot when he recalled how thoughtless he'd been. And how awed at her gift.

She shuddered and moaned, her fingers digging into his back. Encouraging him to greater efforts.

He smiled.

'Why are you laughing?' she asked, her voice husky with passion.

'I'm *smiling* because I am happy.' He licked first one nipple, pausing to watch it bead into a tight little nub, then the other. He cupped her breast in his hand and swirled his tongue around that hard little peak, flicking at it until she squirmed beneath him, then taking it into his mouth, letting her feel his teeth in a gentle graze before suckling.

Her hips rolled against his groin, so sweet an appeal it almost undid his good intentions. He shifted away and let his hand drift down her flat belly to the sweet little triangle of blonde curls, stroking and petting while she moaned and tried to increase the pressure of his hand on her mons.

He pressed down with the heel of his hand and when she sighed her approval he gently parted her folds, one fingertip slipping inside her warm damp heat. Hot silky smooth softness. Still so damned tight. He caressed and stroked until she opened her thighs wider, giving him deeper access.

A quick learner his Rose. He licked and teased the other nipple. She pressed down on his nape, telling him silently what she wanted.

He suckled. Drew hard. She cried out and her body tightened, before climaxing in a rush of heat and dampness and tight muscles around his finger.

Breathing hard, she lay lax, looking up at him from beneath lowered lids, her lips parted in a smile of surprise and pleasure. Something in his chest tugged. As if a part of him had attached itself to her.

Not possible. He had no wish for deep attachments. Never had. People he cared for always abandoned him when he needed them most. His mother, Ralph, even his father. All right, so it wasn't their fault, but the pain of it had been intolerable. He refused to go through that again.

When he married, it would be to a woman to whom he would not be emotionally attached. As long as he liked her, that would be all that mattered.

He didn't like Lady Alicia and her ilk. A woman like her would drive him mad in half a day, but there were other women he'd met who were not so silly. Sensible women. He was sure of it.

But he really liked Rose.

He froze as he realised the depth of that liking. At how deep she had got under his skin in such a short time. The way Georgiana had with Fred. Their happiness was almost painful to watch when one stood on the sidelines.

His father and Ralph would turn in their graves if they knew he was wishing for such a thing. Typical irresponsible Jake, they'd be saying. He could hear their voices in his head.

He could no longer be that man. He had a duty to the title. He'd sworn to do his best. Rose as anything more than a mistress was out of the question.

But he would do his best for Rose, too. Here in this bed and hopefully outside of it where he'd find out what had happened to her family. She'd like that, he was sure. It was something he could give her that no one else could.

Right now, though, he needed to be inside her, buried in her warmth and surrounded by her loving self. Tenderly, he eased his knee between her parted thighs and nudged them farther apart. She welcomed him into the cradle of her hips. Deep satisfaction filled him, a sense of belonging as he entered her body.

'That's better.' She sighed, lifting her legs around his waist, opening to him, arching up to kiss him deeply.

He slid home to the hilt and gave himself up to the pleasure and the bliss and the peace of mind that he only found with Rose.

* * *

Later, when they lay in each other's arms, his mind once more turned to the future. Her future. It seemed he could not prevent himself from being concerned. He spooned around her and knew she was smiling, and she snuggled back against him.

'Have you thought about where you would like to open up your dressmaking shop?' he asked.

'Near Bond Street.' She yawned. 'Somewhere ladies will feel comfortable. Cork Street, perhaps. Nothing too large to start.'

He tucked the information away. 'You will need to advertise.'

She glanced over his shoulder. 'You are very interested in this enterprise that may never come to pass.'

'I have every faith in you, Rose.'

She sighed. 'I will try to get *La Belle Assemblée* to use one of my gowns in their articles on fashion. One can advertise, but their recommendation would be the best.'

'Grandmama would be able to assist you there.'

'Do you think she would?'

'I know so. She is very fond of you.'

'She might not want me to leave.' A little

pause. A little hitch in her breathing. 'But I expect she would see it as for the best, once you marry.'

He wasn't going to touch that with a barge pole. He didn't even want to think about it. 'She will want what is best for you.' Even if he did have to explain.

She sighed. Not unhappily. A sound of contentment. 'Go to sleep, Jake.'

He close his eyes and drifted off.

Chapter Nine

Three days after becoming Jake's mistress, Rose sat with Her Grace in the drawing room. It was the only public room in the house not closed up. And as usual, because the old lady's eyes were failing, Rose read and Her Grace pretended to embroider. A little snore indicated that also, as usual, the old lady had dropped off. Rose stopped reading and let her mind wander.

Her days seemed to so idle now. Writing a few letters to Her Grace's dictation in the mornings. A bit of fetching and carrying during the day. Not to mention the wonderful food she ate at every meal. It was all so very easy. But it was her nights that she lived for. More and more. And each time Jake came to her chamber, he seemed more attentive, more loving.

Yet she always felt a sense of distance, too.

He never shared any other part of his life. A brief mention of the V&V from time to time. An odd reference to other estates in other places as they undressed each other, or lay sated and touching and stroking.

While he listened endlessly to her plans for a dressmaker's shop, he never spoke of his hopes or dreams. And each time they made love, he seemed a little more desperate and each time he left her before the sun rose, he seemed a little more reserved.

Only once, when he'd come to her, had she asked him what troubled his mind. He'd closed up tighter than an oyster tapped with a knife. Clearly, whatever was on his mind, he had decided it was not the business of his mistress to enquire. With a heavy heart, she had passed it off with a smile and a kiss.

He'd relaxed then and been his usual wonderfully attentive lover. What more could she ask? Why should she hurt that he did not want to share? That was not their arrangement.

Yet she was not sure how much longer she could bear their growing distance. Perhaps it was his way of showing he was ready to be done with her.

A commotion at the front door brought the old lady awake with a start. She patted at her hair to see if her cap was straight. Rose put the book aside and went to assist, replacing a couple of pins that had come adrift.

'Great-Grandmama!' A dark-haired little girl lunged across the room and buried her face in the old lady's lap. 'I thought we would never get here, Mama made so many stops along the way.'

Rose retreated behind the Dowager Duchess's chair at the same moment an elegantly tall woman swept into the room. An eyebrow lifted at the sight of Rose, but a sweet smile curved her lips, and her eyes lit up when they fell on Her Grace. 'Grandmother. Here we are at last.'

Rose sidled out of the room. This was a moment for the family, not for her to intrude. Head down, hurrying towards the stairs, she would have collided with Jake had he not caught her by the shoulders.

'Rose? What is it?'

She gazed up into his face, unable to explain why she hurt so bad inside and forced a cheerful smile. 'Good news. Lady Eleanor has arrived.'

He glanced eagerly towards the drawing room from where a high-pitched voice was to be heard, though the words were indistinct.

'And Lucy, too. I'm glad. I thought she might

not bring her, after all.' He frowned. 'But where are you going?'

'On an errand,' she said vaguely, not wanting to admit she was running away from her own feelings. 'I will see you at dinner.' She slipped out of his grasp and headed up the stairs.

He followed after her, then stopped, one foot on the bottom step. 'Rose. Is something wrong?'

'Nothing is wrong, Your Grace,' she said, hoping she sounded calm and sensible instead of full of inexplicable tears. 'Go and greet your sister.' She turned and carried on.

He did not follow. He couldn't. Not with half the household standing in the hall looking on. But she did think she heard him curse softly.

She kept going. She needed a bit of time alone. Time to remember who and what she was.

By the time she needed to help Her Grace down to dinner, she was perfectly composed. As they had when Mr Gregory had joined them, they gathered in the drawing room. Jake was already there with Lady Eleanor. Rose curtsied deeply when he introduced her to his sister. Inside, she winced as the young woman took her hand. What on earth would she think if she knew the truth about her and Jake?

'Rose has been such a help to me these past few weeks,' the Dowager Duchess pronounced. 'I do not know how I managed before she came.' To Rose's ears she sounded a little defensive. Did she know? Cold fingers walked down Rose's spine.

Heat travelled up to her cheeks. 'Thank you, Your Grace.' She risked a glance at the statuesque Lady Eleanor, who seemed to notice nothing amiss.

Strangely, Jake looked rather stiff and starchy. Tense.

If the circumstances had been different, she might have given him a poke in the ribs and told him to relax. But it wasn't her place.

She helped the Dowager to sit and stood behind her with the old lady's shawl over her arm, ready to place it around her shoulders if she showed the least sign of feeling a draught.

Eleanor smiled at her. 'I am so glad to meet you, Miss Nightingale. Someone needs to care for Grandmama. Jake has a great deal to keep him busy, these days.'

'Are you hinting that I am neglecting Her Grace?' Jake asked. There was a twinkle in his eye. Clearly, despite his unbending posture, he was fond of his sister. Rose couldn't help feel a pang of sadness. The man had a family, yet could not seem to fully enjoy it.

A footman walked around with a tray of drinks. Sherry. Rose shook her head when offered a glass, but the others partook and Jake raised his glass. 'Welcome to London, Eleanor.'

'Where is Lady Lucy?' Rose blurted out, realising they were one person short.

Jake frowned.

Eleanor looked down her nose very much in the way Jake did when he was displeased. 'Miss Lucy,' she said, her voice calm. 'No title, Miss Nightingale.'

An awkward silence descended, finally broken by Lady Eleanor. 'My daughter is in the nursery. She was tired after the journey and I gave her an early dinner and put her to bed.' She straightened her shoulders. 'I hope you don't mind, Your Grace, but she does usually eat dinner with me.'

Jake stiffened. 'Do we have to stand on ceremony, Eleanor?'

Rose flinched at his stern tone.

Eleanor seemed to take it in stride, though her expression held sadness. 'The sooner you get used to who you are, Jake, the easier it will be for you and the rest of us, but, no, we do not need to observe the formalities at home if you do not wish it.'

Jake put his drink down with a snap that spoke of irritation. 'Then, since Rose is as good as family, we can all be comfortable without titles and such.'

Rose's heart gave an odd little thump. *As good as family*. How delightful that sounded, yet how foreign. What wouldn't she give for it to be true. She swallowed. She could not imagine calling the Dowager Duchess by her Christian name. Not for a second. She risked a quick glance at Jacob's sister and saw that her smile was encouraging.

'Dinner is served,' the butler announced.

Jake took his grandmother's arm and Rose followed Lady Eleanor into the dining room. No, she *would* think of her as Eleanor, or Jake would be displeased.

Once they were seated, the Dowager at one end, Jake at the other and Rose and Eleanor on each side, the footmen served them their dinner.

'How was your journey?' Jake asked. 'Not too arduous, I hope?'

'Not at all. Lucy was a treasure. Hardly any complaining at all, but I took Grandmama's advice and took it in small stages with lots of walks in between. We even visited a couple of castles along the way. The child is fascinated with the idea of knights and maidens in distress. I fear I have read her too many stories.'

They discussed the proper reading for Miss Lucy, speaking of books Rose could only have dreamed of as a child. Some of them sounded wonderful. She wondered if there were any of them in the library. Not that she'd ever dare venture there again. Jake had made it clear it was out of bounds for everyone.

Towards the end of the meal, Eleanor put down her dessertspoon. 'Why on earth are we eating in here?'

Jacob's eyebrows shot up. 'It may have escaped your notice, sister mine, but this is the dining room.'

'Don't be ridiculous, Jake. This room holds forty people. It is like eating in a mausoleum. We should be using the breakfast room, where we always dined *en famille* when Papa was alive.'

In response Jacob's gaze became frosty, his shoulders stiff.

Her Grace made a face of distaste. 'Most the rooms in this wing, apart from this one and the drawing room, are under holland covers. It *is* like living in a mausoleum. Don't you agree, Rose?'

'Many of the rooms are indeed closed up, Your Grace.' She had asked Jake why it was so and he had shrugged her question off. She certainly wasn't going to offer her unwanted opinion on it. The Quality did what they did and people like her simply accepted it.

'What is the point of opening up a lot of rooms when they are never used?' Jake said.

'This room won't do for Lucy, if she is ever to join us for a meal,' Eleanor said. 'The poor child will be overwhelmed.'

'Jake has taken to using the library for his office,' Her Grace grumbled. She waved off a footman's offer of dessert, though Jake and Eleanor accepted several of the dishes.

Rose also accepted a small portion on her plate. A lovely fruit pudding and custard. She loved the sweets they served after dinner, but tried not to appear too greedy.

Eleanor took a small bite. 'The library, Jake? Is there something wrong with the estate office?' Eleanor sounded scandalised. 'Is it also true you do not yet sleep in the ducal apartments?'

What would his sister think if she knew he slept either at the V&V or in the bed of his grandmother's companion? She'd likely be horrified. Rose wanted the floor to open up and swallow her.

Suddenly the dessert tasted like cardboard.

Jacob's eyes turned bleak. 'Gossiping with the servants, Eleanor? Isn't that beneath you?'

Eleanor flushed.

Jake stiffened even more. 'I beg your pardon, but surely where I sleep is my business.'

'Never fear, he will take over the ducal suite when he marries,' Her Grace said with the certainty of old age. Her gaze flickered to Rose and away. 'His wife will see to it, of that you can be sure.'

For a long moment, Jake stared at his grandmother, his face an expressionless mask. He glanced around the table. 'If everyone is finished, shall you withdraw, Grandmama?'

Her Grace blinked and smiled vaguely. 'Tea in the drawing room, ladies?'

Jake helped his grandmother to her feet. The attending footmen assisted Eleanor and Rose with their chairs. Eleanor took her grandmother's arm.

Jake bowed them out.

When they reached the drawing room, Eleanor took Rose's accustomed placed behind the teapot. She poured with the graceful elegance of one who did not need to give a second's thought to what she was doing or how she did it. Unlike herself, who agonised over each part of the ritual, each movement, fearing she'd display clumsiness or ignorance.

She seated herself a little distant from the other two ladies, not wishing to appear intrusive or above her station.

Jake did not join them and while the two ladies chatted, she heartily wished she had pleaded tiredness and gone to her chamber to await him there.

Jake strode along the deserted corridors. One of the first things he had done when becoming Duke had been to do away with the night-duty footmen. Not because he envisaged needing to sneak about under his own roof in order to visit a lady, but because it made no sense in this day and age.

It was a medieval practice, requiring men to sit on hard chairs at the corner of every corridor in case the sleeping occupants might be in need of some service.

The remaining two took turns below stairs watching for a bell to ring. The rest, he'd either pensioned off or found other positions.

He halted on the landing between the two wings. He had told himself he would not go to her tonight. Not with his sister under his roof. Seeing Eleanor and his niece had reminded him of his own obligations to the dukedom.

It was not fitting for a duke to keep his lover under the same roof as his family. His father would never have done such a thing. Nor would Ralph. He would have set her up in her own little house at the edge of town. In New Town or across the river. Ralph had never put a foot wrong when it came to doing his duty.

Jake gritted his teeth. How could he send Rose away when his grandmother had come to rely on her?

He stopped outside her door, a wry smile twisting his lips. His reluctance was nothing to do with his grandmother. It was his own selfishness. Something his father had accused him of that last day when he had convinced Ralph to go in his place. Selfish and feckless was what his father had called him. It seemed he hadn't changed.

He turned the handle and walked in.

Seated by the fireplace in her nightgown, Rose looked up from her book and smiled. The gladness in her eyes warmed his heart, making the cares of the day disappear. The cold lump in his chest shrank and became less weighty.

She put her book aside. 'I wasn't sure you would come tonight.'

Guilt intensified. 'Would you like me to go?' The hurt in her eyes made him want to kick himself. 'I'm sorry. I'm a little out of sorts.'

She rose and opened her arms to him. 'It is all right. I am a little out of sorts, too.'

'Because of Eleanor's arrival?'

'Your sister is lovely. And her daughter is quite delightful.'

Ignoring her avoidance of his question, he sat in the chair, as he did most nights when he first arrived, and pulled her on to his lap for a lovely satisfying and arousing kiss.

He was relieved to discover not a scrap of hesitation in the way she melded her lips to his. He ran his hand over her back and down over the lovely swell of her hip, feeling the change in her breathing against every inch of his body, sensing her relax into him, bringing her breasts flush with his chest. Her fingers combed through the hair at his nape and his mind seemed to settle, even as his body came awake in a surge of hot blood.

Finally, breathlessly, they broke apart. She rested her head upon his shoulder as she always did. A gesture of trust, but the hand clutching at the lapel of his dressing gown spoke of possession. Of need.

He needed her, too.

The only time he slept well was in her arms. As often as he had tried to tell himself it was ridiculous, it was the truth.

He didn't deserve it. He didn't deserve her. But he could not bring himself to give her up. Not yet.

So often in the past he had found himself bored to tears by a woman within a very short space of time, a week or two, sometimes even within days. With Rose he never had the slightest urge to be anywhere else. Not even when they sat silently as they did now.

Rose released her grip on his dressing gown and patted his chest. 'How was your day?'

Such a small thing to ask, but it always soothed him, let him talk of things he never discussed with anyone else. 'I heard from the steward at Maston. The sheep have foot rot.'

She shuddered. 'That sounds horrible.'

'It is. We are likely to lose the whole flock.'

'Lambs, too?'

He had told her about lambs. The way they pranced around each other and the way their little tails wagged when they nursed. 'All of them.'

'That is…so sad.'

'It is. It is also a financial disaster.'

He hadn't realised until he came into the title how close to the edge of bankruptcy the Duchy operated with its heavy reliance on the land for income.

She frowned. 'One flock can make that much of a difference?'

'It is the same for everyone. Since the war ended, more and more men are leaving the land to work in factories. I have fewer tenants and therefore less income from rents. Not to mention the price of wool has plummeted. A loss like this will make things even worse.'

It was why his father had asked him to go with him to Brighton to charm the Regent into selling them an attaindered estate. It would have added to their financial security for years to come, not because it would allow them to expand their farming, but because of what they suspected lay beneath the soil. Coal.

Perhaps if Father had couched his demand in those terms, Jake might have acquiesced. Instead, Father had simply ordered Jake to accompany him instead of wasting his time on what he called frivolous nonsense. Never mind that his investment in Vitium et Virtus as well as other businesses had resulted in Jake's considerable wealth. Enough for a gentleman to live very well indeed, but a drop in the bucket compared to what the Duchy needed.

It wasn't until he took over that he realised how difficult things had become. His father had done a fine job according to his lights. And Ralph no doubt would have known how to turn things around. While, despite his man of business's assurances to the contrary, Jake felt as if he was floundering on the brink of ruin.

By the time he'd had the reins of the Duchy in hand, the opportunity for that other estate had been snatched up by another. Today his man of business had suggested he sell himself to the highest bidder on the marriage mart as the quickest and easiest financial solution. He'd actually suggested an American heiress.

Was it his just deserts?

'Is there no way of saving them?' Rose asked.

Sheep. She meant the sheep. 'The steward and the shepherd are doing everything they can. I have every faith in them.'

'But you are worried.'

'We need the income. Plus we have a contract. Defaulting is not an option. I will have to buy the wool elsewhere in order to keep our side of the bargain. If word of our loss gets out to the marketplace, we will end up paying a premium on the price of those sheep and lose even more.'

'You will lose money in order to keep your word?'

He nodded. 'A man's word is his bond. And besides, break faith once and no one will ever trust me again.'

She patted his shoulder. 'I read today that the price of wool is depressed.' She wrinkled her nose. 'Is that the right word?'

'It is. But if word of my need gets out, and it will, prices will rise immediately.'

'What if you bought it now, before word gets out.'

'Then I'm left with a load of wool no one may want.'

'Someone must want it, if they contracted for yours.'

He frowned. Kissed the tip of that wrinkled nose. 'You are right. First thing in the morning…' His brain raced ahead. 'You know, I have been thinking of buying a factory to make our own cloth. It is risky. If we lose all our sheep, we will have no wool to weave.' He closed his eyes. 'We won't lose them. I read something somewhere. A way of cutting the losses. An article. Where the devil did I put it…?'

She captured his face in his hands. 'Jake.

It will still be there in the morning. There is nothing you can do tonight.'

'I can send a message.'

'To a man who is likely in his bed. It will get there faster if your messenger sets out in daylight.' She kissed his lips. 'You are exhausted, my dear sweet Jake. Tomorrow is quite soon enough.'

He was exhausted. Had been for weeks. The only time he slept was in here in her arms. He gazed at the expression of concern on her face, the sweetness, and relaxed. Let go with a sigh. 'You are right.'

'Make love to me, Jake. Please.'

What man, least of all him, could refuse such an enticing request? Even if he did not deserve such bounty.

He rose to his feet and carried her to the bed.

Held in Jake's arms, Rose felt treasured. Being held had been a rare enough event in her life. Most of the people at the orphanage had been kind enough. They had done their best for unwanted children, but they'd had families of their own on whom to lavish affection.

This sense of being wanted, of belonging, was completely new. Even though she knew it wouldn't last, she wanted to wallow in it. Pretend that she was the princess in a fairy tale, instead of the example held out to orphans of what would happen to them unless they were good.

While Jake pulled back the sheet, she clung on to his shoulders. When he set her gently on the bed, she opened her arms to him, welcoming him to lay beside her.

And when he untied his robe's belt, she gazed in awe at his beautiful masculine body. Aroused for her. His lips smiling for her. Him needing her. At this moment she could pretend it was only her he wanted.

She welcomed him into the cradle of her hips, drawing him to her with her legs high about his waist.

He dipped a finger into her feminine folds and groaned. 'So wet and hot. So ready.'

'For you, Jake,' she whispered in his ear. Only ever for you, her mind echoed back. She stilled. Was it true? Was he the only one for her? And what did that mean for her future? She pushed the unwanted doubts aside. All would be well, as long as she didn't visit her own needs and desires on an innocent child.

His lips roamed her breasts, his tongue teasing and tormenting, his hands glided over her body in a trail of heat and sensual tingles.

The desire in her built until she could not bear it any longer.

'I need you,' she groaned. 'Inside me.'

'You are impatient tonight.'

Impatient. Yes. He had read her correctly. Meeting his sister, the Lady Eleanor, so beautiful, so cool and reserved, had given her an odd premonition that time was running out for her and Jake and she didn't want to waste a moment.

Likely because his sister had agreed with his grandmother. Jake needed to wed. He seemed to take more notice of his sister's words.

'I want you.' And no matter what happened in the future, one thing she knew for certain, if a child did result, despite all their precautions, she would never ever leave it to grow up alone.

He took her mouth in a searing kiss and she gave herself up to the pleasure she planned to hoard as if it was miser's gold.

He broke the kiss, gazing down into her face. She sensed the deep weariness of soul he tried to hide from the world. Perhaps he, too, was feeling the future closing in. 'Jake, is something wrong?'

He smiled and kissed her forehead. 'What on earth could be wrong when I have you in my arms?'

What indeed. Whatever it was he did not intend for her to know and for some reason that made her feel sad. And distanced.

She wished there was something she could do to share his burdens. There was always this, of course. Whenever they made love he seemed to forget the outside world for a time. But she wanted to do so much more. To lessen the shadows she saw in his eyes.

She recalled the discussions of the girls at the V&V. Some of the naughty things they'd talked about doing with the men at the club.

Perhaps all men liked such things? Would he think her terrible if she offered?

She flattened her hands on his chest and pushed.

A look of disappointment crossed his face, but he obligingly broke the kiss and raised up on his hands. 'Not in the mood tonight, sweet?'

The girls had been right. A real gentleman never forced himself on an unwilling woman, lady or not.

A wicked smile pulled at her mouth. 'It isn't that.'

He frowned and if anything looked more disappointed. 'Indisposed?'

She tilted her head in question.

'It is your time of the month?'

Oh, that. 'Not until next week.' She gave his shoulder a hard push and he rolled on his back, his erection arrowing up against his belly.

'Tired, then,' he said, throwing an arm over his eyes. 'You should have said when I first arrived. I promise, you are entitled to your peace if that is what you want.'

She leaned over him, her hair falling forward to brush over his chest. He moved his arming, frowning up at her. 'Don't tease. It doesn't become you.'

She threw one leg over him and came up on her knees so she straddled his thighs, but not sitting down.

His whole expression changed. No longer disgruntled, but intrigued and hopeful. 'Rose?'

He sounded hopeful, too.

She glanced down to see him beautifully aroused. When they joined she knew it would feel wonderful. But first she wanted to do a little exploring.

Heat rushed to her cheeks at her wanton thoughts.

But when she looked up to see his face, to read his expression, his gaze was fixed on her breasts.

A hand reached out to cup her and it felt wonderful and gentle, tender.

She grazed a thumb over his flat nipple, ran her fingers through the rough smatter of hair in the centre of his chest. His breathing hitched at her touch.

He grinned. 'I see what you are about. Trying to seduce an innocent young man.'

She circled his nipple with a fingertip and watched in fascination at the way the nipple furled up tight the same way hers did when he touched them. She leaned forward and licked. The little bud felt like a bead against her tongue. He moaned softly.

'It is hard to imagine you as innocent,' she said, sitting up to regard the result of her efforts.

He tried to look insulted, but his pout was adorable. 'I was until my brother Ralph introduced me to a local widow looking for a young man to make her happy. She taught me all I needed to know.'

'She pleased you?' She bent forward to lick the other nipple as if she could swipe away memories of that other woman.

He groaned. 'What were you saying?'

The girls had been right. A man with lust on his mind lost the ability to think. 'About the widow.'

He gasped as she grazed the hard nub with her teeth. 'Rose!' He stroked her hair back from her face. 'How sensual you are,' he said. 'She was a kind lovely woman. I was very fond of her. Also very disappointed to come home from university and learn she had married again. But then I hadn't met you.'

Her heart gave an odd little squeeze. 'Don't try your charming ways with me, your Dukeship.'

He laughed and that sound, that rascally look on his face, was what she had been looking for. As a reward, she bent, intending to give his lips a brief kiss before setting about completing her plan, but he caught her around the nape and held her while he deepened the kiss and they both became breathless.

But she wasn't about to be deterred. Once more she rose up on her knees, working her way backwards.

His eyes widened. He reached out as if to stop her, then let his hands fall away. 'Leaving already, Miss Nightingale?'

'I can't leave, this is my bed.' She swooped down to swirl her tongue in his navel.

He gasped. 'Oh, you really don't want to—'

The gravel in his voice made her insides clench. The girls were right about this also. She slid back another few inches, until her prize was right where she needed it. She grasped it firmly, pausing to admire the pulsing life of it, the darkness of the skin, the rigid length, and dipped down to swirl her tongue around the blunt head that gave her so much pleasure.

The taste was remarkable. Salty, male, hot against her tongue. His hips came up in silent plea. She glanced up to see the agony of extreme pleasure etched on his handsome features as he watched her with hot eyes.

She took him into her mouth and he cried out, a rough feral sound from deep in his throat. As she swirled and licked this most pleasurable part of him, she learned what made him gasp and what made his hips buck out of control, and in the end, that when she drew hard on that part of him, learned what drove him to a pitch where he could hold out no longer.

In a flash of movement, he lifted her up and had her beneath him, driving home to the hilt. She gave herself up to his pleasure with an indescribably joy.

Sometime later, as she lay scarcely able to breathe, their hearts pounding in tandem, he cuddled her in his arms and stroked her hair. She felt…blissfully happy. Safe.

A dream, of course, but lovely none the less.

'Rose,' he whispered against her ear.

She smiled. 'Jake.'

'Do you ever think about your parents? Wonder what became of them?'

She tensed. 'I used to wonder about them all the time as a child.'

'And now?'

'Who wouldn't be curious?'

'That is what I thought.'

He sounded oddly pleased. 'Why do you ask?'

'I wondered, that was all.' He rose up on one elbow and kissed the tip of her nose. 'It is time I left.' He slid out of the bed and slipped on his robe.

The chill left by his departure stayed with her for some considerable time. It was the way it had to be, without question, but that didn't mean she liked it. Still, she had him for small snatches of time and those times were all that mattered.

Chapter Ten

Jake entered the bright breakfast room at the back of the house for the first time in six months. As had been the case under his father's rule, chafing dishes were laid out on the sideboard. The occupants, his sister and his grandmother, had already helped themselves.

Where was Rose? He kept the question behind his teeth, discretion being the watchword.

'I'm sorry, Grandmama,' Eleanor was saying as he browsed the offerings on the sideboard, 'but there is nothing I can do. I have no power to cure the ague.'

Jacob's heart clenched. 'Is Lucy ill?' He turned from the scrambled eggs to eye his sister.

'No it is Nanny who is ill. Grandmama and I planned to go shopping, but I refuse to leave Lucy in the care of the upstairs maid as Grandmama suggests. Lucy doesn't know her and, besides, the girl is much too young.'

He spooned scrambled egg on to his plate and added another dollop for good measure. Clearly his appetite had returned. He moved on to the bacon, then frowned. 'We were left with the maids often enough after Mother died.'

'Do not tell me you don't recall the mischief we got up to,' Eleanor said, 'because I won't believe you. If it hadn't been for Ralph that one time, we would have set the house afire.'

His heart clenched painfully at the sound of his brother's name. 'You lit the blasted thing.' He hoped she didn't notice the rough edge to his voice.

'I understand your fears, dearest,' Grandmama said. 'But we won't be gone above a couple of hours, surely?'

'Two hours will run into three.'

'And three to four,' Jake finished. 'Why don't I take care of Lucy?'

Eleanor's doubtful expression cut at him. He'd seen how little trust she placed in men these days. Did she put him in the same category as the man who had abandoned her and her child? Instinctively his fists clenched, not for himself, but in his need to protect his sister.

'It is not that I don't trust you, Jake,' she said

quietly, obviously understanding his reaction. 'There are some things a young lady requires where an uncle cannot be of assistance.'

Of course there were. *Idiot*. 'I will enlist the help of Miss Nightingale, then.'

'A lady's companion, Jake?' Eleanor scoffed. 'I doubt she'd consent to play nursemaid.'

He took his plate to his seat, only to stand up again as Rose entered. She handed his grandmother an amethyst ring.

'You found it.' His grandmother beamed. 'Clever girl.'

'It was under the dressing table caught in the rug's fringe.'

'Oh, thank you so much, I had Parrot on her knees for half an hour with no success.'

'Poor Parrot,' Eleanor said.

His grandmother's dresser was older than his grandmother.

'Not at my request,' his grandmama said. 'She was upset about dropping it.'

'I told her all is well before I came down,' Rose said, going to the sideboard and filling her plate before taking her seat.

Eleanor poured tea for her. It pleased Jake no end to see Rose being treated more like family than employee. More than it should.

'Rose, my dear,' Grandmama said. 'Jake has

offered to look after Lucy while Eleanor and I go shopping, since Nanny is ill. May we impose on you to help him for a few hours?'

As predicted by Eleanor, Rose looked doubtful.

Jake frowned. He hadn't expected that from his Rose. His Rose. He liked the sound of it in his head. If only.... He shook the thought off.

'It is not that I mind, your ladyship... I mean, Eleanor,' Rose said with a regretful smile. 'But I have very little experience with the needs of young children.'

'No need to worry about that,' Jake said, smiling at her. 'I practically raised Eleanor single-handedly after Mother died.'

With Father and Ralph busy with the dukedom, the two younger siblings had been left to manage for themselves.

'You were a wonderful big brother, Jake.'

Jake felt stunned at his sister's compliment. He felt heat sting his cheeks. 'Well, I helped Nanny a bit, anyway.'

'You help me.' She turned to Rose. 'It is all right if you don't wish it, Miss Nightingale. Indeed, it was wrong of us to ask. You have your own duties.'

'It is only for a couple of hours, Rose,' Jake said quickly, then winced. 'Unless you would prefer to accompany Grandmama and Eleanor to the shops?'

Rose shook her head. 'I thought to catch up with my mending.'

'You prefer mending to time spent with Lucy and me?'

'Enough, Jake,' Eleanor said. 'If Rose—'

Rose put up a hand with a smile. 'His Grace is right. Mending pales in comparison to spending the morning with Lucy in the schoolroom. Truly.'

Jake raised his brows at her. 'The schoolroom? Really? What sort of uncle would that make me? We are going out.'

'It needs to be something educational,' Eleanor said sternly, 'If you intend her to forgo her lessons.'

Jake made a face.

'What about the Elgin Marbles?' Grandmama suggested.

Jake winced. 'Some of those might be a little too risqué for an uncle to be explaining.'

'I know the very place!' Eleanor said, her eyes alight. 'Lucy has been learning about famous explorers. The Panorama in Leicester Square is exhibiting the North Coast of Spitzbergen. We talked about it just the other day. Would it interest you, Miss Nightingale?'

Rose looked fascinated, the way she looked fascinated when she discovered a new word.

Mentally he grinned. There was no way her natural curiosity would let her allow such an offer pass her by.

She glanced his way, but he kept his gaze fixed on Eleanor. 'Educational, Eleanor?'

'I would like to see it,' Rose said.

'Everyone should visit Barker's Panorama,' Grandmama pronounced with a stern look at Rose. Dear old stick. If he hadn't known better he might have thought she was championing his cause with Rose. Really? He narrowed his gaze on her, but her expression was completely innocent. Suspiciously so.

'In the upper chamber they have a view of St Petersburg,' Eleanor said, drawing his attention to her. She looked more animated that she had for a while. His offer had pleased her and he could not help but feel glad. Mostly these days she simply looked sad. 'I read in the paper that it is even better than going to visit the actual city,' she continued. 'Apparently one can see the whole thing, though it is quite a climb to the top.'

'You had better eat a hearty breakfast, Rose,' Grandmama said, with a chuckle. 'You are going to have your hands full with those two.'

'Two?' Rose asked.

'Lucy and Jake,' the old lady said, her eyes twinkling with mischief.

Rose smiled such a sweet smile his heart gave a strangely painful little thump. It meant nothing. He was glad for her, that was all. He simply wanted to give her an opportunity that might never present itself again.

What was he letting himself in for? An expedition alone with Lucy and Rose, that was what. Something he was looking forward to far more than he should.

The morning was warm, the sky blue with only a few puffy clouds sailing along on a light breeze when Jake helped Rose into his town carriage. A grand black affair with its wheels picked out in yellow and the ducal crest emblazoned on the door. Once she was settled, he handed Lucy in as if she was a grown-up young lady.

The child spoiled the impression with a giggle. Once inside she hopped up on the forward-facing seat beside Rose, wiggling around until she was comfortable.

After giving instructions to the coachman, Jake climbed aboard and took the seat facing them.

'How long will it take to get there?' Lucy asked.

'Half an hour,' Jake said. 'Depending on the traffic.'

The coach pulled off.

'Exactly what should we expect to see when we visit this Panorama?' Rose asked. 'Perhaps you should explain it to Lucy.' She'd looked up the word, but it hadn't been listed. His grandmother had waved a vague hand and called it a vista, which Rose had learned came from the Italian word for *view*.

Jake gave her a rather mischievous look. 'It's a surprise.'

He looked younger with that expression on his face. More handsome than ever. Somehow more dear.

The nervous flutter in her stomach increased. She had hoped he would give her some guidance as to what to expect. There were so many traps to avoid when moving among the members of the *ton*. But clearly he wanted to surprise his little niece. Who was she to want to spoil the occasion? And, truth to admit, she was really looking forward to accompanying Jake on this adventure. For that is what it would be.

'Oooh!' Lucy exclaimed, bouncing off the seat and lurching towards the window. 'Birdies.' She grabbed the ledge and pulled herself up to lean out, pointing.

In a flash, Jake leaned forward and pulled her back to sit on his knee.

'Uncle, you made me miss the birdies,' Lucy grumbled.

A second later a horse and carriage going in the other direction passed so close Rose recoiled from the noise and the swirl of air that swept into the carriage, raising a cloud of dust in its wake. Her breath caught in her throat as she realised it could easily have hit the little girl's head.

'What did I tell you about leaping about inside a moving vehicle?' Jake growled. He sounded so severe the little girl visibly shrivelled. Poor little thing.

Rose recalled one of the maids telling her that his father and brother had died in a carriage accident. No wonder he looked so fierce.

He cared for this child. Deeply. Rose couldn't help admiring his protective streak even if he had spoken too harshly.

Then she saw that he had softened the effect of his admonition with a gentle touch, one hand holding the little girl gently but safely on his knee while the other rubbed comforting circles on her narrow little shoulders. He shifted so she could once again see out of the window, but this time in safety.

'You know if you stick your head out like that you will frighten the horses coming the other way,' he said.

Lucy gave a nervous little giggle. 'They would be scared of my head?'

'Certainly,' he said. 'Horses are stupid creatures. They are terrified of rabbits and can shy at the mere sight of a ribbon fluttering on a hat.'

'Did Grandpapa's horses see a hat?'

Rose's heart stopped. Jake never talked about his father. He became positively remote if the subject came up.

His hand on the child's back stilled. His shoulders tensed. A little muscle in his lean jaw flickered.

For a long moment, Rose feared he might stop the carriage and walk away.

He inhaled a slow breath and blew it out. 'I don't know. Perhaps they did,' he finally said.

'I miss Grandpapa,' Lucy said quietly, sadly. 'And Uncle Ralph.'

'Me, too, poppet,' he said in a low voice.

The pain in Jacob's eyes was hard for Rose to see. She wanted to offer comfort, but all she could do was look down at her hands so he would not see her sympathy. She did not want to intrude on his grief. She did not have the right.

Oh, but she did understand their sense of loss.

There was an empty space in her heart where a mother and father should have been and perhaps one or two siblings.

She blinked the mist from her eyes. Perhaps she was the lucky one after all. Seeing the depth of Jacob's sorrow made her think it was better to have never known her family, than to have had them wrenched out of her life in such a cruel way.

'How much farther is it?' Lucy asked, returning to her bright eager self in the wink of an eye.

Jake smiled at her fondly. 'Not far now.'

What a wonderful father he would make. Wealthy. Protective. And best of all, loving. The woman he married would be fortunate indeed.

She on the other hand would likely never have children. For that she would need a proper home and husband, but women in service rarely married, because if they did, they lost their positions and income.

No, what she had with Jake was the best she

could ever expect. Sadly, it would not last for ever, but when it was over she would have the most wonderful memories, including those of today.

'Time to go back to your seat, young lady,' Jake said, lifting Lucy as if she was lighter than air and setting her beside Rose as the horses slowed, turned the corner on to Cranbourn Street and halted.

Jake climbed down and helped them to alight to the pavement. He crouched on his haunches so he was eye to eye with Lucy. 'You will hold my hand at all times,' he said, once more his tone stern. 'Your mama will spank my backside so hard I won't be able to sit for a week if I lose you.'

Lucy roared with laughter at the thought. Rose couldn't help smiling at the image her mind conjured up, though she had the feeling Jake meant every word.

The entrance to the rotunda was rather small, though it proudly proclaimed its exhibition and promised delight and amazement. The porter at the door tipped his hat.

'Westmoor,' Jake said. 'I am expected.'

'Indeed, Your Grace.' The man bent almost in half, his bow was so low. 'This way if you please. All is ready for your party.'

Rose frowned at him.

Jake raised a brow. 'I sent word ahead. The place is reserved for us.'

'Reserved for…' She gasped. 'You mean no one else can come in while we are here?'

'One of the benefits of being a duke. Privacy.'

She eyed him with suspicion. There was a little too much smugness in his voice. But with Lucy able to hear every word there was little she could say.

Jake held out his arm, she hooked hers through his and, with Lucy holding his other hand, they followed the porter through a door.

The narrow passage in which they found themselves was dimly lit. There was absolutely nothing at all to see in the chilly gloom of the corridor that twisted and turned like a labyrinth.

'Not much of a vista,' Rose, said savouring the unfamiliar word.

Jake patted her hand. 'Wait. You'll see.'

The shadowy passage arrived at a set of equally badly lit stairs winding upwards. Finally, at the top, they stepped through a black curtain and on to a platform. Rose blinked at the sudden brightness.

Her jaw dropped as her eyes finally focused.

Speechless, she stared at the…the view. She was standing in a blazing white wilderness of ice that was not just in front of them but all around, no matter which way she turned. She shivered, despite that she was not cold. Chills ran down her spine.

'Oh, look,' Lucy cried. 'Mermaids.'

Fearful for the child's safety, Rose made a grab for her, only to realise there was a railing between the edge of the gallery where they stood and what seemed like a gaping black hole beneath them.

She stood behind the child, gazing at the scene spread out before her. 'Oh, my.' There were icy mountains and a ship heeled over, held fast between two blocks of ice, and men in small boats or standing around conversing on the snow. The whole thing made her feel slightly dizzy.

She swayed and Jake put an arm around her waist, steadying her. 'Give it a moment,' he murmured. 'You'll get used to it. They say Princess Charlotte was seasick for a week after viewing a sea panorama.'

The feel of that strong arm supporting her was blissful. She took a deep breath and looked up to find Jake grinning at her, though much of his face was in shadow. 'Now you know what panorama means.'

She took in the scene before her in wonder. 'Yes. Yes, I do.'

'And how would *you* explain it?'

She shook her head. 'I couldn't. Not in a hundred years, if I was to try ever so hard.'

He leaned forward and brushed his lips along her jaw, a fleeting warm touch over almost before it began and shivers broke out all over her body. Pleasure and desire.

Naughty man. She glanced down at Lucy, who for once was silent and clearly transfixed, unaware of the adults behind her. She was terribly tempted to kiss him back. Out of gratitude. Out of deep affection. Out of love.

It could not be. She forced herself to remain still.

Lucy turned and tugged at her skirts. 'What are those things there?' She pointed through the railing.

Jake pulled a sheet of paper from his pocket. 'I have a guide.' He angled the paper towards the light that somehow seemed to emanate from the scene itself. 'The ship you see is the *Dorothea*, caught in the ice.'

'But the creatures, Uncle Jake.'

'Give me a moment, child.' He scanned the

paper. 'Those are walruses. See their curving tusks.'

'Where are their legs?'

'No legs, pet. They don't need them for swimming.'

Lucy ran a little farther along to take in another part of the scene. Jake tucked Rose's hand beneath his arm and they strolled after her, he reading from the guide and pointing out the items of interest.

'They have dogs,' Lucy announced.

'Not dogs,' Jake said. 'Polar bears.'

'Bears aren't white.'

'These are.' He went on to describe the explorers and their ships as they promenaded around the railing, until they had gone full circle.

To Rose, it felt as if they were a real family. A man and his wife and their child. A lump forced its way into her throat. Longing. She wanted to weep for longing. She turned her face to the panorama, hoping Jake would not see.

She took a deep breath. Swallowed past the lump and pinned a smile on her lips. 'Why is some of the ice blue?' Her voice sounded brittle.

Luckily in the dim light, Jake seemed to notice nothing amiss.

'Honestly, I don't know. I would have to read more about it. It is hard to believe this happened last August. The middle of summer, no less. They were lucky to survive a huge storm, I understand.'

'They are very brave men.'

'I'm going to be an explorer when I grow up,' Lucy said. 'And go on a ship. And get stuck in the ice.'

Jake glanced down at her.

Rose expected him to tell her that women did not undertake such daring adventures. Instead he merely smiled. 'I expect you will, pet.'

And then they were back where they came in. 'Shall we go down?' Jake asked. 'There is another staircase leading up to the other view, but it is a very long climb to get a view of St. Petersburg. Not nearly as exciting as this.'

In other words, not something that would interest a child. 'No, I think it might be best saved it for another day.'

'I want to go,' Lucy said, pouting.

Jake crouched down. 'Very well, I will give you a choice. A long hot climb for a view of an old city with streets and buildings or ices at Gunter's.'

'Ices. I want raspberry.'

Jake chuckled and came to his feet.

Rose breathed a sigh of relief, having expected floods of tears or a tantrum. The man was so lovely with the little girl. He would indeed make a wonderful father.

Again her heart squeezed.

'Shall I carry you down the stairs, Lucy?' he asked.

'I can do it myself,' the little girl said. She bustled ahead.

'Hold on to the banister,' Rose reminded just before Jake spun her around and kissed her on the lips.

She melted against him and kissed him back. When they finally broke apart, she smiled up at him. 'Thank you.'

His eyes sparkled. 'Thank you. Now, *you* will allow me to help you down the stairs, will you not?'

Chapter Eleven

To Jacob's disgruntlement, the heat of the day had brought every member of the *ton* left in London to Gunter's Tea Shop. Didn't they know they were supposed to be residing in the country at this time of year?

Glancing around him as he stepped out of the carriage, he realised he had made a fatal error. The place was riddled with biddies who would have a field day when they saw him escorting Rose without the company of his grandmother.

He could bring the ices into the coach, but it was far too hot to be sitting inside a stuffy carriage. And besides, he didn't want the seat cushions ruined just because of a lot of gossipy old besoms.

To hell with them. He had promised Lucy an ice and he wasn't going back on his word.

With the skill born of long practice, along with the newly acquired ducal stare, he contrived a seat in a corner beside an open window where what breeze there was would help keep them cool until their ices arrived.

He made his ladies comfortable, seating himself between them and relaxed. Sitting here beside Rose seemed right somehow. With her at his side, he felt more settled inside himself than he had for months.

He smiled down at his niece, who was sitting with her hands folded in her lap as if ice cream would never melt in her mouth, let alone on her frock. 'I know Lucy wants a raspberry ice, but what about you, Rose?'

Rose looked thoroughly uncomfortable. He turned in his seat. Blast it.

Everyone present was looking at them, some covertly, others openly interested. 'Don't worry about them,' he said with an encouraging smile. 'I can assure you, they are ogling me.' Probably regurgitating the stories around the accident, if he knew them. He handed her the menu.

She gazed at it with what he could only describe as awe. 'I have no idea what to choose.'

'Have raspberry. It is the best,' Lucy pronounced.

Rose lifted her gaze to meet his. 'Is that your opinion also?'

'I like them all.' A wicked idea formed in his head. 'Trust me?'

She nodded.

He hailed a passing waiter and turned aside so Rose could not hear while he placed his order.

Lucy frowned. 'Raspberry, Uncle Jake.'

He grinned. 'I didn't forget.'

'What a lovely place this is,' Rose said. 'They are even taking ices out to that carriage.'

'An open carriage is the only place a gentleman can be alone with a single lady of marriageable age,' Jake said, 'and not cause talk. On a hot day like today an ice will make a gentleman very popular with his lady.'

A moment later, the waiter returned with a tray full of small glass dishes, each containing a different flavour, and one large one with red ice cream. He arranged them on the table, making sure Lucy had her favourite, the smart observant chap.

Rose gasped and looked at Jake in dismay. 'They must have made a mistake. These can't all be for us?'

'They are. There is one of every flavour for you to try. You like tasting things.'

Her face went fiery red and her expression became mortified.

He cursed. He'd meant to tease, not embarrass. What was the matter with him? He seemed to be behaving like an awkward schoolboy. 'Rose, I mean it as a treat. These are samples. Look, over there, they are doing the same at that table.'

Her eyes widened. 'Oh.'

The other table did not have quite as many dishes, but they had several. Her feathers settled. She picked up her spoon and he breathed a sigh of relief.

Lucy was already tucking in to her ice. He grabbed her napkin and tied it beneath her chin. 'Your mama won't be pleased if you ruin your dress.'

Lucy nodded. 'Which one will you try first, Miss Nightingale?' she asked.

'This one.' Rose drew the white one closer and inhaled. 'Vanilla?'

'Indeed,' Jake said and the next moment, watching her scoop a small amount into her mouth and seeing her eyes go particularly dreamy, he was as hard as a rock.

'Oh, my word,' she breathed, staring at him. She gave a little shiver. 'It is cold, but it simply melts on my tongue.

He wanted to melt on her tongue. He couldn't stop recalling how she had licked…

He looked down at the dishes, trying not to shift on his seat. 'Try that one. It is strawberry.'

And so it continued, the sensual torture of Rose's first experience of ice cream.

Her surprise at the taste of lemon made him laugh.

One or two people sent startled glances their way and Rose's face mirrored worry.

'I told you,' he said. 'Pay them no mind.'

'It is not that,' she whispered. 'Mr Challenger just walked in, with a lady.' She swallowed. 'What if he…?' She glanced at Lucy and winced.

'People only see what they expect to see.' He shifted so he could see the door. 'Mr Challenger is my friend. He won't say a thing. The lady with him is his wife.'

They made a lovely couple, too. Imagine, Frederick married. The first of the founders of Vitium et Virtus leg-shackled. And happily so. Times were changing. He, too, would have to marry. But not for a long while yet.

'What flavour will you choose next, Rose?'

'Have the raspberry,' Lucy said with the wisdom of the very young. 'You will like it the best of all, I promise. It tastes just like raspberries and it is pink. The first time I came here, Uncle Jake said raspberry was the best.'

He gave Rose's hand a squeeze where it rested on her lap out of sight of any of the watching crows. 'Why not let Miss Nightingale choose for herself.'

'It is all so extravagant,' Rose said.

He loved the way she rolled the word of her tongue as if tasting its meaning.

'But I hate to think of it going to waste, when it must have cost a fortune.' Her spoon hovered over the raspberry ice.

He also loved it that she was considerate about spending his money. So different from any other lady of his acquaintance, he realised with a sense of deep admiration.

'Do not worry. I'll eat anything you don't want, so nothing will go to waste.' He wanted to kiss her again. Taste all those flavours on her tongue. And not a sneaking kiss in the dark as he had at the rotunda, but a possessive this-lady-is-mine sort of kiss for all the world to see. Wouldn't that be scandalous? He grinned inwardly at the thought, even knowing he would never embarrass her that way.

'Westmoor.' Fred stood looking down at him. Jake rose to his feet.

'Challenger.'

'Well met, old chap. Can we impose ourselves on you? There's not a table to be had and we walked over, so I cannot even offer my lady a carriage in which to partake of her ice.'

'Please, do join us.'

While Fred went for a couple of chairs, Jake bowed over Georgiana's hand. 'It is good to see you again, Georgiana. Please, allow me to introduce my grandmother's companion, Miss Rose Nightingale, and my sister's daughter, Miss Lucinda Robertson. Ladies, this is Mrs Challenger.'

Georgiana smiled warmly at both of his ladies. 'How lovely to meet you. And please, call me George. Everyone does. What luck for us, meeting you here, Jacob. I feared we would have to leave without our ices and I would have been most disappointed.'

Rose visibly swallowed and took Georgiana's outstretched hand. 'I am pleased to meet you, Mrs um… George.'

A flush stained her cheeks and she looked nervous, her gaze flitting to his face and back to Georgiana as if the sky was about to fall. A feeling of impatience took Jake by surprise. He didn't want her feeling embarrassed when meeting his friends. He wanted her to feel… comfortable. At ease.

'I am pleased to meet you, too,' Lucy added. 'Can I have another ice, Uncle Jake, if the waiter ever comes back? I am still hot.'

Jake gave her a mock-stern look. She had been such a good girl today and he didn't want to crush her high spirits as long as they stayed within bounds.

Georgiana, bless her, looked indulgent. 'It is hot,' she said.

He became aware of Fred giving Rose a narrow-eyed stare and his stomach knotted. Not much slipped by Fred.

'Why don't I go and order at the counter?' Fred said. 'It might be faster.' He gave Jake a pointed stare.

'I'll come with you,' Jake said. Might as well hear what he had to say.

He followed in Fred's wake, the man's shoulders militarily straight and an aura of disapproval distinctly visible. When they reached the counter, Fred gave him a chilly stare. 'Nightingale? I recognise her name. She's employed at Vitium et Virtus. Damn it all, I'm sure I have seen her there. You certainly have a nerve to introduce her to my wife?'

'To the devil with you, Fred,' he said in a

low voice. 'You joined us. Don't you think that if she's good enough for my niece, she's good enough for your wife? And besides, she worked there as a maid, nothing else.'

His friend looked mollified. Slightly. 'What on earth is she doing as the Dowager's companion?'

'My grandmother likes her and she is doing a very good job. First one the old lady has agreed to tolerate, in fact.'

'If that's the case, where is your grandmother?'

'I don't see that it is any of your business.'

'I saw the way you were looking at her when we came in.'

'The way… Blast your eyes, man. You are as bad as all the other gossips in this place.'

'So you don't have seduction on your mind? Or do you plan to make an honest woman of her?'

That was the question, wasn't it? He'd promised his father he would be the Duke his brother would have been. Sworn it. His brother, Ralph, would have done his duty. Married for political or financial advantage, for the sake of the title. He would not have married a scullery maid, even if he had fallen in— He froze. Cut off his thought before it could fully form. Love was not an option for him.

He'd keep his promise.

Fred thrust out his chin, wanting an answer.

Jake glared at his friend. 'Miss Nightingale is a perfectly respectable young woman, Fred, and if you say one more word suggesting otherwise, I swear I will draw your cork.'

Fred stared at him for a long moment. He let out a long sigh. 'Have it your way, Jake. But I advise you to be very careful. She seems like a nice girl.'

Rose was a nice girl. Very nice. The nicest girl he had ever met. Fred was right. Much too nice for him. He ground his back teeth.

Across the room, the ladies were engaged in a lively conversation.

Rose really was amazing. It didn't matter where he took her, she could hold her own.

He had never felt prouder.

Or, given Fred's admonition, more miserable as reality struck home.

Rose had spoken of children and family and he had heard the longing in her voice. Under the circumstances in which he found himself, he could never give her that. And children out of wedlock were out of the question. No child of his would suffer the way Oliver had.

He ought to stop what he should never have started. Send her on her way with a generous gift and wish her happy when she found a good and decent man who could make her an honest woman.

The thought of Rose in the arms of another did not sit well in his gut as he maintained his outward calm beneath Fred's stare.

Fred waved at one of the servers behind the counter who was looking around for his next customer. 'Over here, man.'

They placed their order and returned to the table, but all through the chatter and pleasantries, Jake could only worry about Rose and what he should do.

On the way home in the carriage, Lucy leaned against Rose's arm and closed her eyes. Rose pulled her close and made her comfortable. 'Dear little soul. She's fast asleep.'

'It has been an exciting day for her.'

Rose raised a worried glance to his face. 'I met Mrs Challenger once before, you know. At the club. I don't think she remembered me.'

'You did what?' He realised he had raised his voice when her eyes widened.

'I helped her dress. Mr Challenger was most annoyed with her at the time.'

Jake could only imagine. Good for George. Perhaps she'd shake Fred up a bit. He'd become far too stuffy since coming back from the war. 'You must never mention the club again and especially in relation to Mrs Challenger.'

She paled. 'Oh, I would never…' She turned her face away. 'I would not want to put you to shame.'

Dash it, now he'd upset her. Fred was right, he was bad for Rose. He could never offer her what she truly deserved. Things could not continue as they were. The resolution came to him in a flash. 'I have to go to Hertfordshire. To my estate. Something has come up there that requires my attention.'

Surprise filled Rose's expression. 'Has something gone wrong there? I thought you seemed distracted.'

He might have known she would sense his mood, though he'd been careful to keep his thoughts hidden. But her concern was misplaced. She should be worrying about herself. Guilt twisted in his gut. He really did have to make this right. 'My steward has written concerning problems with the harvest. I need to see for myself.'

Her brow cleared. An understanding smile

curved her pretty lips. Her gaze softened. 'Will you be gone long?'

The longing not to go at all shook him to his core. Never before had he had any trouble parting from a woman. He took a deep breath, kept his expression cool. 'I am not sure how long I will be away, actually. A week or two. Maybe longer.'

'Oh.' She looked nonplussed. 'I see.'

'I am relying on you to care for Grandmama in my absence. She depends on you.'

She gave a nod. 'Anything I can do to help, I will.'

'I am most grateful.' The words sounded stilted and formal and he saw the hurt in her eyes, but he could not let that sway him. The risks were too great no matter what precautions they took. He needed to make a clean break of it. To set her free of any obligation she might feel to him so she could get on with the life she had planned for herself. 'I will leave the moment we arrive at the house.'

Rose's little gasp of shock, quickly hidden, cut his heart to ribbons. He ignored the pain. 'If I leave right away, I can make it there before it is dark.'

The evenings were already drawing in, but he could do it, if he rode hard. The staff would be surprised to see him, but it was a ducal household and they were always prepared.

The days after Jake left were the longest of Rose's life. There had been one letter from him, a single line to his grandmother announcing his safe arrival in Hertfordshire and no mention of when he might return.

The household had continued in its usual routine, despite the strange emptiness the house evoked without him. She missed him terribly.

On the third afternoon, Rose sat with Eleanor and her grandmother in the drawing room, the other two ladies sewing and chatting as if nothing had changed, while an uncomfortable thought kept going around and around in Rose's mind.

Did Jake's departure mean something more than a need to visit one of his estates? He'd decided so suddenly. And had been so distracted in the carriage ride home from Gunter's. Had he intended that she should hand in her notice in his absence?

Every time that thought crossed her mind, as it had several times since he'd bid her farewell, her heart squeezed with a pang so painful she couldn't breathe. Over the past few weeks, she had grown to love his grandmother as if she was her own. She adored Lucy. And wondrously, Eleanor treated her as an equal. She had the feeling they might have become friends if things had been different.

But she could not allow it. Not when she was living a lie.

Eleanor would be disgusted if she knew the truth of her history, what she was. Not to mention her horror if she learned of Rose's relationship with Jake. What decent mother would want someone like her near their child?

Shame rose up in a horrid wave. She ought to leave before Jake returned. A voice inside her, a niggling discomfort, kept reminding her that as sure as eggs were eggs, the truth would come out. A servant would see him entering her room. Or Mr Challenger would say something. Or…

'Your Grace,' the butler said, walking in with a silver salver. 'A note came for you. Hand delivered. The messenger said it was urgent.'

The Dowager Duchess took the paper with a smile of thanks and spread the paper open. 'Well, fancy that.'

'What is it, Grandmama?' Eleanor asked.

'We are all invited to a musicale evening at Lady Buckhurst's.'

Rose rested her embroidery frame in her

lap, intending to refuse any attempt to take her along.

Eleanor frowned. 'Why would that be considered urgent? When is it?'

'Tonight. A last-minute affair. Lady Buckhurst discovered that Signora Calvetti, a brilliant soprano fêted in Paris and Rome, is visiting London. She is due to depart on the morrow. Lady Buckhurst has managed to get her to agree to one performance only. Quite the coup, from her note. Shall we go and add to the consequence of the evening?'

'You may go if you wish, Grandmama,' Eleanor said softly. 'I prefer not.'

'You need to go about more, my dear, now that we have put off black gloves. It is not right for someone so young to be cloistered away.'

Eleanor sighed. 'I am perfectly happy as I am, Grandmama. You will not flex your matchmaking muscles on my behalf. You have enough to do with Jake.'

Her Grace frowned mightily. 'Rose, you *will* add your pleas to mine.' The old lady turned to Rose. Her hopeful expression pulled at Rose's heartstrings more than it should. The old lady was right, though. Eleanor was too young to remain a widow. She ought to be out among society, seeking enjoyment.

'You told me you like music, Eleanor,' Rose said, a little weakly even to her own ears. She forced confidence into her voice, along with a dab of persuasion. 'You might regret not hearing this singer if she is as good as your grandmother says.'

Eleanor grimaced. 'I don't know.' Her face brightened. 'I will go, if you will. You have been moping about, since my brother left.'

Jake. She meant Jake. Shock hit her hard. She couldn't believe Eleanor would have noticed. And now her cheeks were hot and she couldn't meet the other woman's gaze for fear she would give herself away. More than she already had.

'It is true, Rose,' the Dowager Duchess said. 'You have not been your usual cheerful self. An outing will do you good.'

Oh, no. She had noticed, too. Why was she not demanding she leave? Instead she looked… sympathetic?

'I know nothing about opera, my lady,' she managed to mumble. 'It would be better if I stayed here with Lucy.'

Eleanor looked startled. Perhaps even shocked.

Oh, dear. Was opera a part of every young lady's curriculum? The only thing close to what she thought might be opera were the bawdy ditties at the V&V.

Her Grace wagged a gnarled finger in her direction. 'A lack of education in a young lady such as you will not do, Rose. The sooner you add music to your repertoire the better, my gel.'

Her repa— *What?* A young lady such as her would likely be on the next ship to Botany Bay if Her Grace ever guessed the lies she'd been told.

She opened her mouth to refuse again.

'Please, Rose,' the Dowager said and the hope in her old wise eyes made Rose feel as if she'd stepped into a bog and was floundering around for an excuse when Her Grace knew Rose would never refuse her anything she wanted. As an employee, she didn't have the right.

Still she tried. 'I don't think—'

'Oh, please don't say no,' Eleanor said. 'Grandmama is going to insist I go, I can see she is. Having you with me will make it bearable. It doesn't matter in the least that you don't speak Italian. It is the music that counts.'

Italian? Heaven help her.

How could she refuse? These people had been good to her. So good that sometimes she forgot herself and thought of them as family.

And to have the chance to hear such music… What a treat it would be. She raised a hand. 'I give in. I will go.'

Hopefully they would not run into Mr Challenger. As kindly as his smile seemed, that man unnerved her.

Seated between Her Grace and Lady Eleanor in Lady Buckhurst's opulent music room, Rose had never heard anything quite so beautiful as Signora Calvetti's singing. True, she did not understand the words—but, oh, the feelings her voice evoked. They tore at her heartstrings in nameless ways. Sorrow. Loss. Joy. It was all there in the music. Rose sat entranced. Thrilled they had persuaded her to accept the invitation.

Nothing in her life had prepared her for the sounds issuing from the woman who stood at the front of the room with diamonds glittering in her hair, at her throat and on her eloquent hands.

The music came to a close and the audience clapped heartily.

The dark-haired voluptuous flashing-eyed singer, curtseyed and blew kisses to her audience.

'Encore!' someone shouted.

The cry was picked up around the room.

The singer smiled but shook her head.

Lady Buckhurst hustled up to stand beside the woman, signalling for silence. 'Thank you everyone. I promised the *signora* we would understand that she has a long journey tomorrow and must guard her voice for a performance in Paris booked many months ago. If you would like to follow my major-domo, refreshments are served in the conservatory.'

The crowd, good-natured if disappointed, began to shuffle their way out. Someone tapped Rose on the shoulder with a fan.

Wondering who it could be, she turned around. It was the girl who had played croquet with Jake. 'Oh,' she said surprised. 'Lady Alicia.'

The girl's smile was less than friendly. 'He won't marry you, you know.'

Rose blinked. 'I beg your pardon?'

'The Duke.' She nodded to the back of the room. Jake was standing there, talking to another gentleman.

Rose's heart soared.

He was looking a little haggard. Something like the way he had looked when they first met. What could have happened during the past few days to make him appear so? Or was it merely weariness from his journey?

'He won't marry a nobody from the country,' the girl hissed in her ear as people shuffled around them as if they were an island in the middle of a fast-flowing river. 'A libertine and a rake he may have been, but he will do his duty by the title. You'll see.'

Rose glared at her, her hackles rising at the scornful tone. 'You don't think he will marry you, do you?'

The girl primped the cluster of curls resting on her cheek. 'If my father has anything to say to it he will. After all, it is his fault I didn't get to marry his brother.'

'His fault.' Rose's jaw dropped. 'What on earth do you mean?'

'He wanted the title and he arranged to get it. Everyone says so.'

Rose's fists clenched. Was one allowed to strike a horrid girl in the face at a musicale evening? Likely not. But, oh, how she was tempted.

'How could you believe such horrid gossip?'

The girl sniffed. 'There's no smoke without a fire. He owes my family a marriage. And my papa isn't one to leave a debt unpaid.'

She flounced away to join an older lady who was looking daggers at Rose. The girl's mother.

Instead of shrinking beneath that stare as she

might have a few weeks ago, Rose straightened her shoulders. Poor Jake, if that young woman was his ultimate fate.

A horrid suspicion crossed her mind. Was he aware of this family's expectations? Was that why he had played croquet with the girl?

Rose sat in the chair beside the window, looking over the gardens. Night had fallen a good two hours before and still Jake had not come to her.

Not only that, while he'd been his usually gentlemanly self in the carriage on the way home from the musicale, he'd returned to his former coolness. He'd barely spoken to her and only answered his grandmother's enquiries as to the affairs at his estate with brusque brevity. In the end, Eleanor had taken him to task for his rudeness and he'd made more of an effort.

Had he finally realised how unsuitable she was as a companion for his grandmother and was trying to pluck up the courage to let her go? Mr Challenger had recognised her. She was sure of it. And if he had not, she had certainly seen the reservation in his gaze, despite that he'd been the soul of politeness and his wife had been lovely.

And noble.

Her hands clenched in her lap. That was the sort of woman Jake would marry. A girl of good family. One who would not cause him to be ashamed. She just hoped he didn't choose Lady Alicia for a bride. That girl would not make him happy. And no matter what happened, she did want him to be happy.

A knock at the door startled her. She shot to her feet.

Jake strode in. Fully clothed.

He usually came in a dressing gown of green silk covered in golden dragons.

Her stomach fell away at the grim look on his face, the intensity in his eyes as he took in her *dishabille*.

'Rose.' His voice had a rough edge to it.

'Jake?'

'I came to tell you…'

She held her breath, her heart balanced on a knife-edge of expectation, ready, but in no way prepared for the pain of his words of parting.

He closed his eyes briefly, stepped into the room and closed the door behind him.

'You came to tell me?' she prompted in a whisper, tipping her face to meet his gaze, seeing heat there, desire flaring between them as it always did.

He kissed her, hard and deep, a low growl

rising up from his throat. Feral. Not tender, not sweet, but wild and hungry. Full of dark passion.

A rush of desire ran hot through her blood, her heart picked up speed, her body trembled. She twined her arms around his neck and kissed him back hard. How could she have thought she had lost him?

Their tongues tangled, her heart pounded against her breastbone making it hard to breath and she sank into the fire of a blazing kiss. Moments seemed like for ever until they fell apart, breathless.

He attacked the ties of her robe, she tore at the buttons of his coat. He shrugged out of his jacket, then his waistcoat; she let the dressing robe slide to the floor. He tore off his neckcloth. Ripped his shirt off over his head.

She jerked at the ribbon holding her bodice closed.

He groaned as the gown dipped down one shoulder, pulled her close and kissed her again. In a movement so swift and effortless she felt weightless, he picked her up and carried her to the bed, depositing her carefully on the mattress. It took him mere seconds to strip out of his nether garments and, gloriously naked, he joined her on the bed, giving her no time to admire his rampant erection and manly physique.

Never had she seen him so demanding, so urgent, so fierce.

It called to something inside her she had not known existed. The need to be overpowered, to feel vulnerable, yet powerful in a different way. As if in breaking through his control, he had given her something strange and wonderfully exhilarating.

Without thought, without modesty, she drew her nightdress off over her head and brought his mouth to her aching breast.

He drew deeply on the aching nub. A pain of such piercing sweetness arrowed deep to the heart of her femininity. She cried out. Her hips arched, pressing into him, feeling his hardness against her mons. Seeking him inside her.

A knee pressed between her thighs and the pleasure of opening herself to him made her heart lift and soar.

He settled himself between her legs and drove into her body with a groan that welled from deep in his chest.

She shattered, melting around him, surrendering beneath him.

He stilled. A shudder ran through him, so strong it resonated in her bones.

Him, too? Never had he shown such urgency.

But, no. She could feel him inside her, still hard.

He slowly rocked his hips. Tension inside her began to build. A ripple of pleasure spread outward from her core, intense, soul stirring. Again?

And still he had not—

He moved again, slow easy thrusts of his hips, gradually increasing the tempo. The restlessness started up again, tightening every nerve in her body. He drove deeper and again she reached the pinnacle and let go.

Overwhelmed by the beauty of the sensations he instilled, a joy so vast filled her and tears leaked from the corner of her eyes. Supported on his hands, looming over her, the rigid tension of his body, the ripple of hard muscle and the straining of tendons in his neck left her in awe.

Balancing on one hand, he lifted her buttocks, opening her more to his penetration, filling her completely.

Somehow she managed to lift her head to nibble at his earlobe, to trace the outer ear with delicate strokes of her tongue, then plunged into the depths of it, tasting salt and inhaling the scent of his soap.

His hiss of indrawn breath sent shivers across her skin.

He raised his head, gazing down at her, his eyes dark with passion, his expression strained by longing and need. The same longing and need echoing in her heart.

As if their souls had merged into one.

'You undo me,' he rasped, driving into her harder.

I love you, she whispered in her mind, finally recognising the truth of the depths of her feelings and revelling in them even as she grieved that he would never be fully hers.

She closed her lips on the words, held them tight to her heart, for she had a shred of wit left to know that to admit them out loud and see rejection in his eyes would tear her apart.

Instead, she showed him all she could never say with her hands and her body and her lips.

Feeling him unravelling inside her body was the greatest joy of all. And the saddest moment of her life. Because in a moment of clarity at the moment before she followed him into bliss, she sensed he was saying goodbye. *'I will always love you.'*

They lay tangled together, damp with sweat, hearts beating a wild rhythm, breathing harsh in the quiet room.

After several moments he shifted. Moving away. She reached to hold him, but he slipped from her grasp, leaving the bed in a surge of movement. She rose up on her elbows and was startled to see him hastily dressing. He glanced over his shoulder.

'I am so damned sorry, Rose. I did not intend this.'

Her heart stopped beating. Her breath caught in her throat. 'What is it? What did I do?'

He straightened, now fully clothed, his expression stern, closed off. 'You did nothing wrong, Rose. You are everything that is—' He choked the words off, made a slicing gesture with his hand. 'I actually came to tell you I have business at Vitium et Virtus this evening and cannot stay.' He closed his eyes against her surprised gaze. 'I am sorry.'

He bowed and, with his shoulders straight and his steps determined, he left.

While he had said nothing of any import, Rose had a strange feeling that everything between had changed.

He'd donned the reserve he'd worn when they first met like a coat, or some sort of suit of armour, as if he sought protection.

Protection from her?

Chapter Twelve

Jake could not stop thinking about the expression of Rose's face when he had left her last evening.

Flushed, sated, seductive. Words of love barely discernible above their pounding heartbeats and ragged breathing. He wasn't sure she'd realised what she'd said. But the words had carved a path through his heart to his very soul.

He had tried to convince himself that the words meant nothing, that she had spoken them in the heat of passion. After all, other women had said similar things in the same circumstances, but he knew deep within him that Rose wasn't like other women. She did not say things that were not true.

She'd given him everything and he had been so stunned, he'd been unable to think, let alone speak what was in his own heart.

Thank God he had not.

In bringing her into his home, he'd made a grave mistake. The sort of mistake he might have made as a green boy new upon the town. Feeling more than he should for a lover. Wanting to keep her, when all he could do was keep her safe. Not only that, he'd stolen her innocence. Stolen her lack of worldliness which had made her so attractive to him in the first place.

His heart twisted. He did not deserve a woman like Rose. He could not allow his own feeling to colour his decisions. His life was not his own.

If things had been different— He squashed a thought that kept intruding where Rose was concerned.

Things, he thought bitterly, would have been different had he been a little less selfish. A little less headstrong. A little more willing to do his father's bidding instead of leaving it to Ralph to fill the breach. As he always had.

On the other hand, had he done as he'd been asked that day six months ago, he might never have met Rose. Anger balled in his chest. A hot, hard lump. At himself. At whatever fate had decided his world should be turned on its head.

The stupidest part of all of it? He'd never

been happier than he had been these past few weeks. A happiness he did not deserve.

Last night, seeing her waiting for him in her nightgown, her skin golden in the glow of the candles, he'd been unable to resist her allure.

She loved him. The wonder of it had shaken him to his core. Left him speechless and wanting what he could not have.

Today, in the cold light of day, he would lay out the future. The best he could offer, given his circumstances. A carte blanche.

A house of her own across the river, where they could be together whenever they wished. A house where he could entertain his friends and they could be themselves, instead of sneaking around late at night. She'd have a carriage and clothes as befitted her beauty. He'd settle her financial affairs so when it was over, perhaps when he married, she would be comfortable for the rest of her life. Able to do just as she pleased. Perhaps find herself a husband.

Icy fingers clutched at his heart.

He fought off their chill. It was only fair. Because the one thing she wanted, the one thing he could not give her, were children. No child of his would suffer the taint of bastardy, though as a duke he could likely get away with it more easily than Oliver's father had.

He steeled himself for the coming interview. Fortunately, his grandmother and sister had taken Lucy shopping for clothes. It was the perfect opportunity for him to talk to Rose without the fear of interruption.

He entered the drawing room with a smile and a yawning pit of dread in his gut.

Rose had her back to him, concentrating on—

'What are you doing?' His voice was loud, harsh, in the silence. He kept his gaze fixed on her, not on the portrait above the mantel.

She spun around. Put a hand to her heart. 'Jake. You startled me.' She turned back to the painting, denuded of crepe, which she must have pulled down and now held in her hand.

'In this painting, you look more like your sister than your father or your brother,' she mused with a smile in her voice. 'They seem quite stern, the way you do most of the time, whereas here you look ready for any kind of adventure. A right proper rascal. You can't hide it, though. Sometimes that rascal peeks out and you seem more like this boy.' She turned back to face him, her face alight with interest in the truth she'd instantly seen.

Her words struck a blow at his heart. At the essence of everything he'd tried to be these past few months. A flash of unreasoning rage raced along his veins. 'How dare you remove that without permission.'

Her face blanched. She glanced guiltily over her shoulder and winced. 'I wanted to see the other members of your family. This is the only likeness of them in the house.'

Unable to stop himself, he glanced up. The faces of his brother and father gazed down on him with their usual self-assured gravity.

The Duke in his regalia and his heir, squaring his shoulders beneath the weight of the father's hand and the responsibilities he would bear with dignity when his turn came around. And Eleanor, little more than a baby, holding her father's hand. A hand that had been ripped from her grasp.

And then there was himself. Looking out with the expression of devil-may-care that had always been an irritant to his brother. After all, he was the younger son with all the privilege and none of the duty. A careless attitude that had destroyed everything he and Eleanor had held dear. A stark reminder of his failings.

He snatched the crepe from her hand, intending to replace it, but could not reach the top of the frame. Cursing under his breath, he went for a chair.

'Why do you hide it?' Rose asked from behind him, her voice full of puzzlement. 'It is a beautiful portrait. Your father's obvious pride in his children is heart-warming. Surely—?'

His hands gripped the chair arms, his knuckles white, his heart beating an unsteady rhythm. He didn't need the portrait in order to recall his father's face, it was there in his mind's eye every time he took a decision on behalf of the Duchy, every time he drew a breath he had denied his brother.

Along with the shame he felt every time he thought about his father's request and the way he had sloughed it off on to good old dutiful Ralph so he could go to a masked ball at Vitium et Virtus. It made him feel ill. How could he tell her what he had done? How could he ever explain what the look on his father's face did to him when he couldn't explain it to himself?

He chilled the heat of his emotions. Slowed the beat of his heart. Turned to face her. 'You don't understand.'

She stood her ground, eyeing him with concern and confusion. 'How can I understand? You always keep me and everyone else at a distance. I do understand one thing. I would give anything to have a likeness of my family even though they didn't care enough about me to keep me.' Her voice filled with tears. She swallowed them down, fumbling with the hem of her sleeve to produce a dingy bit of linen tied in a knot, which she undid. The little half of mother-of-pearl button dropped into her palm. She held it up between forefinger and thumb, her hand shaking. 'This is all *I* have of *my* family. No memories, only this. And I had to beg for it to get it. I keep it to remind me that I did once belong to someone.'

She turned to look up at the picture. 'I thought that if you saw them it might help you feel better about—'

'This really is not your concern.' The words were hard and cruel and intended to stop her questions. Intended to maintain his appearance of strength in the face of the guilt eating away at his insides.

Her eyes filled with hurt. The same hurt he'd seen the previous evening when he'd left her so abruptly.

Her shoulders straightened. Her chin came up. Amazed, nonplussed, by her dignity, he could only stare in silence. This woman was no longer the little maid who had polished the floors at Vitium et Virtus or the giddy girl who had laughed on the swing, she was a woman with a sense of herself.

Such strength. She put him to shame.

'I apologise. I should not have put myself forward,' she said coolly. She glanced up at the picture and back at him. 'You are right. It really is none of my business, but if I had had a family like yours, I would want the world to see them. To celebrate their lives, not hide them like some shameful secret. You don't deserve a family at all, if you cannot see that. I am done with you.'

He froze, waiting for the next words out of her mouth. The words that would part them for ever. But he could not allow it. 'You are not leaving. We have a bargain.'

Anger sparked amid the sadness in her eyes. 'I know my responsibility as well as my position.' She took a deep breath. 'I am your grandmother's paid companion. Nothing more. Henceforth, my chamber door will be locked.'

It was as if an arrow had struck his heart. She'd seen him for what he was and she no longer wanted him.

'I apologise if my words were overly harsh, Miss Nightingale.' His gaze slid up to the portrait. 'I—' The gesture of his hand expressed the impossibility of trying to explain. 'It is complicated.'

She nodded. 'Too complicated for someone

like me. I understand perfectly. Please excuse my transgression, it will not happen again.'

She bobbed a curtsy much like the first one she had given him. This time, she knew it was an insult and he could only admire her nerve. 'I bid you good afternoon, Your Grace.' She swept out of the room.

He closed his eyes at the odd painful pang in his chest and the sense of emptiness left by her departure. When he opened them again his gaze fell upon the portrait everyone had said was a perfect likeness. Everyone had agreed that the artist had perfectly captured the character of his subjects.

Rose had seen it, too. What he lacked. It didn't matter that he'd done everything in his power to emulate his father and his brother, his relationship with Rose was proof he could never live up to their example. He didn't have it in him.

No wonder disappointment had lurked in the grey depths of his father's pain-filled eyes that last night. 'You really didn't expect me to make a go of this, did you, Pater?' he said to those eyes looking down on him now. 'You must have known I'd muck it up.'

He was a terrible substitute for his brother. He glanced down at the fabric in his hand. He balled up the scrap of cloth and threw it into the empty coal scuttle. 'To hell with it.' It wasn't like he could hide the truth from himself. 'I'm for the club.' And a nice bottle of Nicholas's best brandy.

Thank God he had work to do. There were always mountains of paperwork, both here and at Vitium et Virtus.

Again his unwilling gaze was drawn back to the portrait. He remembered the endless sittings, the admonishments from his father to stand his ground like a man, and Eleanor's chatter. He frowned at it.

He would leave the picture undraped as a reminder of his shortcomings and the promise to his father.

More to the point, what was he to do about Rose?

Seated at the escritoire in Her Grace's private sitting room, Rose waited, pen poised, while Her Grace reread the letter in her hand. This was their usual after-breakfast ritual. Replying to Her Grace's correspondents. For an elderly lady Her Grace certainly had plenty of letters in want of reply.

'My dearest Wellington…' the old lady said.

Rose's eyes widened. She was writing to the

Duke of Wellington? The most famous man in England, after the King and the Prince of Wales? She carefully formed the salutation below the date.

After a long pause, she looked up to find her employer regarding her somewhat sadly.

'Is something wrong, Your Grace?'

The old lady's lower lip trembled. 'It is Jacob. For three days now he has been shut up in the library with his papers and his man of affairs. He doesn't even come to dinner any more and I thought things were improving.' Her brow furrowed. 'Did something happen, Rose? You seemed to be getting along so well and now you rarely look at each other, let alone speak? I had hoped…'

Rose's fingers clenched on the pen. A large drop of ink dribbled off the nib on to the paper. 'Bother.' She snatched up the sheet of blotting paper. Too late. The blot had already spread across the words she had written. 'I am sorry, Your Grace. I am afraid I shall have to start again.' She set the sheet aside to be cut smaller and used for notes and lists and drew another sheet from the pigeonhole in front of her. She readied her pen.

'You did not answer my question,' Her Grace said gently. While her eyes might be old and short-sighted, they were not in the least bit vague. She wanted a reply.

What could she say? That she had tossed him out of her bed? Hardly. Indeed, she had missed him so badly she was scarcely able to force food past her lips. Had Her Grace noticed that too?

'We had an argument.' It was the truth.

Her Grace tipped her head on one side. 'Put him in his place, did you? Hmm. Well, it might serve, I suppose.'

'I do not understand.'

The old lady's lips pursed, the wrinkles around her mouth deepening. 'I have my hopes pinned on you, Rose. Now, where were we? Ah yes. My Dearest Wellington—have you got that?'

Her hopes? What did she mean? 'Yes, Your Grace.'

'Very well, then. Let us continue.'

And continue she did for another hour. Rose's hand was cramped by the time she had returned the writing implements to their proper places and closed up the writing table. 'Will there be anything else, Your Grace?'

'Yes, Rose. I have come to a decision.' Her voice was strangely tight as if she was holding back some sort of emotion. 'I am going with Eleanor to Hertfordshire. I wish to spend more time with Lucy.' She picked up her fan and waved it briskly. 'Not to mention, it is far too hot at this time of year to remain in town.'

'We are going to Hertfordshire?'

The old lady shook her head, her gaze piercing. 'I am sorry, Rose. I will not need a companion in the country.'

Her heart shrank. The pain of it made her gasp. 'You are letting me go?'

The old lady looked determined. 'I feel it might be the best thing I can do at this point. I will let Jacob know. In the meantime, will you ask Eleanor to come and see me?'

Blinded by the hot rush of tears and unable to speak another word, Rose made her curtsy and escaped. On her way to her room, she sent the message to Eleanor by way of a footman. She knew she would never keep her composure if she had gone herself.

Did Jake know she'd been dismissed? He must do. He was the Duke. Pain carved an empty space in her chest. Loss. This was what he must have felt when his father and brother had died. How could she not have realised the extent of his pain?

She should not have interfered. She'd only

made things worse when all she wanted was his happiness.

Emptiness filled her. She would always miss him.

She drew a deep breath. There was nothing she could do to change what had always been inevitable. As heartbroken as she felt, she had to think of her future, not wallow in misery.

And she could do anything she wished. Jake had shown her a different world and she had proved to herself she could be more than a scullery maid. She just wished there had been something more she could have done for him, to make him happy.

She was packing and mulling over what her next step should be when a knock came at the chamber door.

To her surprise a footman stood outside. He handed her a package. 'From His Grace.' He bowed and marched away.

Slowly she closed the door and then unrolled the fancy scroll tied with a red ribbon. It took her a while to understand what its contents meant. She sat in stunned silence. He'd bought a dressmaker's establishment and put it in her name.

Why on earth would he do such a terrible thing?

* * *

Footsore and weary, Rose arrived in the alley behind the V&V. She'd slipped out the moment she'd heard Jake leave the house at eleven. Night was a dangerous time for a well-dressed woman to be wandering the streets near St James's. But she knew her way around here far better than she had ever known her way around the fancy houses in Mayfair.

And at least she'd had the presence of mind to pick up an umbrella on her way out. It would serve to remind any man who thought to accost her of his manners. Fortunately, she knew where she was going and as always her determined stride and confident manner stood her in good stead. What a fool she had been to think Jake might actually care for her.

She'd been a convenience. His mistress. She meant nothing to him but sexual gratification.

The ache in her chest was pure foolishness.

She couldn't even blame him. She'd offered herself. No wonder he'd no respect for her or her opinions and thoughts.

She shuddered.

For years she'd convinced herself that she could earn a living as a servant and not be led astray by some handsome gentleman, as her mother must have been.

More fool her. At least the precautions she had taken meant no children would result from her foolishness. Apart from their last encounter. There had been no time. No thinking.

Surely fate would not be so cruel as to punish her for one night's forgetfulness. She wrapped her arms around her waist, huddling deeper into the shadows, thinking better of this foolish plan of hers. The familiar odours of the gutters filled her nostrils. Offal and stale food and the taste of coal smoke. This was where she belonged, not in a mansion that smelled of beeswax and lemon and roses in vases.

Which was why she was back where she had first met Jake. It was where impossible dreams had started to build themselves like castles amid the clouds. Those dreams now lay in tumbled ruins about her feet.

She almost wished she'd never met him. Never experienced the kind of joy he had brought to her life. Yet, she didn't. Not really. No matter what happened to her in the future, he would remain in her heart. There would never be another man for her. Only Jake.

A sad realisation.

With a deep breath to bolster her courage, she stepped up to the door and knocked. The porter, Ben, opened it with a cheeky grin. 'Back, are yer? Get ye in.'

When the saucy lad gave her an up-and-down look, she ignored him and kept going. Attractive in a rough sort of way, he wasn't above a bit of flirting with the girls who worked at the V&V, but he'd never previously given her a second glance. Was he somehow aware of what she had become? Could Jake have boasted of his conquest? No. She would not believe that of him. The porter was simply being himself.

She made her way down to the Green Room where a couple of dancers she didn't recognise were practising their twirls. No sign of Flo. Music and feet pounded above her head. She must be on stage. She ducked into her old quiet corner. She didn't want Mr Bell seeing her, or Mrs Parker for that matter. They'd quite likely find her something to do. She set her reticule down on the arm of the sofa and took in the cobwebs and dust. It looked as if no one had been here since she left. She picked up the broom leaning in the corner and tidied up.

The rousing crescendo above signalled the end of the act. It wasn't more than a few minutes before a torrent of girls streamed through the door with a chorus of out-of-breath giggles and the usual mutter of complaints. It felt good to be here.

Or it would, if it were not for her mission.

She poked her head out when she heard Flo's voice, grabbed her and dragged her into the secluded corner.

'Rose!' Flo shrieked. She thrust her head back out into the room. 'Hey, everyone, Rose is back.' So much for seclusion.

Several of the girls crowded into the little space. 'Rose, I missed you,' Ginny said. 'No one does hair as good as you.'

'And it's costing a fortune to get the mending done,' someone moaned.

'Where have you been?' asked a third.

'I found a new position,' she said, blushing.

A girl called Lanie, who had never been all that friendly, tipped her chin. 'I should think you did. On your back, if your clothes are any kind of clue.'

The other girls shouted her down.

'I came to speak to Flo,' Rose said. 'If you ladies do not mind.'

'Go on, the lot of you,' Flo said. 'You've had your look-see. If you don't hurry you'll be late for the next act. Rose will help me dress.' She winked at Rose.

There was some good-natured shoving and

elbowing as the girls squeezed out. And from one squeak, Rose surmised there had been a pinch delivered to Lanie as well.

Flo turned her back for Rose to untie the tapes. 'How can I help you? That nob of yours treating you right?'

'He's been very kind.' She got the knot undone and started pulling the tapes free of the holes down Flo's back. She stopped at the sight of ugly bruises between her shoulder blades. 'Flo, what happened?'

'Oh, nothing. Tripped down the stairs.' She waved an airy hand.

Rose didn't believe her. 'Flo—'

'Wot about you, missy? Not got a bun in the oven, I hope?' Flo pulled the pins from her headpiece.

'A bun—' Rose gasped at the implication. 'No.'

'That's good, then. Wot did you want?'

'I don't know what to do. We argued and now I'm to leave.'

'He's probably got another girl.'

Her heart wrenched. 'Do you think so?'

'That's usually wot happens.'

Did that explain his sudden withdrawal? The picture had been an excuse. Rose eased the gown down Flo's arms and helped her to step out of it. 'Did you…? Have you seen him with someone?'

'Me?' Flo turned around. 'How would I have seen…? Who is he?'

Rose swallowed and leaned close to her friend's ear. 'Westmoor.'

'The Duke?'

'Hush. Someone will hear you.'

Flo wriggled the next costume up her body and stood waiting for Rose to fasten her up. 'Oh, Rose, you couldn't have picked a worse 'un, I can tell you.'

Her heart sank. 'Why?'

'He's a right one for the ladies, he is. Always a new one on his arm, they say.'

'You *have* seen him, then?'

'Well,' Flo said grudgingly, 'not recently. But a leopard don't change its spots, you know. Off with the old, on with the new.'

Feeling sick to her stomach, she tied the tapes off. 'Do you know if he's here tonight?'

'Oh, he's here every night, according to what I heard Mr Bell say to Mrs Parker. Stays in the office all night. Working.'

Rose knew where the office was. She'd cleaned its grate on many occasions when the gentlemen were absent. They demanded their privacy. But she had to speak to Jake. She just must. She finished Flo's hair and attached the feather plume. 'There you are. All done.'

'I really do miss you,' Flo said, giving her a hug. 'Is there anything I can do for you?'

'You can keep old Mr Bell busy while I sneak past him to have a word with the Duke.'

'Employees aren't supposed to go in there.'

'Well I am not an employee any more, so the rule doesn't apply to me.'

Flo chuckled. 'All right then. And by the way, thanks for that lovely hamper you sent over. It were a proper treat.'

'It was simply a thank you for all your kindness when I first started working here.'

A bell jangled in the corridor.

'Are you ready?' Flo asked. 'I'll have to go up in a minute.'

'As ready as I will ever be.

Flo whisked out of the door and Rose followed a few moments later. As she passed the housekeeper's door, she could hear Flo complaining loudly inside. A moment or two later and she was up the stairs and passing through the green-baize-covered door that led to the owners' inner sanctum.

When she entered the office, a weary-looking Jacob looked up. His eyes flared with something warm and welcoming. But as he shot to his feet, his expression shuttered, revealing only the cold, remote facade she had come to dread.

What little hope she had nurtured around the coming interview dwindled. So be it.

'You should not be here.' Jacob was appalled at the harshness of his tone.

Rose gave him a cold glare. 'Why not? I used to work here. Remember?'

He raked the hair that would insist on falling forward back from his face, using the time to get his brain into some sort of working order. 'You are no longer employed here.'

She flung a bundle of documents down in front of him. 'Apparently, I am no longer employed anywhere.'

She sounded angry. Bitter. He frowned at the papers in their neat red ribbon, the seal dangling off the edge of the table.

'Please, Rose, sit down so we can discuss this like sensible adults.'

For a moment, from the stubborn set of her jaw, he thought she would refuse, but then, to his inordinate relief, she sat.

He followed suit, leaning back, trying to look relaxed. As if nothing was wrong. As if he didn't want to leap across the table and kiss away her anger.

He deserved her anger.

'Tell me why you are here.' He kept his voice cool, distant, barely interested. He could not afford to show any emotion where she was concerned. When it came to Rose, passion begot yet more passion. He could not allow it ever again.

She stiffened. A scowl formed on her face. 'I came about that.' She pointed at the papers.

He curled his lips into a hard smile. 'What, isn't it enough?' An unexpected pang of disappointment struck him behind the sternum. He'd thought she'd be pleased.

She gestured impatiently. 'I want to know why you are giving it me.'

She must be more upset than he'd realised if her grammar was failing her. He wanted to hold her and tell her everything would be all right. He couldn't do it. Not if he were to retain any semblance of common sense. What he had to do was make her take his offer and go away.

Then he might be able to introduce some normality into his life.

'It is a gift, Rose,' he said with a hint of irony he despised the moment he used it. He ploughed on. 'A gentleman always gives a lady a gift when they part company. Most of my other ladies preferred jewels.'

She flinched.

He wanted to hit someone. Or have someone hit him as he deserved for causing her pain. This was for the best, though. He had to keep that in mind. He shrugged with what he hoped was idle nonchalance, though his shoulders felt tight. 'I thought you might like that better. If I am wrong, I would be happy to provide something else. Or more. Name it.' He'd do anything to make sure she was happy. Even let her go.

The fury in her eyes was a good thing, but not the underlying hurt. His fist clenched on his thighs beneath the table. Carefully he relaxed them. It would not do to show his inner turmoil.

He watched her gaze drop to the package, saw her frown. He held his breath, wondering what she would say, hoping she would take his gift. It was what she had said she wanted. That and her family which as yet he'd been unable to find. He had not given up hope on that front, but he would not say anything until he was sure.

Not that he would be saying anything to Rose on any matter. It would be dealt with through his man of business.

'So,' she said, musingly, 'when you decided on this, you thought to give me my heart's desire.'

His heart stuttered in his chest. How easily she saw through him. 'Something of the sort, I suppose. You did mention your dream to open a dressmaker's shop more than once.'

She gave a little nod of acknowledgement.

He started to relax. To feel a sense of satisfaction. She would accept his gift. Relief trickled warm along his veins.

'But you see, Westmoor,' she continued, 'it was a dream I wanted to earn by my own efforts, not have it handed to me on a plate at a mere whim.'

'You did earn it.'

The moment the words came out of his mouth he knew he had fallen into a fatal error. Knew it with every fibre of his being. He didn't have to see the scorn on her face. The repudiation. 'You have been a wonderful companion to my grandmother.' He spoke before she could get out a word.

'I received wages for that,' she spat. 'No, you said only a moment ago that this was a parting gift from you.'

'If you do not find it acceptable on those terms, then look on it as a bonus for your work with my grandmother.'

She shook her head. 'No, thank you.'

No, thank you? Just like that she was turning down a lucrative business in the heart of Mayfair? The terms were so generous, she wouldn't even need to set foot in the shop to make a profit. A manager could handle it all. He wanted to howl. He took a deep calming breath. 'You cannot have read it properly. Perhaps I should explain.'

'Do not patronise me, Jake. I do not want your parting gift.'

'Then what do you want?' Damn. He hadn't meant to ask that. Hadn't intended to give her an opportunity to set her own terms of departure. It was the sort of mistake old Prinny had made with Mrs Robinson. That of a green boy. But the words were out and he waited for what sort of punishment she had devised for him, for she was clearly furious.

It was no more than he deserved.

The wry thought pulled at his lips.

Suspicion filled her eyes. 'Are you laughing at me?'

'No. I am laughing at my own foolishness.' Bitterly.

'Wishing you'd never met me, more like.'

Never that. He had memories of her that he never wanted to forget. He had the feeling they would comfort him into his old age. As long as he knew she was happy. And safe.

'I want you to tell me why you are sending me away with this…this gift. I want to know what I did wrong. It was the picture, wasn't it? I apologised for that and you didn't even cover it up again.'

'You did nothing wrong.'

She shook her head. 'I must have.' She rose to her feet and paced in a small circle. 'But if not, then why?'

She stopped pacing, staring at the back of the door. Spun around to face him. 'That's my bonnet. The one I wore the day I met you in the garden. When I was on the swing. Why is it here?'

He stared at the bonnet. God knew he had been staring at it for days, remembering how she had laughed when he had pushed her on the swing. It was only later that he realised she must never have experienced such a thing before. And she'd let him kiss her. It had been the loveliest kiss of his life. Innocent and fresh and utterly entrancing.

'I meant to return it to you. You can take it if you like.'

Then he would have nothing of hers. Something wrenched at his chest. He pushed the thought back where it belonged. Buried it beneath the cold he used to keep pain at bay.

'You kept my bonnet.' Something glimmered in the back of her eyes. Something suspiciously bright. And come to think of it, her voice seemed a little husky.

God help him, tears would leave him undone and defenceless.

'What of it?'

She returned to her chair and sat down with her hands folded in her lap. 'You haven't yet answered my question.'

'Which was?'

'You know what I am asking. Why would you toss me out on my ear and yet give me everything I said I ever wanted?'

To make you happy.

But it hadn't made her happy, had it? For some unfathomable reason he'd made her angry. And sad.

The only way to make sure she left was to tell her the truth. Make it so she wanted to leave *him.*

'You really want the answer? You want to understand the sort of man I am?'

She said nothing, but her eyes widened. He forged ahead. 'I presume you have heard the rumour about me killing my father and brother in order to take the title?'

Her complexion paled. 'I—it was mentioned. I didn't believe a—'

'It is true.'

Her gasp of shock did not make him feel one iota better. In fact, it felt like an arrow through his heart.

But at least now she would leave him in peace.

Rose stared at him in shock. She couldn't believe, would not believe such a thing about him. 'You are just saying that to make me go away.'

His expression darkened, became grim, hard. He stared down at the desk. 'I wish that were the case.'

Why was she even bothering with him if he was going to lie through his teeth to be rid of her? Then he shot a glance at her from beneath his lowered brows and she saw the pain in his eyes. And the despair.

Why would he want her to believe such an awful thing about him? It didn't make any sense. 'How did you kill them?'

He recoiled. His expression stark with shock. 'What?'

'I heard they were on the way to Brighton when their carriage turned over. You were here at the V&V that night. The girls said so.'

'How would they know? It was a masked ball.'

'Really? You and your friends come and go from this place every day and you think no one knows who you are? They don't blab about you or the goings-on in this place because they are protecting their livelihoods. Not that it's the sort of thing a duke should be doing.'

He grimaced. 'I don't need telling what a duke should or should not do.'

'Nor are you the sort of man who would kill members of his family to gain a title.'

'It's the last thing I ever wanted.' The words came out like a sigh, as if speaking them gave him relief. His shoulders tightened almost immediately. 'But I am responsible for my brother's death.'

The misery in his gaze made her want to hold him. 'I don't understand.'

He squeezed his eyes shut and rubbed a palm down his face as if to wipe away an unpleasant image. 'It was supposed to be me in that carriage,' he said in so low a tone she could scarcely hear him.

She leaned forward in order to hear the softly spoken words and he looked down at the desk, as if too ashamed to meet her gaze.

'I should have been with my father that night,' he said. 'He asked me to go with him to Brighton to visit Prinny.'

'Prinny as in the Prince of Wales?'

'The same. The Prince needed money as usual. Father saw the chance to get him to hand over an estate that had fallen into the Crown's hands when the title died out. My father knew what Prinny did not. The value of that estate. According to Ralph, who was sent to fetch me, I was to go in his place because he had a prior engagement.

'As usual, I was my father's second choice, despite the fact that I read law at university. I'd offered my services on numerous occasions only to be told the Duchy was not my affair. Father only wanted me along to distract Prinny with gossip. One fashionable fribble entertaining another.'

Her eyes widened. Oh, yes, she would be shocked at his callousness.

'To cut a miserable story short, I told Ralph I had invited a lady guest to the annual Vitium et Virtus masked ball and was dashed if I was going to go back on my word.' He clenched his fists. 'That was the last time I saw Ralph alive. Father sent round a pretty stiff note before he and Ralph departed for Brighton. He noted my lack of filial duty, saying as usual Ralph had put the dukedom before his own amusements. Ralph died in the accident, and Father shortly after, but not before he made me promise to do my duty to the title in my brother's place. He could scarcely look me in the eye. He knew as well as I did, it was my fault Ralph died that night. It is my fault they are dead.'

He sat watching her, his expression haughty, indifferent. Defensive. No doubt he expected her to heap coals upon his head.

As if she would blame him. 'I'm so sorry.'

He frowned.

'But you know...' she glanced down at her fingers twisting around themselves in her lap '...you can never replace your brother.'

His jaw dropped. The pain in his eyes intensified. He looked away. 'I know that.'

The despair in his deep voice made her heart contract painfully.

'You should go. Take that with you.' He made a dismissive gesture with his hand at the documents.

How easily he shut her out. But somehow, before she left, she had to make him see what had become so obvious now she knew the whole story. 'Jake, you cannot spend your life thinking about the what if, but only about the what is. I learned long ago not to wonder what my life might have been like if my mother hadn't left me behind. I might have had brothers and sisters. My parents might have been cruel. Or poor. Or rich. I could imagine them for hours on end. But it wouldn't change the fact they never wanted me. All I can do is take my life as it is now.'

His eyes lifted to her face, his gaze intense. Piercing. Almost frightening. She forced herself to continue. 'I never knew your brother. But in the portrait, you seem so different from him.'

He let out an impatient sound. 'You said that before. It is not relevant.' He started to rise.

'Jake, you wear your brother like a mask.' Oh, now that really sounded as if she was a bedlamite.

It stilled him, though. He sank back into his seat. 'Rose—'

'No. The man *you* are is the man who took pity on a lonely girl waltzing in the dead of night. You are the man who gave an innocent miss her first turn on a swing and was not bored by her simple joy in one of the most amazing moments in her life. You are the man who spent an afternoon with his niece explaining a Panorama and eating ices and who made her feel loved. You are the man who took me out of the squalor of the rookeries and asked nothing in return. You are you. No one else. And who you are is a good, kind man.'

At that last, he frowned. 'I am also the man who seduced you.'

She relaxed a little. At last, he was listening. She cast him an arch smile, because he certainly did not want her pity. 'Oh? And did you hear any protests?'

He shook his head.

'And would you have seduced me had I said no?'

He grimaced.

'Of course not. You are who you are, Jake. And life can be hard. Impossibly so. But you have been given an opportunity to use yours for the good of others. To make a difference. But how can you, if you cut yourself off from who you really are?'

His face shuttered.

She unclenched her hands and realised her whole body was tense. Shaking with the passion in her words. She collapsed against the chair back. He must think her such a fool. But she would say what was in her heart or regret it for the rest of her life.

'I understand you cannot love me. Our worlds are too far apart. But please, Jake, do not hate yourself for what happened to your family. Forcing yourself to be someone you are not is hurting you badly. You are no worse or better than your brother. You are different.'

The distant expression remained on his face.

He didn't understand and she wasn't clever enough to make it any plainer. Her throat felt raw from all the talking. Almost as raw as her heart.

A sense of defeat filled her. She pushed to her feet. 'I thank you for your gift. It was thoughtful and kind, but I cannot accept it.' It was worth a king's ransom. 'I will always treasure the time we spent together.' She choked on the words and swallowed. 'I would not spoil those precious memories for anything.'

She turned to leave.

'Rose.' His voice was harsh.

She turned, expecting to see anger. His expression was tortured.

He had risen to his feet, his hands clenched at his sides. His eyes were fixed on her face again. 'Rose,' he said softly. 'If I promised to do better, will you stay?'

Startled, she could only stare. He wanted her to stay? Her heart leaped, driving the breath from her throat.

'Rose?' He came around the desk, holding his hands out for hers.

Reason overcame her joy. She whipped her hands behind her back. 'I cannot.' She shook her head and backed away. She would not stay as his mistress. One day soon he would marry. Must marry. She would not be able to bear parting from him again. She just wanted him to be happy. To be himself.

'I love you, Rose,' he said hoarsely.

'No.' Not this. Not now. 'You are a duke. You cannot be with someone like me.'

'I love you more than my own life, Rose. I should never have told you to go. Marry me.'

She turned to run for the door. On a hook on the back of it was that sad-looking little straw bonnet with blue ribbons. She turned back to face him.

She frowned. The hat meant something. It had to. 'For a duke, you are a hopeless romantic.'

'It would seem so.' He went down on one knee and took both her hands in his, kissing each one in turn. He looked up at her with a spark of mischief in his eyes, but there was something else there, too. A great deal of love. 'I love you, Rose. You see *me*. I need you to remind me who I am. I cannot do this without you. Will you marry me? Please?'

Longing filled her chest. It was so tight it hurt. Tears filled her eyes, blurring her vision. 'How can I? I'm not even a lady.'

'You are the most beautiful, wonderful, amazing lady in the world to me and that is all that counts. Isn't that what you said only moments ago?'

'But this is different. I can't—'

'You can. You can do anything you want. Rose. Darling, dearest Rose. Can't you see? You are what I needed. Without you, I was lost.'

Blinking away the mist, she looked down into his lovely face, saw the love and slowly sank to her knees before him, throwing her arms around his neck and weeping on his shoulder. 'Oh, Jake,' she said through her sobs.

'Is that a yes?' he asked, half-joking, half-serious.

'Yes.'

He swept her up in his arms and carried to the nearest armchair where she curled up on his lap the way she always did. He proceeded to kiss away her tears, until they were both breathless.

'Darling Rose,' he murmured against her lips, 'I love you so damned much.'

'I love you to bits, Jake,' she said tipping her chin to look into his face. 'I always will.

Chapter Thirteen

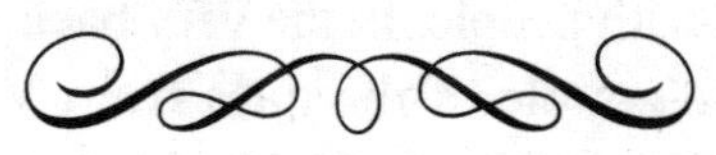

The Church of St George was packed to the gunnels. After all, it wasn't every day a duke got married to a lady's companion and former scullery maid at the most debauched club in London. Though no one but Frederick had recognised her, Rose had insisted his family be told the full truth before they got married.

Jake had been worried they might not accept her.

To his surprise, Grandmother had taken it all in stride. Indeed, she had taken quite a bit of pride in her matchmaking efforts and said she always knew Jake would come to his senses and marry the gel.

Bless the old dear.

Jake couldn't have been more proud to walk down the aisle towards the waiting vicar with his bride on his arm. Lucy trailed behind them, ready to hold Rose's posy when it was time to say their vows. The pews rising up on either side of them were festooned with flowers, roses of course at this late season, and crowded with well-wishers, as well as others who simply came to gawk. The galleries above were also teaming with people. In the very back row he'd spotted a couple of the girls from Vitium et Virtus. Rose's friends. He'd laid on a carriage for them, but he wasn't sure they would come. He was delighted that they had. Rose had so few people to call her own.

'I told you we should have had a quiet wedding at home,' Rose whispered as they approached the altar with its magnificent Venetian window letting the light flow over the awe-inspiring altar piece showing the Last Supper. Her hand trembled beneath his. While any of his friends would have been more than happy to escort her down the aisle, he'd been terrified she might turn tail and run at the last moment and he knew she wouldn't with him at her side.

He smiled at her encouragingly. 'I wanted everyone to see what a lucky man I am.'

She blushed.

The urge to kiss her welled up inside him. He glanced around. There was one person he didn't see. He'd tried everything in his power to get her to come, but she wouldn't promise. Didn't want to intrude. She had also wept copiously.

Then, as they approached the altar, he saw her sitting on the left side of the Church directly opposite from Grandmama and hemmed in between Fred and Georgiana. Today she was smiling mistily. Georgiana apparently had her in hand and shook her head at him.

She was probably right. Better to wait until after the wedding.

Oliver, serving as best man, stood waiting for them. Fred left Georgiana to join them at the steps to the altar, his task to give Rose away in place of a father.

The service went by in a blur. All he could do was watch the woman who had agreed to become his Duchess in wonder and awe. Her courage nigh unmanned him, for he had been daunted by the idea of becoming a duke and he had at least known something about it.

The vicar joined their hands and the feel of her skin through the lacy glove was icy cold. Perhaps she was not feeling quite so brave after all. He slipped the ring over her finger as they had practised and they repeated their vows.

He'd made the vicar promise not to drag it out. He didn't want Rose suffering unduly, for the scrutiny of the crowds was like a hail of arrows. Yet he didn't want anyone thinking there was something havey-cavey about their marriage, either. And finally the vicar stopped droning on and they were married. They were ushered towards the vestry to sign the register.

He caught Georgiana's eye and nodded. She helped the woman beside her to her feet.

Once they were safely away from prying eyes, Jake took that woman by the arm and led her to Rose.

The woman, a neatly dressed lady with a tidy grey bun and the attire of a gentlewoman, hung back, tears forming in her eyes.

'Rose, I want you to meet someone,' Jacob said firmly.

His bride gave him a startled look. Perhaps he had spoken a little too firmly, but he needed her attention. 'Rose, this lady is your long-lost mother.'

For a moment, he thought she might faint, her face went so pale, and her chest rose and fell so rapidly. He reached out to hold her by the elbow. 'Rose, it is all right. Sit down for a moment.'

'Mother?' she said, looking at the modestly gowned woman. 'You are my mother?'

The woman nodded. 'I am.'

Rose sought his gaze. 'You found her?'

'I did. Rose, your mother did come to the orphanage to find you. She has the other half of your token. They told her you had died. Some sort of error in record keeping. Your mother was heartbroken when they gave her the news.'

Still the woman held back. 'I should never have left you in that place.'

Rose lifted her chin. 'Why did you?'

'Your father died at sea. I had another child on the way and I had no way to feed either one. I had to work to support myself. I was a dressmaker before I married, but no one would hire me with a child. The people at the Foundling Hospital promised to care for you until I returned. Five years later, you were gone. Died, they said.'

Rose frowned. 'I was there when I was eight. Did you not ask for me? Rose Nightingale?'

'My married name is Fairclough. Your name was given as Fairclough.'

Understanding dawned on Rose's face. 'A girl around my age named Fairclough died of pleurisy.'

Jacob stemmed the fury rising in his veins all over again. 'Someone made a bad mistake. Muddled the records. It was only my man's digging around that discovered it. Rose, I am sorry.'

Rose stared at the small woman standing so hesitantly beside him, then opened her arms. 'Mother,' she said softly.

The two women clung together, weeping.

He felt awkward. He patted her back. 'I'm sorry I didn't find her before. It took time to get to the bottom of it.' Perhaps she wouldn't have wanted to marry him if she had known she had family who cared.

He stifled the thought, but Rose, as if she sensed his concern, raised her head and drew him into the circle with her mother. 'Oh, Jake, you could not have given me a better gift on my wedding day. Surely, you could not.'

And as quick as that, all was right with his world.

'Now then,' Grandmama said, moving in like a tiger ready to defend her young. 'You and your mother will have many weeks to spend together once you return from your honeymoon. Right now there is a congregation waiting to greet the Duke and his Duchess.'

Her mother stepped back. 'Indeed, Rose. Indeed. You go on. I will be here when you return.'

'You promise?' Rose visibly choked back tears.

'She will,' Jacob said. 'You can be sure of it.' Fred and Oliver would make sure of it, he could see it on their faces.

Mrs Fairclough bobbed a curtsy and smiled. 'No need, Your Grace. Never again will I be parted from my little girl.'

Rose dried her eyes on a handkerchief provided by Georgiana, and together they ran the gauntlet of the waiting congregation.

Sated and lax and lying in her husband's arms later that evening Rose pressed a kiss to her husband's raspy cheek. They had arrived without incident at Dover. Tomorrow they would take the *paquet* to Calais and from there travel to Paris.

'Thank you,' she whispered.

He rolled on his side and drew her closer to his naked body. She sighed at how well they fit together.

'All I want is your happiness,' he said.

A gentle thrill wandered its way along her spine. 'And I yours.'

A vision of the gin-raddled women of St Giles appeared before her eyes. She yawned. 'Jake, what would you have done if she had been absolutely awful?'

'Exactly what I did. No matter what, she is

your mother. I despaired of finding her, to be honest. Then my man of business suggested asking the Hospital to open their records and we saw that two girl children were admitted on the same day, Rose Nightingale and Rosalyn Fairclough. After looking at both records, we interviewed one of the older wardens. She admitted the clerk at the time had been a drunkard and had messed up several entries, but that she thought they had caught all of his errors.

'But the more we looked into it, the clearer it became there might have been one mistake they had not seen. The Nightingale child was brown-eyed, for example.'

A heavy weight lifted from her heart and finally, finally she dared to believe. 'All this time I thought they didn't want me.'

'When I found her yesterday, she was so shocked, I honestly wasn't sure she believed me. I have never seen a woman so confused. She didn't know whether to laugh or to cry.'

Rose felt like laughing and crying, too. She kissed her husband's shoulder and hoped he would know how much he had eased her pain. She forced lightness into her voice, for after all, this was her honeymoon. 'It will be interesting getting to know my family when we return.'

'The other half of your family,' he corrected,

kissing the tip of her nose. 'You are part of my family now, too.'

She snuggled closer to his warmth and strength. 'I really am the luckiest woman alive.'

'And I the happiest man because of you, my love.'

'I do love you, Jake.'

'I know. I love you more, though.'

She laughed.

They kissed and... Well, anyone could guess what happened next...

* * * * *

If you missed the first book in
THE SOCIETY OF
WICKED GENTLEMEN
quartet, check out

A CONVENIENT BRIDE FOR
THE SOLDIER
by Christine Merrill

And look out for the next two titles in the
quartet, coming soon!

'This most certainly isn't a waltz.' Nell laughed as he swung her out of the way of a portly couple who were clearly interpreting the music as a reel.

Her laugh collapsed into a gasp as her attempt to avoid stepping on his boot brought her sharply against him and somehow his leg slid between hers, straining her skirts against her thighs in a manner that definitely didn't happen in a waltz.

'I never said it was. No, don't pull back yet. Trust me.' His voice was as warm as the cider still tumbling through her and she didn't even manage to scoff at this outrageous demand, too stunned by the sensation of being held there in the middle of the chaos, just swaying gently against his thigh, his head bent next to hers.

She had ridden astride more times than she could count; she knew what it felt to have something firm and muscular between her thighs, the pull of fabric over that sensitive inner flesh. But not this. They continued to

1017_1

move, with no regard to the rhythm, his leg shifting between hers, hard and muscled, scraping and pressing in a way that should have been thoroughly uncomfortable and it was, it was, just not in any way that she wanted to stop. It made her skin heat and tingle and begin to shake and for one mad moment, still misted in the fumes of the cider, she thought it might be the return of that horrible fear, but that thought passed immediately. It wasn't that kind of shaking. It was… She was coming apart and reforming around a completely new heat at her centre, that burst of sun had sunk from her chest and stomach and settled between her legs, insistent and aggravating and in a dialogue with his body she could barely follow.

He bent his head, his mouth beside her ear as if talking to her, and perhaps he was, if talking was that gentle slide of breath over the curve of her ear and every now and then his lips brushed its tip and the heat between her legs would gather in and prepare to shoot up through her to capture that caress and out into the heavens.